Janet's Repentance

George Eliot

ET REMOTISSIMA PROPE

Hesperus Classics

Hesperus Classics
Published by Hesperus Press Limited
4 Rickett Street, London sw6 1ru
www.hesperuspress.com

First published in *Blackwood's Edinburgh Magazine* in 1857; published together with
'Amos Barton' and 'Mr Gilfil's Love Story' as *Scenes of Clerical Life* in 1858.
First published by Hesperus Press Limited, 2007

Foreword © Kathryn Hughes, 2007

Designed and typeset by Fraser Muggeridge studio
Printed in Jordan by Jordan National Press

isbn: 1-84391-158-2
isbn13: 978-1-84391-158-6

CONTENTS

FOREWORD

The thing that immediately strikes you about *Janet's Repentance* is its absolute modernity. The heroine is a battered woman who has taken to drink as a way of softening the horror of her daily existence. Her husband's alcohol-fuelled rages are less about any particular tensions in the marriage than his bullying need to control the person closest to hand. One day, after years of feeling she deserves no better, Janet Dempster finally finds the courage to leave her tormentor and admit to outsiders what has really been going on for the past fifteen years. Following a period of psychological struggle, during which she learns to depend on the support of her friends and family, our heroine finally conquers her cravings for the bottle.

So far, so neatly analogous: you can read this kind of redemptive tale in any mid-market newspaper or magazine today. This, though, is not the only contemporary echo in the concluding part of George Eliot's *Scenes of Clerical Life*. At first reading, the background story of a community coming to blows – literally – over religious doctrine might seem to have little to do with modern Britain. However, you have only to look at the way that the worldwide Anglican Communion is in danger of splitting over the ordination of female and gay clergy to see a parallel. Far from being a whiskery controversy with no possible application to life in the twenty-first century, the vicious falling-out between the Tryanites and the rest of church-going Milby becomes a cautionary tale about what happens when true religion gets perverted by arid sectarianism.

Of course, this is not to suggest that *Janet's Repentance* springs crisply off the page like a modern novel. Much of the writing, especially when concerned with the spiritual struggles of Janet Dempster and Edgar Tryan, has the kind of melodramatic quality that instantly marks it out as 'Victorian'. You lose count of the times that Janet – a provincial lawyer's wife – is described in terms that turn her into a madonna, albeit a childless one. Tryan, meanwhile, with his fevered willingness to sacrifice his life for the sake of his flock, is as close as you can get to Christ while still remaining an Evangelical clergyman of gentlemanly stock. Both figures seem to hover several inches off the ground as they move through a landscape that reverently arranges itself to amplify their every fleeting mood. Thus a smile on Janet's face 'plays like the sunbeams on the storm-beaten beauty of the full and ripened corn' while Mr Tryan makes his first appearance wearing a halo of sunshine. Sun and storm, trees and flowers, clouds and cold are pressed into service by the narrator to create two characters who start to feel, in some key sense, supernatural.

What is so odd about this elevated and highly wrought prose is that it lies in direct opposition to the kind of writing that Eliot was self-consciously trying to do. Smarting under a suggestion from her conventionally minded publisher John Blackwood that she soften what he saw as a rather coarse story about a drunken married woman forming an inappropriately close relationship with her pastor, Eliot declared defensively that her art was 'real and concrete' rather than 'ideal and eclectic'. In other words, she intended to paint people and communities as they really were, rather than how sentimental readers, including Blackwood, wished them to be.

It is not fanciful, I think, to see *Janet's Repentance* – the last piece of short fiction Eliot produced before embarking upon the full-length novels she had waited so long to write – as the place where she begins to wrestle with the challenges inherent in the literary genre that she has chosen to pursue. Her avowed intention is to show the life of the provincial lower middle classes of thirty years ago in all their unloveliness. Here are the people from whom she has sprung with their dropped aitches, silly feuds over small properties and, on the distaff side at least, an obsession with the minutiae of good housekeeping. In the masculine bluster of the Red Lion and the competitive chit-chat of Mrs Linnet's parlour you feel Eliot working from memory, summoning up the flat vowels and petty concerns that furnished her own childhood community in the Midlands. Even if you did not know that the controversy surrounding Mr Tryan's robust ministry was based on actual events recalled from Eliot's youth, you would still feel that you are in the hands of a narrator who has seen at first hand the impact of the Evangelical revival of the early nineteenth century on the small urbanising communities of provincial Britain.

Yet, simultaneously, it is also clear that Eliot has not yet worked out how to get her main story-bearing characters to interact with this minutely realised background. Instead, as we have seen, Janet and Tryan appear to have all the qualities of slightly damaged saints. Janet, for all she is supposed to be an alcoholic, is never seen the least bit tipsy. Her beauty, we are told, is only enhanced by the faint physical traces of her addiction. There are references to her earlier 'satire', but we see none of that in the luminous and bountiful figure whose 'purest enjoyment' is visiting the poor. Mr Tryan's saintliness, meanwhile, is barely dented by an unconvincing back-story, in which he is revealed as being a corruptor of women, or at least one woman in particular. (So clunky and unlikely was this inserted narrative that even Lewes, Eliot's normally loyal partner, privately admitted that it was a mistake.)

The overall effect of *Janet's Repentance*, then, is of a minutely realised social landscape against which a spiritual love affair between two monumental figures is played out. If the background and the foreground refuse ever quite to meet, and indeed seem to be always out of scale, it is less to do with Eliot's status as a literary beginner than the problems inherent in the kind of fiction that she was trying to write. Creating a chorus of red-nosed bigots and thin-lipped matrons is one thing, but Eliot quickly found that there were limits to the aesthetic pleasures of strict realism. When it came to creating a hero and heroine Eliot, like her readers, wanted comparative youth, beauty and goodness. In the end Janet Dempster and Edgar Tryan are the first of a whole series of heroic and idealised central characters – Adam Bede, Dinah Morris, Felix Holt, Daniel Deronda and even the incomparable Dorothea Brooke – who wander through George Eliot's ruined universe, unable quite to comprehend the littleness of the world in which they have been set down.

– Kathryn Hughes, 2007

Janet's Repentance

1

'No!' said Lawyer Dempster, in a loud, rasping, oratorical tone, struggling against chronic huskiness, 'as long as my Maker grants me power of voice and power of intellect, I will take every legal means to resist the introduction of demoralising, Methodistical[1] doctrine into this parish; I will not supinely suffer an insult to be inflicted on our venerable pastor, who has given us sound instruction for half a century.'

It was very warm everywhere that evening, but especially in the bar of the Red Lion at Milby, where Mr Dempster was seated mixing his third glass of brandy and water. He was a tall and rather massive man, and the front half of his large surface was so well dredged with snuff, that the cat, having inadvertently come near him, had been seized with a severe fit of sneezing – an accident which, being cruelly misunderstood, had caused her to be driven contumeliously from the bar. Mr Dempster habitually held his chin tucked in, and his head hanging forward, weighed down, perhaps, by a preponderant occiput and a bulging forehead, between which his closely clipped coronal surface lay like a flat and new-mown table land.[2] The only other observable features were puffy cheeks and a protruding yet lipless mouth. Of his nose I can only say that it was snuffy; and as Mr Dempster was never caught in the act of looking at anything in particular, it would have been difficult to swear to the colour of his eyes.

'Well! I'll not stick at giving myself trouble to put down such hypocritical cant,' said Mr Tomlinson, the rich miller. 'I know well enough what your Sunday evening lectures are good for – for wenches to meet their sweethearts, and brew mischief. There's work enough with the servant-maids as it is – such as I never heard the like of in my mother's time, and it's all along o' your schooling and newfangled plans. Give me a servant as can nayther read nor write, I say, and doesn't know the year o' the Lord as she was born in. I should like to know what good those Sunday schools have done, now. Why, the boys used to go a-birds-nesting of a Sunday morning; and a capital thing too – ask any farmer; and very pretty it was to see the strings o' heggs hanging up in poor people's houses. You'll not see 'em nowhere now.'

'Pooh!' said Mr Luke Byles, who piqued himself on his reading, and was in the habit of asking casual acquaintances if they knew anything of Hobbes.[3] 'It is right enough that the lower orders should be instructed. But this sectarianism within the Church ought to be put down. In point of fact, these Evangelicals are not churchmen at all; they're no better than Presbyterians.'

'Presbyterians? what are they?' enquired Mr Tomlinson, who often said his father had given him 'no eddication, and he didn't care who knowed it; he could buy up most o' th' eddicated men he'd ever come across.'

'The Presbyterians,' said Mr Dempster, in rather a louder tone than before, holding that every appeal for information must naturally be addressed to him, 'are a sect founded in the reign of Charles I, by a man named John Presbyter, who hatched all the brood of Dissenting[4] vermin that crawl about in dirty alleys, and circumvent the lord of the manor in order to get a few yards of ground for their pigeon-house conventicles.'

'No, no, Dempster,' said Mr Luke Byles, 'you're out there. Presbyterianism is derived from the word presbyter, meaning an elder.'[5]

'Don't contradict *me*, sir!' stormed Dempster. 'I say the word presbyterian is derived from John Presbyter, a miserable fanatic who wore a suit of leather, and went about from town to village,

4

and from village to hamlet, inoculating the vulgar with the asinine virus of Dissent.'

'Come, Byles, that seems a deal more likely,' said Mr Tomlinson, in a conciliatory tone, apparently of opinion that history was a process of ingenious guessing. 'It's not a question of likelihood; it's a known fact. I could fetch you my Encyclopaedia, and show it you this moment.'

'I don't care a straw, sir, either for you or your Encyclopaedia,' said Mr Dempster, 'a farrago of false information, of which you picked up an imperfect copy in a cargo of waste paper. Will you tell *me*, sir, that I don't know the origin of Presbyterianism? I, sir, a man known through the county, entrusted with the affairs of half a score parishes; while you, sir, are ignored by the very fleas that infest the miserable alley in which you were bred.'

A loud and general laugh, with 'You'd better let him alone Byles'; 'You'll not get the better of Dempster in a hurry', drowned the retort of the too well-informed Mr Byles, who, white with rage, rose and walked out of the bar.

'A meddlesome, upstart, Jacobinical fellow, gentlemen,' continued Mr Dempster. 'I was determined to be rid of him. What does he mean by thrusting himself into our company? A man with about as much principle as he has property, which, to my knowledge, is considerably less than none. An insolvent atheist, gentlemen. A deistical prater, fit to sit in the chimney-corner of a pot-house, and make blasphemous comments on the one greasy newspaper fingered by beer-swilling tinkers. I will not suffer in my company a man who speaks lightly of religion. The signature of a fellow like Byles would be a blot on our protest.'

'And how do you get on with your signatures?' said Mr Pilgrim, the doctor, who had presented his large top-booted person within the bar while Mr Dempster was speaking. Mr Pilgrim had just returned from one of his long day's rounds among the farmhouses, in the course of which he had sat down to two hearty meals that might have been mistaken for dinners if he had not declared them to be 'snaps'; and as each snap had been followed by a few glasses of 'mixture', containing a less liberal proportion of water than the articles he himself labelled with that broadly generic name, he was in that condition which his groom indicated with poetic ambiguity by saying that 'master had been in the sunshine'. Under these circumstances, after a hard day, in which he had really had no regular meal, it seemed a natural relaxation to step into the bar of the Red Lion, where, as it was Saturday evening, he should be sure to find Dempster, and hear the latest news about the protest against the evening lecture.

'Have you hooked Ben Landor yet?' he continued, as he took two chairs, one for his body, and the other for his right leg.

'No,' said Mr Budd, the churchwarden, shaking his head; 'Ben Landor has a way of keeping himself neutral in everything, and he doesn't like to oppose his father. Old Landor is a regular Tryanite. But we haven't got your name yet, Pilgrim.'

'Tut tut, Budd,' said Mr Dempster, sarcastically, 'you don't expect Pilgrim to sign? He's got a dozen Tryanite livers under his treatment. Nothing like cant and Methodism for producing a superfluity of bile.'

'Oh, I thought, as Pratt had declared himself a Tryanite, we should be sure to get Pilgrim on our side.'

Mr Pilgrim was not a man to sit quiet under a sarcasm, nature having endowed him with a considerable share of self-defensive wit. In his most sober moments he had an impediment in his speech, and as copious gin and water stimulated not the speech but the impediment, he had time to make his retort sufficiently bitter.

'Why, to tell you the truth, Budd,' he spluttered, 'there's a report all over the town that Deb Traunter swears you shall take her with you as one of the delegates, and they say there's to be a fine crowd at your door the morning you start, to see the row. Knowing your tenderness for that member of the fair sex, I thought you might find it impossible to deny her. I hang back a little from signing on that account, as Prendergast might not take the protest well if Deb Traunter went with you.'

Mr Budd was a small, sleek-headed bachelor of five-and-forty, whose scandalous life had long furnished his more moral neighbours with an after-dinner joke. He had no other striking characteristic, except that he was a currier of choleric temperament, so that you might wonder why he had been chosen as clergyman's churchwarden, if I did not tell you that he had recently been elected through Mr Dempster's exertions, in order that his zeal against the threatened evening lecture might be backed by the dignity of office.

'Come, come, Pilgrim,' said Mr Tomlinson, covering Mr Budd's retreat, 'you know you like to wear the crier's coat, green o' one side and red o' the other. You've been to hear Tryan preach at Paddiford Common – you know you have.'

'To be sure I have; and a capital sermon too. It's a pity you were not there. It was addressed to those "void of understanding".'

'No, no, you'll never catch me there,' returned Mr Tomlinson, not in the least stung: 'he preaches without book, they say, just like a Dissenter. It must be a rambling sort of a concern.'

'That's not the worst,' said Mr Dempster; 'he preaches against good works; says good works are not necessary to salvation – a sectarian, antinomian, Anabaptist doctrine.[6] Tell a man he is not to be saved by his works, and you open the floodgates of all immorality. You see it in all these canting innovators; they're all bad ones by the sly – smooth-faced, drawling, hypocritical fellows, who pretend ginger isn't hot in their mouths, and cry down all innocent pleasures; their hearts are all the blacker for their sanctimonious outsides. Haven't we been warned against those who make clean the outside of the cup and the platter? There's this Tryan, now, he goes about praying with old women, and singing with charity children; but what has he really got his eye on all the while? A domineering ambitious Jesuit,[7] gentlemen; all he wants is to get his foot far enough into the parish to step into Crewe's shoes when the old gentleman dies. Depend upon it, whenever you see a man pretending to be better than his neighbours, that man has either some cunning end to serve, or his heart is rotten with spiritual pride.'

As if to guarantee himself against this awful sin, Mr Dempster seized his glass of brandy and water, and tossed off the contents with even greater rapidity than usual.

'Have you fixed on your third delegate yet?' said Mr Pilgrim, whose taste was for detail rather than for dissertation.

'That's the man,' answered Dempster, pointing to Mr Tomlinson. 'We start for Elmstoke Rectory on Tuesday morning, so, if you mean to give us your signature, you must make up your mind pretty quickly, Pilgrim.'

Mr Pilgrim did not in the least mean it, so he only said, 'I shouldn't wonder if Tryan turns out too many for you, after all. He's got a well-oiled tongue of his own, and has perhaps talked over Prendergast into a determination to stand by him.'

'Ve-ry little fear of that,' said Dempster, in a confident tone. 'I'll soon bring him round. Tryan has got his match. I've plenty of rods in pickle for Tryan.'

At this moment Boots entered the bar, and put a letter into the lawyer's hands, saying, 'There's Trower's man just come into the yard wi' a gig, sir, an' he's brought this here letter.'

Mr Dempster read the letter and said, 'Tell him to turn the gig – I'll be with him in a minute. Here, run to Gruby's and get this snuffbox filled – quick!'

'Trower's worse, I suppose; eh, Dempster? Wants you to alter his will, eh?' said Mr Pilgrim.

'Business – business – business – I don't know exactly what,' answered the cautious Dempster, rising deliberately from his chair, thrusting on his low-crowned hat, and walking with a slow but not unsteady step out of the bar.

'I never see Dempster's equal; if I did I'll be shot,' said Mr Tomlinson, looking after the lawyer admiringly. 'Why, he's drunk the best part of a bottle o' brandy since here we've been sitting, and I'll bet a guinea, when he's got to Trower's his head'll be as clear as mine. He knows more about law when he's drunk than all the rest on 'em when they're sober.'

'Ay, and other things too, besides law,' said Mr Budd. 'Did you notice how he took up Byles about the Presbyterians? Bless your heart, he knows everything, Dempster does. He studied very hard when he was a young man.'

2

The conversation just recorded is not, I am aware, remarkably refined or witty, but if it had been, it could hardly have taken place in Milby when Mr Dempster flourished there, and old Mr Crewe, the curate, was yet alive.

More than a quarter of a century has slipped by since then, and in the interval Milby has advanced at as rapid a pace as other market towns in Her Majesty's dominions. By this time it has a handsome railway station, where the drowsy London traveller may look out by the brilliant gaslight and see perfectly sober papas and husbands alighting with their leather bags after transacting their day's business at the county town. There is a resident rector, who appeals to the consciences of his hearers with all the immense advantages of a divine who keeps his own carriage; the church is enlarged by at least five hundred sittings; and the grammar school, conducted on reformed principles, has its upper forms crowded with the genteel youth of Milby. The gentlemen there fall into no other excess at dinner parties than the perfectly well-bred and virtuous excess of stupidity, and though the ladies are still said sometimes to take too much upon themselves, they are never known to take too much in any other way. The conversation is sometimes quite literary, for there is a flourishing book club, and many of the younger ladies have carried their studies so far as to have forgotten a little German. In short, Milby is now a refined, moral and enlightened town, no more resembling the Milby of former days than the huge, long-skirted, drab greatcoat that embarrassed the ankles of our grandfathers resembled the light paletot[8] in which we tread jauntily through the muddiest streets, or than the bottle-nosed Britons, rejoicing over a tankard, in the old sign of the Two Travellers at Milby, resembled the severe-looking gentleman in straps and high collars whom a modern artist has represented as sipping the imaginary port of that well-known commercial house.

But pray, reader, dismiss from your mind all the refined and fashionable ideas associated with this advanced state of things, and transport your imagination to a time when Milby had no gaslights; when the mail drove up dusty or bespattered to the door of the Red Lion; when old Mr Crewe, the curate, in a brown Brutus wig, delivered inaudible sermons on a Sunday, and on a weekday imparted the education of a gentleman – that is to say, an arduous inacquaintance with Latin through the medium of the Eton Grammar – to three pupils in the upper grammar school.

If you had passed through Milby on the coach at that time, you would have had no idea what important people lived there, and how very high a sense of rank was prevalent among them. It was a dingy-looking town, with a strong smell of tanning up one street and a great shaking of handlooms up another; and even in that focus of aristocracy, Friar's Gate, the houses would not have seemed very imposing to the hasty and superficial glance of a passenger. You might still less have suspected that the figure in light fustian and large grey whiskers, leaning against the grocer's doorpost in High Street, was no less a person than Mr Lowme, one of the most aristocratic men in Milby, said to have been 'brought up a gentleman', and to have had the gay habits accordant with that station, keeping his harriers and other expensive animals. He was now quite an elderly Lothario, reduced to the most economical sins; the prominent form of his gaiety being this of lounging at Mr Gruby's door, embarrassing the servant-maids who came for grocery, and talking scandal with the rare passers-by. Still, it was generally understood that Mr Lowme belonged to the highest circle of Milby society; his sons and daughters held up their heads very high indeed; and in spite of his condescending way of chatting and drinking with inferior people, he would himself have scorned any closer identification with them. It must be admitted that he was of some service to the town in this station at Mr Gruby's door, for he and Mr Landor's Newfoundland dog, who stretched himself and gaped on the opposite causeway, took something from the lifeless air that belonged to the High Street on every day except Saturday.

Certainly, in spite of three assemblies and a charity ball in the winter, the occasional advent of a ventriloquist, or a company of itinerant players, some of whom were very highly thought of in London, and the annual three-days' fair in June, Milby might be considered dull by people of a hypochondriacal temperament; and perhaps this was one reason why many of the middle-aged inhabitants, male and female, often found it impossible to keep up their spirits without a very abundant supply of stimulants. It is true there were several substantial men who had a reputation for exceptional sobriety, so that Milby habits were really not as bad as possible; and no one is warranted in saying that old Mr Crewe's flock could not have been worse without any clergyman at all.

The well-dressed parishioners generally were very regular churchgoers, and to the younger ladies and gentlemen I am inclined to think that the Sunday morning service was the most exciting event of the week; for few places could present a more brilliant show of outdoor toilettes than might be seen issuing from Milby Church at one o'clock. There were the four tall Miss Pittmans, old lawyer Pittman's daughters, with cannon curls surmounted by large hats, and long, drooping ostrich feathers of parrot green. There was Miss Phipps, with a crimson bonnet, very much tilted up behind, and a cockade of stiff feathers on the summit. There was Miss Landor, the belle of Milby, clad regally in purple and ermine, with a plume of feathers neither drooping nor erect, but maintaining a discreet medium. There were the three Miss Tomlinsons, who imitated Miss Landor, and also wore ermine and feathers, but their beauty was considered of a coarse order, and their square forms were quite unsuited to the round tippet which fell with such remarkable grace on Miss Landor's sloping shoulders. Looking at this plumed procession of ladies, you would have formed rather a high idea of Milby wealth; yet there was only one close carriage in the place, and that was old Mr Landor's, the banker, who, I think, never drove more than one horse. These sumptuously attired ladies flashed past the vulgar eye in one-horse chaises, by no means of a superior build.

The young gentlemen, too, were not without their little Sunday displays of costume, of a limited masculine kind. Mr Eustace Landor, being nearly of age, had recently acquired a diamond ring, together with the habit of rubbing his hand through his hair. He was tall and dark, and thus had an advantage which Mr Alfred Phipps, who, like his sister, was blond and stumpy, found it difficult to overtake, even by the severest attention to shirt-studs, and the particular shade of brown that was best relieved by gilt buttons.

The respect for the Sabbath, manifested in this attention to costume, was unhappily counterbalanced by considerable levity of behaviour during the prayers and sermon; for the young ladies and gentlemen of Milby were of a very satirical turn, Miss Landor especially being considered remarkably clever, and a terrible quiz, and the large congregation necessarily containing many persons inferior in dress and demeanour to the distinguished aristocratic minority, divine service offered irresistible temptations to joking, through the medium of telegraphic communications from the galleries to the aisles and back again. I remember blushing very much, and thinking Miss Landor was laughing at me, because I was appearing in coat-tails for the first time, when I saw her look down slyly towards where I sat, and then turn with a titter to handsome Mr Bob Lowme, who had such beautiful whiskers meeting under his chin. But perhaps she was not thinking of me, after all, for our pew was near the pulpit, and there was almost always something funny about old Mr Crewe. His brown wig was hardly ever put on quite right, and he had a way of raising his voice for three or four words, and lowering it again to a mumble, so that we could scarcely make out a word he said, though, as my mother observed, that was of no consequence in the prayers, since everyone had a prayer-book, and as for the sermon, she continued with some causticity, we all of us heard more of it than we could remember when we got home.

This youthful generation was not particularly literary. The young ladies who frizzed their hair and gathered it all into large barricades in front of their heads, leaving their occipital region exposed without ornament, as if that, being a back view, was of no consequence, dreamed as little that their daughters would read a selection of German poetry and be able to express an admiration for Schiller, as that they would turn all their hair the other way – that instead of threatening us with barricades in front, they would be most killing in retreat,

And, like the Parthian, wound us as they fly.[9]

Those charming well-frizzed ladies spoke French indeed with considerable facility, unshackled by any timid regard to idiom, and were in the habit of conducting conversations in that language in the presence of their less instructed elders, for according to the standard of those backward days, their education had been very lavish, such young ladies as Miss Landor, Miss Phipps, and the Miss Pittmans, having been 'finished' at distant and expensive schools.

Old lawyer Pittman had once been a very important person indeed, having in his earlier days managed the affairs of several gentlemen in those parts, who had subsequently been obliged to sell everything and leave the country, in which crisis Mr Pittman accommodatingly stepped in as a purchaser of their estates, taking on himself the risk and trouble of a more leisurely sale, which, however, happened to turn out very much to his advantage. Such opportunities occur quite unexpectedly in the way of business. But I think Mr Pittman must have been unlucky in his later speculations, for now, in his old age, he had not the reputation of being very rich, and though he rode slowly to his office in Milby every morning on an old white hackney, he had to resign the chief profits, as well as the active business of the firm, to his younger partner, Dempster. No one in Milby considered old Pittman a virtuous man, and the elder townspeople were not at all backward in narrating the least advantageous portions of his biography in a very round unvarnished manner. Yet I could never observe that they trusted him any the less, or liked him any the worse. Indeed, Pittman and Dempster were the popular lawyers of Milby and its neighbourhood, and Mr Benjamin Landor, whom no one had anything particular to say against, had a very meagre business in comparison. Hardly a landholder, hardly a farmer, hardly a parish within ten miles of Milby, whose affairs were not under the legal guardianship of Pittman and Dempster; and I think the clients were proud of their lawyers' unscrupulousness, as the patrons of the Fancy[10] are proud of their champion's 'condition'. It was not, to be sure, the thing for ordinary life, but it was the thing to be bet on in a lawyer. Dempster's talent in 'bringing through' a client was a very common topic of conversation with the farmers, over an incidental glass of grog at the Red Lion. 'He's a long-headed feller, Dempster; why, it shows yer what a headpiece Dempster has, as he can drink a bottle o' brandy at a sittin', an' yit see further through a stone wall when he's done, than other folks'll see through a glass winder.' Even Mr Jerome, chief member of the congregation at Salem Chapel, an elderly man of very strict life, was one of Dempster's clients, and had quite an exceptional indulgence for his attorney's foibles, perhaps attributing them to the inevitable incompatibility of law and Gospel.

The standard of morality at Milby, you perceive, was not inconveniently high in those good old times, and an ingenuous vice or two was what every man expected of his neighbour. Old Mr Crewe, the curate, for example, was allowed to enjoy his avarice in comfort, without fear of sarcastic parish demagogues; and his flock liked him all the better for having scraped together a large fortune out of his school and curacy, and the proceeds of the three thousand pounds he had with his little deaf wife. It was clear he must be a learned man, for he had once had a large private school in connection with the grammar school, and had even numbered a young nobleman or two among his pupils. The fact that he read nothing at all now, and that his mind seemed absorbed in the commonest matters, was doubtless due to his having exhausted the resources of erudition earlier in life. It is true he was not spoken of in terms of high respect, and old Crewe's stingy housekeeping was a frequent subject of jesting, but this was a good old-fashioned characteristic in a parson who had been part of Milby life for half a century: it was like the dents and disfigurements in an old family tankard, which no one would like to part with for a smart new piece of plate fresh from Birmingham. The parishioners saw no reason at all why it should be desirable to venerate the parson or anyone else; they were much more comfortable to look down a little on their fellow creatures.

Even the Dissent in Milby was then of a lax and indifferent kind. The doctrine of adult baptism, struggling under a heavy load of debt, had let off half its chapel area as a ribbon shop, and Methodism was only to be detected, as you detect curious larvae, by diligent search in dirty corners. The Independents[11] were the only Dissenters of whose existence Milby gentility was at all conscious, and it had a vague idea that the salient points of their creed were prayer without book, red brick and hypocrisy. The Independent chapel, known as Salem, stood red and conspicuous in a broad street; more than one pew-holder kept a brass-bound gig; and Mr Jerome, a retired corn factor, and the most eminent member of the congregation, was one of the richest men in the parish. But in spite of this apparent prosperity, together with the usual amount of extemporaneous preaching mitigated by furtive notes, Salem belied its name, and was not always the abode of peace.[12] For some reason or other, it was unfortunate in the choice of its ministers. The Rev. Mr Horner, elected with brilliant hopes, was discovered to be given to tippling and quarrelling with his wife; the Rev. Mr Rose's doctrine was a little too 'high', verging on antinomianism; the Rev. Mr Stickney's gift as a preacher was found to be less striking on a more extended acquaintance; and the Rev. Mr Smith, a distinguished minister much sought after in the iron districts, with a talent for poetry, became objectionable from an inclination to exchange verses with the young ladies of his congregation. It was reasonably argued that such verses as Mr Smith's must take a long time for their composition, and the habit alluded to might entrench seriously on his pastoral duties. These reverend gentlemen, one and all, gave it as their opinion that the Salem church members were among the least enlightened of the Lord's people, and that Milby was a low place, where they would have found it a severe lot to have their lines fall for any long period; though to see the smart and crowded congregation assembled on occasion of the annual charity sermon, anyone might have supposed that the minister of Salem had rather a brilliant position in the ranks of Dissent. Several Church families used to attend on that occasion, for Milby, in those uninstructed days, had not yet heard that the schismatic ministers of Salem were obviously typified by Korah, Dathan and Abiram,[13] and many Church people there were of opinion that Dissent might be a weakness, but, after all, had no great harm in it. These lax episcopalians were, I believe, chiefly tradespeople, who held that, inasmuch as Congregationalism[14] consumed candles, it ought to be supported, and accordingly made a point of presenting themselves at Salem for the afternoon charity sermon, with the expectation of being asked to hold a plate. Mr Pilgrim, too, was always there with his half-sovereign, for as there was no Dissenting doctor in Milby, Mr Pilgrim looked with great tolerance on all shades of religious opinion that did not include a belief in cures by miracle.

On this point he had the concurrence of Mr Pratt, the only other medical man of the same standing in Milby. Otherwise, it was remarkable how strongly these two clever men were contrasted. Pratt was middle-sized, insinuating and silvery-voiced; Pilgrim was tall, heavy, rough-mannered and spluttering. Both were considered to have great powers of conversation, but Pratt's anecdotes were of the fine old crusted quality to be procured only of Joe Miller; Pilgrim's had the full fruity flavour of the most recent scandal. Pratt elegantly referred all diseases to debility, and, with a proper contempt for symptomatic treatment, went to the root of the matter with port wine and bark; Pilgrim was persuaded that the evil principle in the human system was plethora, and he made war against it with cupping, blistering and cathartics. They had both been long established in Milby, and as each had a sufficient practice, there was no very malignant rivalry between them; on the contrary, they had that sort of friendly contempt for each other which is always conducive to a good understanding between professional men; and when any new surgeon attempted, in an ill-advised hour, to settle himself in the town, it was strikingly demonstrated how slight and trivial are theoretic differences compared with the broad basis of common human feeling. There was the most perfect unanimity between Pratt and Pilgrim in the determination to drive away the obnoxious and too probably unqualified intruder as soon as possible. Whether the first wonderful cure he effected was on a patient of Pratt's or of Pilgrim's, one was as ready as the other to pull the interloper by the nose, and both alike directed their remarkable powers of conversation towards making the town too hot for him. But by their respective patients these two distinguished men were pitted against each other with great virulence. Mrs Lowme could not conceal her amazement that Mrs Phipps should trust her life in the hands of Pratt, who let her feed herself up to that degree, it was really shocking to hear how short her breath was; and Mrs Phipps had no patience with Mrs Lowme, living, as she did, on tea and broth, and looking as yellow as any crow-flower, and yet letting Pilgrim bleed and blister her and give her lowering medicine till her clothes hung on her like a scarecrow's. On the whole, perhaps, Mr Pilgrim's reputation was at the higher pitch, and when any lady under Mr Pratt's care was doing ill, she was half disposed to think that a little more 'active treatment' might suit her better. But without very definite provocation no one would take so serious a step as to part with the family doctor, for in those remote days there were few varieties of human hatred more formidable than the medical. The doctor's estimate, even of a confiding patient, was apt to rise and fall with the entries in the day-book, and I have known Mr Pilgrim discover the most unexpected virtues in a patient seized with a promising illness. At such times you might have been glad to perceive that there were some of Mr Pilgrim's fellow creatures of whom he entertained a high opinion, and that he was liable to the amiable weakness of a too-admiring estimate. A good inflammation fired his enthusiasm, and a lingering dropsy dissolved him into charity. Doubtless this *crescendo* of benevolence was partly due to feelings not at all represented by the entries in the day-book, for in Mr Pilgrim's heart, too, there was a latent store of tenderness and pity which flowed forth at the sight of suffering. Gradually, however, as his patients became convalescent, his view of their characters became more dispassionate; when they could relish mutton chops, he began to admit that they had foibles, and by the time they had swallowed their last dose of tonic, he was alive to their most inexcusable faults. After this, the thermometer of his regard rested at the moderate point of friendly back-biting, which sufficed to make him agreeable in his morning visits to the amiable and worthy persons who were yet far from convalescent.

Pratt's patients were profoundly uninteresting to Pilgrim: their very diseases were despicable, and he would hardly have thought their bodies worth dissecting. But of all Pratt's patients, Mr Jerome was the one on whom Mr Pilgrim heaped the most unmitigated contempt. In spite of the surgeon's wise tolerance, Dissent became odious to him in the person of Mr Jerome. Perhaps it was because that old gentleman, being rich, and having very large yearly bills for medical attendance on himself and his wife, nevertheless employed Pratt – neglected all the advantages of 'active treatment', and paid away his money without getting his system lowered. On any other ground it is hard to explain a feeling of hostility to Mr Jerome, who was an excellent old gentleman, expressing a great deal of good will towards his neighbours, not only in imperfect English, but in loans of money to the ostensibly rich, and in sacks of potatoes to the obviously poor.

Assuredly Milby had that salt of goodness which keeps the world together, in greater abundance than was visible on the surface: innocent babes were born there, sweetening their parents' hearts with simple joys; men and women withering in disappointed worldliness, or bloated with sensual ease, had better moments in which they pressed the hand of suffering with sympathy, and were moved to deeds of neighbourly kindness. In church and in chapel there were honest-hearted worshippers who strove to keep a conscience void of offence; and even up the dimmest alleys you might have found here and there a Wesleyan to whom Methodism was the vehicle of peace on earth and good will to men. To a superficial glance, Milby was nothing but dreary prose: a dingy town, surrounded by flat fields, lopped elms and sprawling manufacturing villages, which crept on and on with their weaving-shops, till they threatened to graft themselves on the town. But the sweet spring came to Milby notwithstanding: the elm-tops were red with buds; the churchyard was starred with daisies; the lark showered his love-music on the flat fields; the rainbows hung over the dingy town, clothing the very roofs and chimneys in a strange transfiguring beauty. And so it was with the human life there, which at first seemed a dismal mixture of griping worldliness, vanity, ostrich feathers and the fumes of brandy; looking closer, you found some purity, gentleness and unselfishness, as you may have observed a scented geranium giving forth its wholesome odours amidst blasphemy and gin in a noisy pot-house. Little deaf Mrs

Crewe would often carry half her own spare dinner to the sick and hungry; Miss Phipps, with her cockade of red feathers, had a filial heart, and lighted her father's pipe with a pleasant smile; and there were grey-haired men in drab gaiters, not at all noticeable as you passed them in the street, whose integrity had been the basis of their rich neighbour's wealth.

Such as the place was, the people there were entirely contented with it. They fancied life must be but a dull affair for that large portion of mankind who were necessarily shut out from an acquaintance with Milby families, and that it must be an advantage to London and Liverpool that Milby gentlemen occasionally visited those places on business. But the inhabitants became more intensely conscious of the value they set upon all their advantages, when innovation made its appearance in the person of the Rev. Mr Tryan, the new curate, at the chapel of ease[15] on Paddiford Common. It was soon notorious in Milby that Mr Tryan held peculiar opinions; that he preached extempore; that he was founding a religious lending library in his remote corner of the parish; that he expounded the Scriptures in cottages; and that his preaching was attracting the Dissenters, and filling the very aisles of his church. The rumour sprang up that Evangelicalism had invaded Milby parish – a murrain or blight all the more terrible, because its nature was but dimly conjectured. Perhaps Milby was one of the last spots to be reached by the wave of a new movement and it was only now, when the tide was just on the turn, that the limpets there got a sprinkling. Mr Tryan was the first Evangelical clergyman who had risen above the Milby horizon: hitherto that obnoxious adjective had been unknown to the townspeople of any gentility, and there were even many Dissenters who considered 'Evangelical' simply a sort of baptismal name to the magazine which circulated among the congregation of Salem Chapel. But now, at length, the disease had been imported, when the parishioners were expecting it as little as the innocent Red Indians expected smallpox. As long as Mr Tryan's hearers were confined to Paddiford Common – which, by the by, was hardly recognisable as a common at all, but was a dismal district where you heard the rattle of the handloom, and breathed the smoke of coal-pits – the 'canting parson' could be treated as a joke. Not so when a number of single ladies in the town appeared to be infected, and even one or two men of substantial property, with old Mr Landor, the banker, at their head, seemed to be 'giving in' to the new movement – when Mr Tryan was known to be well received in several good houses, where he was in the habit of finishing the evening with exhortation and prayer. Evangelicalism was no longer a nuisance existing merely in by-corners, which any well-clad person could avoid; it was invading the very drawing rooms, mingling itself with the comfortable fumes of port wine and brandy, threatening to deaden with its murky breath all the splendour of the ostrich feathers, and to stifle Milby ingenuousness, not pretending to be better than its neighbours, with a cloud of cant and lugubrious hypocrisy. The alarm reached its climax when it was reported that Mr Tryan was endeavouring to obtain authority from Mr Prendergast, the non-resident rector, to establish a Sunday evening lecture in the parish church, on the ground that old Mr Crewe did not preach the Gospel.

It now first appeared how surprisingly high a value Milby in general set on the ministrations of Mr Crewe; how convinced it was that Mr Crewe was the model of a parish priest, and his sermons the soundest and most edifying that had ever remained unheard by a churchgoing population. All allusions to his brown wig were suppressed, and by a rhetorical figure his name was associated with venerable grey hairs; the attempted intrusion of Mr Tryan was an insult to a man deep in years and learning; moreover, it was an insolent effort to thrust himself forward in a parish where he was clearly distasteful to the superior portion of its inhabitants. The town was divided into two zealous parties, the Tryanites and anti-Tryanites; and by the exertions of the eloquent Dempster, the anti-Tryanite virulence was soon developed into an organised opposition. A protest against the meditated evening lecture was framed by that orthodox attorney, and, after being numerously signed, was to be carried to Mr Prendergast by three delegates representing the intellect, morality and wealth of Milby. The intellect, you perceive, was to be personified in Mr Dempster, the morality in Mr Budd, and the wealth in Mr Tomlinson; and the distinguished triad was to set out on its great mission, as we have seen, on the third day from that warm Saturday evening when the conversation recorded in the previous chapter took place in the bar of the Red Lion.

3

It was quite as warm on the following Thursday evening, when Mr Dempster and his colleagues were to return from their mission to Elmstoke Rectory, but it was much pleasanter in Mrs Linnet's parlour than in the bar of the Red Lion. Through the open window came the scent of mignonette and honeysuckle; the grass plot in front of the house was shaded by a little plantation of Gueldres roses, syringas and laburnums; the noise of looms and carts and unmelodious voices reached the ear simply as an agreeable murmur, for

Mrs Linnet's house was situated quite on the outskirts of Paddiford Common, and the only sound likely to disturb the serenity of the feminine party assembled there, was the occasional buzz of intrusive wasps, apparently mistaking each lady's head for a sugar basin. No sugar basin was visible in Mrs Linnet's parlour, for the time of tea was not yet, and the round table was littered with books which the ladies were covering with black canvas as a reinforcement of the new Paddiford Lending Library. Miss Linnet, whose manuscript was the neatest type of zigzag, was seated at a small table apart, writing on green paper tickets, which were to be pasted on the covers. Miss Linnet had other accomplishments besides that of a neat manuscript, and an index to some of them might be found in the ornaments of the room. She had always combined a love of serious and poetical reading with her skill in fancy-work, and the neatly bound copies of Dryden's *Virgil*, Hannah More's *Sacred Dramas*, Falconer's *Shipwreck*, Mason *On Self-Knowledge*, *Rasselas* and Burke *On the Sublime and Beautiful*,[16] which were the chief ornaments of the bookcase, were all inscribed with her name, and had been bought with her pocket money when she was in her teens. It must have been at least fifteen years since the latest of those purchases, but Miss Linnet's skill in fancy-work appeared to have gone through more numerous phases than her literary taste, for the japanned boxes, the alum and sealing-wax baskets, the fan-dolls, the 'transferred' landscapes on the fire screens, and the recent bouquets of wax flowers, showed a disparity in freshness which made them referable to widely different periods. Wax flowers presuppose delicate fingers and robust patience, but there are still many points of mind and person which they leave vague and problematic; so I must tell you that Miss Linnet had dark ringlets, a sallow complexion and an amiable disposition. As to her features, there was not much to criticise in them, for she had little nose, less lip and no eyebrow; and as to her intellect, her friend Mrs Pettifer often said, 'She didn't know a more sensible person to talk to than Mary Linnet. There was no one she liked better to come and take a quiet cup of tea with her, and read a little of Klopstock's *Messiah*.[17] Mary Linnet had often told her a great deal of her mind when they were sitting together: she said there were many things to bear in every condition of life, and nothing should induce her to marry without a prospect of happiness. Once, when Mrs Pettifer admired her wax flowers, she said, "Ah, Mrs Pettifer, think of the beauties of nature!" She always spoke very prettily, did Mary Linnet; very different, indeed, from Rebecca.'

Miss Rebecca Linnet, indeed, was not a general favourite. While most people thought it a pity that a sensible woman like Mary had not found a good husband – and even her female friends said nothing more ill-natured of her than that her face was like a piece of putty with two Scotch pebbles stuck in it – Rebecca was always spoken of sarcastically, and it was a customary kind of banter with young ladies to recommend her as a wife to any gentleman they happened to be flirting with – her fat, her finery and her thick ankles sufficing to give piquancy to the joke, notwithstanding the absence of novelty. Miss Rebecca, however, possessed the accomplishment of music, and her singing of 'Oh no, we never mention her', and 'The Soldier's Tear', was so desirable an accession to the pleasures of a tea party that no one cared to offend her, especially as Rebecca had a high spirit of her own, and in spite of her expansively rounded contour, had a particularly sharp tongue. Her reading had been more extensive than her sister's, embracing most of the fiction in Mr Procter's circulating library, and nothing but an acquaintance with the course of her studies could afford a clue to the rapid transitions in her dress, which were suggested by the style of beauty, whether sentimental, sprightly or severe, possessed by the heroine of the three volumes actually in perusal. A piece of lace, which drooped round the edge of her white bonnet one week, had been rejected by the next; and her cheeks, which, on Whitsunday, loomed through a Turnerian haze of network, were, on Trinity Sunday, seen reposing in distinct red outline on her shelving bust, like the sun on a fog bank. The black velvet, meeting with a crystal clasp, which one evening encircled her head, had on another descended to her neck, and on a third to her waist, suggesting to an active imagination either a magical contraction of the ornament, or a fearful ratio of expansion in Miss Rebecca's person. With this constant application of art to dress, she could have had little time for fancy-work, even if she had not been destitute of her sister's taste for that delightful and truly feminine occupation. And here, at least, you perceive the justice of the Milby opinion as to the relative suitability of the two Miss Linnets for matrimony. When a man is happy enough to win the affections of a sweet girl, who can soothe his cares with crochet, and respond to all his most cherished ideas with beaded urn rugs and chair covers in German wool, he has, at least, a guarantee of domestic comfort, whatever trials may await him out of doors. What a resource it is under fatigue and irritation to have your drawing room well supplied with small mats, which would always be ready if you ever wanted to set anything on them! And what styptic for a bleeding heart can equal copious squares of crochet, which are useful for slipping down the moment you touch them? How our fathers managed without crochet is the wonder, but I believe some small and feeble substitute existed in their time under the name of 'tatting'. Rebecca Linnet, however, had neglected tatting as well as other forms of fancy-work. At school, to be sure, she had spent a great deal of time in acquiring flower painting, according to the ingenious method, then fashionable, of applying the shapes of leaves and flowers cut out in cardboard, and scrubbing a brush over the surface thus conveniently marked out; but even the spill cases and hand screens which were her last half-year's performances in that way were not considered eminently successful, and had long been consigned to the retirement of the best bedroom. Thus there was a good deal of family unlikeness between Rebecca and her sister, and I am afraid there was also a little family dislike, but Mary's disapproval had usually been kept imprisoned behind her thin lips, for Rebecca was not only of a headstrong disposition, but was her mother's pet; the old lady being herself stout, and preferring a more showy style of cap than she could prevail on her daughter Mary to make up for her.

But I have been describing Miss Rebecca as she was in former days only, for her appearance this evening, as she sits pasting on the green tickets, is in striking contrast with what it was three or four months ago. Her plain grey gingham dress and plain white collar could never have belonged to her wardrobe before that date, and though she is not reduced in size, and her brown hair will do nothing but hang in crisp ringlets down her large cheeks, there is a change in her air and expression which seems to shed a softened light over her person, and make her look like a peony in the shade, instead of the same flower flaunting in a parterre in the hot sunlight.

No one could deny that Evangelicalism had wrought a change for the better in Rebecca Linnet's person – not even Miss Pratt, the thin stiff lady in spectacles, seated opposite to her, who always had a peculiar repulsion for 'females with a gross habit of body'. Miss Pratt was an old maid, but that is a no more definite description than if I had said she was in the autumn of life. Was it autumn when the orchards are fragrant with apples, or autumn when the oaks are brown, or autumn when the last yellow leaves are fluttering in the chill breeze? The young ladies in Milby would have told you that the Miss Linnets were old maids, but the Miss Linnets were to Miss Pratt what the apple-scented September is to the bare, nipping days of late November. The Miss Linnets were in that temperate zone of old-maidism, when a woman will not say but that if a man of suitable years and character were to offer himself, she might be induced to tread the remainder of life's vale in company with him; Miss Pratt was in that arctic region where a woman is confident that at no time of life would she have consented to give up her liberty, and that she has never seen the man whom she would engage to honour and obey. If the Miss Linnets were old maids, they were old maids with natural ringlets and embonpoint, not to say obesity; Miss Pratt was an old maid with a cap, a braided 'front', a backbone and appendages. Miss Pratt was the one bluestocking of Milby, possessing, she said, no less than five hundred volumes, competent, as her brother the doctor often observed, to conduct a conversation on any topic whatever, and occasionally dabbling a little in authorship, though it was understood that she had never put forth the full powers of her mind in print. Her 'Letters to a Young Man on his Entrance into Life', and 'De Courcy, or the Rash Promise, a Tale for Youth', were mere trifles which she had been induced to publish because they were calculated for popular utility, but they were nothing to what she had for years had by her in manuscript. Her latest production had been Six Stanzas, addressed to the Rev. Edgar Tryan, printed on glazed paper with a neat border, and beginning, 'Forward, young wrestler for the truth!'

Miss Pratt having kept her brother's house during his long widowhood, his daughter, Miss Eliza, had had the advantage of being educated by her aunt, and thus of imbibing a very strong antipathy to all that remarkable woman's tastes and opinions. The silent handsome girl of two-and-twenty, who is covering the *Memoirs of Felix Neff*,[18] is Miss Eliza Pratt, and the small elderly lady in dowdy clothing, who is also working diligently, is Mrs Pettifer, a superior-minded widow, much valued in Milby, being such a very respectable person to have in the house in case of illness, and of quite too good a family to receive any money payment – you could always send her garden stuff that would make her ample amends. Miss Pratt has enough to do in commenting on the heap of volumes before her, feeling it a responsibility entailed on her by her great powers of mind to leave nothing without the advantage of her opinion. Whatever was good must be sprinkled with the chrism of her approval; whatever was evil must be blighted by her condemnation.

'Upon my word,' she said, in a deliberate high voice, as if she were dictating to an amanuensis, 'it is a most admirable selection of works for popular reading, this that our excellent Mr Tryan has made. I do not know whether, if the task had been confided to me, I could have made a selection, combining in a higher degree religious instruction and edification with a due admixture of the purer species of amusement. This story of *Father Clement* is a library in itself on the errors of Romanism.[19] I have ever considered fiction a suitable form for conveying moral and religious instruction, as I have shown in my little work "De Courcy", which, as a very clever writer in the Crompton *Argus* said at the time of its appearance, is the light vehicle of a weighty moral.'

'One 'ud think,' said Mrs Linnet, who also had her spectacles on, but chiefly for the purpose of seeing what the others were doing, 'there didn't want much to drive people away from a religion as makes 'em walk barefoot over stone floors, like that girl in *Father Clement* – sending the blood up to the head frightful. Anybody might see that was an unnat'ral creed.'

'Yes,' said Miss Pratt, 'but asceticism is not the root of the error, as Mr Tryan was telling us the other evening – it is the denial of the great doctrine of justification by faith.[20] Much as I had reflected on all subjects in the course of my life, I am indebted to Mr Tryan for opening my eyes to the full importance of that cardinal doctrine of the Reformation. From a child I had a deep sense of religion, but in my early days the Gospel light was obscured in the English Church, notwithstanding the possession of our incomparable Liturgy, than which I know no human composition more faultless and sublime. As I tell Eliza, I was not blest as she is at the age of two-and-twenty, in knowing a clergyman who unites all that is great and admirable in intellect with the highest spiritual gifts. I am no contemptible judge of a man's acquirements, and I assure you I have tested Mr Tryan's by questions which are a pretty severe touchstone. It is true, I sometimes carry him a little beyond the depth of the other listeners. Profound learning,' continued Miss Pratt, shutting her spectacles, and tapping them on the book before her, 'has not many to estimate it in Milby.'

'Miss Pratt,' said Rebecca, 'will you please give me Scott's *Force of Truth*? There – that small book lying against the *Life of Legh Richmond*.[21]

'That's a book I'm very fond of – the *Life of Legh Richmond*,' said Mrs Linnet. 'He found out all about that woman at Tutbury as pretended to live without eating. Stuff and nonsense!'

Mrs Linnet had become a reader of religious books since Mr Tryan's advent, and as she was in the habit of confining her perusal to the purely secular portions, which bore a very small proportion to the whole, she could make rapid progress through a large number of volumes. On taking up the biography of a celebrated preacher, she immediately turned to the end to see what disease he died of, and if his legs swelled, as her own occasionally did, she felt a stronger interest in ascertaining any earlier facts in the history of the dropsical divine – whether he had ever fallen off a stage coach, whether he had married more than one wife, and, in general, any adventures or repartees recorded of him previous to the epoch of his conversion. She then glanced over the letters and diary, and wherever there was a predominance of Zion, the River of Life, and notes of exclamation, she turned over to the next page, but any passage in which she saw such promising nouns as 'smallpox', 'pony', or 'boots and shoes', at once arrested her.

'It is half-past six now,' said Miss Linnet, looking at her watch as the servant appeared with the tea tray. 'I suppose the delegates are come back by this time. If Mr Tryan had not so kindly promised to call and let us know, I should hardly rest without walking to Milby myself to know what answer they have brought back. It is a great privilege for us, Mr Tryan living at Mrs Wagstaff's, for he is often able to take us on his way backwards and forwards into the town.'

'I wonder if there's another man in the world who has been brought up as Mr Tryan has, that would choose to live in those small close rooms on the common, among heaps of dirty cottages, for the sake of being near the poor people,' said Mrs Pettifer. 'I'm afraid he hurts his health by it; he looks to me far from strong.'

'Ah,' said Miss Pratt, 'I understand he is of a highly respectable family indeed, in Huntingdonshire. I heard him myself speak of his father's carriage – quite incidentally, you know – and Eliza tells me what very fine cambric handkerchiefs he uses. My eyes are not good enough to see such things, but I know what breeding is as well as most people, and it is easy to see that Mr Tryan is quite *comme il faw*,[22] to use a French expression.'

'I should like to tell him better nor use fine cambric i' this place, where there's such washing, it's a shame to be seen,' said Mrs Linnet; 'he'll get 'em tore to pieces. Good lawn 'ud be far better. I saw what a colour his linen looked at the sacrament last Sunday. Mary's making him a black silk case to hold his bands, but I told her she'd more need wash 'em for him.'

'Oh, mother!' said Rebecca, with solemn severity, 'pray don't think of pocket handkerchiefs and linen, when we are talking of such a man. And at this moment, too, when he is perhaps having to bear a heavy blow. We have more need to help him by prayer, as Aaron and Hur held up the hands of Moses. We don't know but wickedness may have triumphed, and Mr Prendergast may have consented to forbid the lecture. There have been dispensations quite as mysterious, and Satan is evidently putting forth all his strength to resist the entrance of the Gospel into Milby Church.'

'You niver spoke a truer word than that, my dear,' said Mrs Linnet, who accepted all religious phrases, but was extremely rationalistic in her interpretation, 'for if iver Old Harry appeared in a human form, it's that Dempster. It was all through him as we got cheated out o' Pye's Croft, making out

33

as the title wasn't good. Such lawyer's villainy! As if paying good money wasn't title enough to anything. If your father as is dead and gone had been worthy to know it! But he'll have a fall some day, Dempster will. Mark my words.'

'Ah, out of his carriage, you mean,' said Miss Pratt, who, in the movement occasioned by the clearing of the table, had lost the first part of Mrs Linnet's speech. 'It certainly is alarming to see him driving home from Rotherby, flogging his galloping horse like a madman. My brother has often said he expected every Thursday evening to be called in to set some of Dempster's bones, but I suppose he may drop that expectation now, for we are given to understand from good authority that he has forbidden his wife to call my brother in again either to herself or her mother. He swears no Tryanite doctor shall attend his family. I have reason to believe that Pilgrim was called in to Mrs Dempster's mother the other day.'

'Poor Mrs Raynor! She's glad to do anything for the sake of peace and quietness,' said Mrs Pettifer, 'but it's no trifle at her time of life to part with a doctor who knows her constitution.'

'What trouble that poor woman has to bear in her old age!' said Mary Linnet, 'to see her daughter leading such a life! – an only daughter, too, that she dotes on.'

'Yes, indeed,' said Miss Pratt. 'We, of course, know more about it than most people, my brother having attended the family so many years. For my part, I never thought well of the marriage, and I endeavoured to dissuade my brother when Mrs Raynor asked him to give Janet away at the wedding. 'If you will take my advice, Richard,' I said, 'you will have nothing to do with that marriage.' And he has seen the justice of my opinion since. Mrs Raynor herself was against the connection at first, but she always spoiled Janet, and I fear, too, she was won over by a foolish pride in having her daughter marry a professional man. I fear it was so. No one but myself, I think, foresaw the extent of the evil.'

'Well,' said Mrs Pettifer, 'Janet had nothing to look forward to but being a governess, and it was hard for Mrs Raynor to have to work at millinering – a woman well brought up, and her husband a man who held his head as high as any man in Thurston. And it isn't everybody that sees everything fifteen years beforehand. Robert Dempster was the cleverest man in Milby, and there weren't many young men fit to talk to Janet.'

'It is a thousand pities,' said Miss Pratt, choosing to ignore Mrs Pettifer's slight sarcasm, 'for I certainly did consider Janet Raynor the most promising young woman of my acquaintance – a little too much lifted up, perhaps, by her superior education, and too much given to satire, but able to express herself very well indeed about any book I recommended to her perusal. There is no young woman in Milby now who can be compared with what Janet was when she was married, either in mind or person. I consider Miss Landor far, far below her. Indeed, I cannot say much for the mental superiority of the young ladies in our first families. They are superficial – very superficial.'

'She made the handsomest bride that ever came out of Milby Church, too,' said Mrs Pettifer. 'Such a very fine figure! And it showed off her white poplin so well. And what a pretty smile Janet always had! Poor thing, she keeps that now for all her old friends. I never see her but she has something pretty to say to me – living in the same street, you know, I can't help seeing her often, though I've never been to the house since Dempster broke out on me in one of his drunken fits. She comes to me sometimes, poor thing, looking so strange, anybody passing her in the street may see plain enough what's the matter, but she's always got some little good-natured plan in her head for all that. Only last night I met her, I saw five yards off she wasn't fit to be out, but she had a basin in her hand, full of something she was carrying to Sally Martin, the deformed girl that's in a consumption.'

'But she is just as bitter against Mr Tryan as her husband is, I understand,' said Rebecca. 'Her heart is very much set against the truth, for I understand she bought Mr Tryan's sermons on purpose to ridicule them to Mrs Crewe.'

'Well, poor thing,' said Mrs Pettifer, 'you know she stands up for everything her husband says and does. She never will admit to anybody that he is not a good husband.'

'That is her pride,' said Miss Pratt. 'She married him in opposition to the advice of her best friends, and now she is not willing to admit that she was wrong. Why, even to my brother – and a medical attendant, you know, can hardly fail to be acquainted with family secrets – she has always pretended to have the highest respect for her husband's qualities. Poor Mrs Raynor, however, is very well aware that everyone knows the real state of things. Latterly, she has not even avoided the subject with me. The very last time I called on her she said, "Have you been to see my poor daughter?" and burst into tears.'

'Pride or no pride,' said Mrs Pettifer, 'I shall always stand up for Janet Dempster. She sat up with me night after night when I had that attack of rheumatic fever six years ago. There's great excuses for her. When a woman can't think of her husband coming home without trembling, it's enough to make her drink something to blunt her feelings – and no children either, to keep her from it. You and me might do the same, if we were in her place.'

'Speak for yourself, Mrs Pettifer,' said Miss Pratt. 'Under no circumstances can I imagine myself resorting to a practice so degrading. A woman should find support in her own strength of mind.'

'I think,' said Rebecca, who considered Miss Pratt still very blind in spiritual things, notwithstanding her assumption of enlightenment, 'she will find poor support if she trusts only to her own strength. She must seek aid elsewhere than in herself.'

Happily the removal of the tea things just then created a little confusion, which aided Miss Pratt to repress her resentment at Rebecca's presumption in correcting her – a person like Rebecca Linnet! who six months ago was as flighty and vain a woman as Miss Pratt had ever known – so very unconscious of her unfortunate person!

The ladies had scarcely been seated at their work another hour, when the sun was sinking, and the clouds that flecked the sky to the very zenith were every moment taking on a brighter gold. The gate of the little garden opened, and Miss Linnet, seated at her small table near the window, saw Mr Tryan enter.

'There is Mr Tryan,' she said, and her pale cheek was lighted up with a little blush that would have made her look more attractive to almost anyone except Miss Eliza Pratt, whose fine grey eyes allowed few things to escape her silent observation. 'Mary Linnet gets more and more in love with Mr Tryan,' thought Miss Eliza; 'it is really pitiable to see such feelings in a woman of her age, with those old-maidish little ringlets. I daresay she flatters herself Mr Tryan may fall in love with her, because he makes her useful among the poor.' At the same time, Miss Eliza, as she bent her handsome head and large cannon curls with apparent calmness over her work, felt a considerable internal flutter when she heard the knock at the door. Rebecca had less self-command. She felt too much agitated to go on with her pasting, and clutched the leg of the table to counteract the trembling in her hands.

Poor women's hearts! Heaven forbid that I should laugh at you, and make cheap jests on your susceptibility towards the clerical sex, as if it had nothing deeper or more lovely in it than the mere vulgar angling for a husband. Even in these enlightened days, many a curate who, considered abstractedly, is nothing more than a sleek bimanous animal in a white neckcloth, with views more or less Anglican, and furtively addicted to the flute, is adored by a girl who has coarse brothers, or by a solitary woman who would like to be a helpmate in good works beyond her own means, simply because he seems to them the model of refinement and of public usefulness. What wonder, then, that in Milby society, such as I have told you it was a very long while ago, a zealous Evangelical clergyman, aged thirty-three, called forth all the little agitations that belong to the divine necessity of loving, implanted in the Miss Linnets, with their seven or eight lustrums and their unfashionable ringlets, no less than in Miss Eliza Pratt, with her youthful bloom and her ample cannon curls.

But Mr Tryan has entered the room, and the strange light from the golden sky falling on his light-brown hair, which is brushed high up round his head, makes it look almost like an aureole. His grey eyes, too, shine with unwonted brilliancy this evening. They were not remarkable eyes, but they accorded completely in their changing light with the changing expression of his person, which indicated the paradoxical character often observable in a large-limbed sanguine blond, at once mild and irritable, gentle and overbearing, indolent and resolute, self-conscious and dreamy. Except that the well-filled lips had something of the artificially compressed look which is often the sign of a struggle to keep the dragon undermost, and that the complexion was rather pallid, giving the idea of imperfect health, Mr Tryan's face in repose was that of an ordinary whiskerless blond, and it seemed difficult to refer a certain air of distinction about him to anything in particular, unless it were his delicate hands and well-shapen feet.

It was a great anomaly to the Milby mind that a canting Evangelical parson, who would take tea with tradespeople, and make friends of vulgar women like the Linnets, should have so much the air of a gentleman, and be so little like the splay-footed Mr Stickney of Salem, to whom he approximated so closely in doctrine. And this want of correspondence between the physique and the creed had excited no less surprise in the larger town of Laxeter, where Mr Tryan had formerly held a curacy, for of the two other Low Church clergymen in the neighbourhood, one was a Welshman of globose figure and unctuous complexion, and the other a man of atrabiliar aspect, with lank black hair, and a redundance of limp cravat – in fact, the sort of thing you might expect in men who distributed the publications of the Religious Tract Society,[23] and introduced Dissenting hymns into the Church.

Mr Tryan shook hands with Mrs Linnet, bowed with rather a preoccupied air to the other ladies, and seated himself in the large horsehair easy chair which had been drawn forward for him, while the ladies ceased from their work, and fixed their eyes on him, awaiting the news he had to tell them.

'It seems,' he began, in a low and silvery tone, 'I need a lesson of patience; there has been something wrong in my thought or action about this evening lecture. I have been too much bent on doing good to Milby after my own plan – too reliant on my own wisdom.'

Mr Tryan paused. He was struggling against inward irritation.

'The delegates are come back, then?' 'Has Mr Prendergast given way?' 'Has Dempster succeeded?' – were the eager questions of three ladies at once.

'Yes; the town is in an uproar. As we were sitting in Mr Landor's drawing room we heard a loud cheering, and presently Mr Thrupp, the clerk at the bank, who had been waiting at the Red Lion to hear the result, came to let us know. He said Dempster had been making a speech to the mob out the window. They were distributing drink to the people, and hoisting placards in great letters – "Down with the Tryanites!" "Down with cant!" They had a hideous caricature of me being tripped up and pitched head-foremost out of the pulpit. Good old Mr Landor would insist on sending me round in the carriage; he thought I should not be safe from the mob, but I got down at the Crossways. The row was evidently pre-concerted by Dempster before he set out. He made sure of succeeding.'

Mr Tryan's utterance had been getting rather louder and more rapid in the course of this speech, and he now added, in the energetic chest-voice, which, both in and out of the pulpit, alternated continually with his more silvery notes, 'But his triumph will be a short one. If he thinks he can intimidate me by obloquy or threats, he has mistaken the man he has to deal with. Mr Dempster and his colleagues will find themselves checkmated after all. Mr Prendergast has been false to his own conscience in this business. He knows as well as I do that he is throwing away the souls of the people by leaving things as they are in the parish. But I shall appeal to the Bishop – I am confident of his sympathy.'

'The Bishop will be coming shortly, I suppose,' said Miss Pratt, 'to hold a confirmation?'

'Yes, but I shall write to him at once, and lay the case before him. Indeed, I must hurry away now, for I have many matters to attend to. You, ladies, have been kindly helping me with your labours, I see,' continued Mr Tryan, politely, glancing at the canvas-covered books as he rose from his seat. Then, turning to Mary Linnet, 'Our library is really getting on, I think. You and your sister have quite a heavy task of distribution now.'

Poor Rebecca felt it very hard to bear that Mr Tryan did not turn towards her too. If he knew how much she entered into his feelings about the lecture, and the interest she took in the library. Well! perhaps it was her lot to be overlooked – and it might be a token of mercy. Even a good man might not always know the heart that was most with him. But the next moment poor Mary had a pang, when Mr Tryan turned to Miss Eliza Pratt, and the preoccupied expression of his face melted into that beaming timidity with which a man almost always addresses a pretty woman.

'I have to thank you, too, Miss Eliza, for seconding me so well in your visits to Joseph Mercer. The old man tells me how precious he finds your reading to him, now he is no longer able to go to church.'

Miss Eliza only answered by a blush, which made her look all the handsomer, but her aunt said, 'Yes, Mr Tryan, I have ever inculcated on my dear Eliza the importance of spending her leisure in being useful to her fellow creatures. Your example and instruction have been quite in the spirit of the system which I have always pursued, though we are indebted to you for a clearer view of the motives that should actuate us in our pursuit of good works. Not that I can accuse myself of having ever had a self-righteous spirit, but my humility was rather instinctive than based on a firm ground of doctrinal knowledge, such as you so admirably impart to us.'

Mrs Linnet's usual entreaty that Mr Tryan would 'have something – some wine and water and a biscuit' was just here a welcome relief from the necessity of answering Miss Pratt's oration.

'Not anything, my dear Mrs Linnet, thank you. You forget what a Rechabite[24] I am. By the by, when I went this morning to see a poor girl in Butcher's Lane, whom I had heard of as being in a consumption, I found Mrs Dempster there. I had often met her in the street, but did not know it was Mrs Dempster. It seems she goes among the poor a good deal. She is really an interesting-looking woman. I was quite surprised, for I have heard the worst account of her habits – that she is almost as bad as her husband. She went out hastily as soon as I entered. But' (apologetically) 'I am keeping you all standing, and I must really hurry away. Mrs Pettifer, I have not had the pleasure of calling on you for some time; I shall take an early opportunity of going your way. Good evening, good evening.'

4

Mr Tryan was right in saying that the 'row' in Milby had been preconcerted by Dempster. The placards and the caricature were prepared before the departure of the delegates, and it had been settled that Mat Paine, Dempster's clerk, should ride out on Thursday morning to meet them at Whitlow, the last place where they would change horses, that he might gallop back and prepare an ovation for the triumvirate in case of their success. Dempster had determined to dine at Whitlow, so that Mat Paine was in Milby again two hours before the entrance of the delegates, and had time to send a whisper up the back streets that there was promise of a 'spree' in the Bridge Way, as well as to assemble two knots of picked men – one to feed the flame of orthodox zeal with gin and water, at the Green Man, near High Street, the other to solidify their Church principles with heady beer at the Bear and Ragged Staff in the Bridge Way.

The Bridge Way was an irregular straggling street, where the town fringed off raggedly into the Whitlow road: rows of new red-brick houses, in which ribbon looms were rattling behind long lines of window, alternating with old, half-thatched, half-tiled cottages – one of those dismal wide streets where dirt and misery have no long shadows thrown on them to soften their ugliness. Here, about half-past five o'clock, Silly Caleb, an idiot well known in Dog Lane, but more of a stranger in the Bridge Way, was seen slouching along with a string of boys hooting at his heels; presently another group, for the most part out at elbows, came briskly in the same direction, looking round them with an air of expectation; and at no long interval, Deb Traunter, in a pink flounced gown and floating ribbons, was observed talking with great affability to two men in sealskin caps and fustian, who formed her cortège. The Bridge Way began to have a presentiment of something in the wind. Phib Cook left her evening washtub and appeared at her door in soapsuds, a bonnet-poke, and general dampness; three narrow-chested ribbon weavers, in rusty black streaked with shreds of many-coloured silk, sauntered out with their hands in their pockets; and Molly Beale, a brawny old virago, descrying wiry Dame Ricketts peeping out from her entry, seized the opportunity of renewing the morning's skirmish. In short, the Bridge Way was in that state of excitement which is understood to announce a 'demonstration' on the part of the British public; and the afflux of remote townsmen increasing, there was soon so large a crowd that it was time for Bill Powers, a plethoric Goliath, who presided over the knot of beer drinkers at the Bear and Ragged Staff, to issue forth with his companions, and, like the enunciator of the ancient myth, make the assemblage distinctly conscious of the common sentiment that had drawn them together. The expectation of the delegates' chaise, added to the fight between Molly Beale and Dame Ricketts, and the ill-advised appearance of a lean bull terrier, were a sufficient safety valve to the popular excitement during the remaining quarter of an hour, at the end of which the chaise was seen approaching along the Whitlow road, with oak boughs ornamenting the horses' heads; and, to quote the account of this interesting scene which was sent to the *Rotherby Guardian*, 'loud cheers immediately testified to the sympathy of the honest fellows collected there, with the public-spirited exertions of their fellow-townsmen.' Bill Powers, whose bloodshot eyes, bent hat, and protuberant altitude, marked him out as the natural leader of the assemblage, undertook to interpret the common sentiment by stopping the chaise, advancing to the door with raised hat, and begging to know of Mr Dempster, whether the Rector had forbidden the 'canting lecture'.

'Yes, yes,' said Mr Dempster. 'Keep up a jolly good hurray.'

No public duty could have been more easy and agreeable to Mr Powers and his associates, and the chorus swelled all the way to the High Street, where, by a mysterious coincidence often observable in these spontaneous 'demonstrations', large placards on long poles were observed to shoot upwards from among the crowd, principally in the direction of Tucker's Lane, where the Green Man was situated. One bore, 'Down with the Tryanites!' another, 'No Cant!' another, 'Long live our venerable Curate!' and one in still larger letters, 'Sound Church Principles and no Hypocrisy!' But a still more remarkable impromptu was a huge caricature of Mr Tryan in gown and band, with an enormous aureole of yellow hair and upturned eyes, standing on the pulpit stairs and trying to pull down old Mr Crewe. Groans, yells and hisses – hisses, yells and groans – only stemmed by the appearance of another caricature representing Mr Tryan being pitched head-foremost from the pulpit stairs by a hand which the artist, either from subtlety of intention or want of space, had left unindicated. In the midst of the tremendous cheering that saluted this piece of symbolical art, the chaise had reached the door of the Red Lion, and loud cries of 'Dempster for ever!' with a feebler cheer now and then for Tomlinson and Budd, were presently responded to by the appearance of the public-spirited attorney at the large upper window, where also were visible a little in the background the small sleek head of Mr Budd, and the blinking countenance of Mr Tomlinson.

Mr Dempster held his hat in his hand, and poked his head forward with a butting motion by way of bow. A storm of cheers subsided at last into dropping sounds of 'Silence!' 'Hear him!' 'Go it, Dempster!' and the lawyer's rasping voice became distinctly audible.

'Fellow-townsmen! It gives us the sincerest pleasure – I speak for my respected colleagues as well as myself – to witness these strong proofs of your attachment to the principles of our excellent Church, and your zeal for the honour of our venerable pastor. But it is no more than I expected of you. I know you well. I've known you for the last twenty years to be as honest and respectable a set of ratepayers as any in this county. Your hearts are sound to the core! No man had better try to thrust his cant and hypocrisy down *your* throats. You're used to wash them with liquor of a better flavour. This is the proudest moment in my own life, and I think I may say in that of my colleagues, in which I have to tell you that our exertions in the cause of sound religion and manly morality have been crowned with success. Yes, my fellow-townsmen! I have the gratification of announcing to you thus formally what you have already learned indirectly. The pulpit from which our venerable pastor has fed us with sound doctrine for half a century is not to be invaded by a fanatical, sectarian, double-faced, Jesuitical interloper! We are not to have our young people demoralised and corrupted by the temptations to vice, notoriously connected with Sunday evening lectures! We are not to have a preacher obtruding himself upon us, who decries good works, and sneaks into our homes perverting the faith of our wives and daughters! We are not to be poisoned with doctrines which damp every innocent enjoyment, and pick a poor man's pocket of the sixpence with which he might buy himself a cheerful glass after a hard day's work, under pretence of paying for bibles to send to the Chicktaws!

'But I'm not going to waste your valuable time with unnecessary words. I am a man of deeds' ('Ay, damn you, that you are, and you charge well for 'em too,' said a voice from the crowd, probably that of a gentleman who was immediately afterwards observed with his hat crushed over his head.) 'I shall always be at the service of my fellow-townsmen, and whoever dares to hector over you, or interfere with your innocent pleasures, shall have an account to settle with Robert Dempster.

'Now, my boys! you can't do better than disperse and carry the good news to all your fellow-townsmen, whose hearts are as sound as your own. Let some of you go one way and some another, that every man, woman and child in Milby may know what you know yourselves. But before we part, let us have three cheers for True Religion, and down with Cant!'

When the last cheer was dying, Mr Dempster closed the window, and the judiciously instructed placards and caricatures moved off in divers directions, followed by larger or smaller divisions of the crowd. The greatest attraction apparently lay in the direction of Dog Lane, the outlet towards

Paddiford Common, whither the caricatures were moving; and you foresee, of course, that those works of symbolical art were consumed with a liberal expenditure of dry gorse bushes and vague shouting.

After these great public exertions, it was natural that Mr Dempster and his colleagues should feel more in need than usual of a little social relaxation; and a party of their friends was already beginning to assemble in the large parlour of the Red Lion, convened partly by their own curiosity, and partly by the invaluable Mat Paine. The most capacious punch bowl was put in requisition, and that born gentleman, Mr Lowme, seated opposite Mr Dempster as 'Vice', undertook to brew the punch, defying the criticisms of the envious men out of office, who with the readiness of irresponsibility, ignorantly suggested more lemons. The social festivities were continued till long past midnight, when several friends of sound religion were conveyed home with some difficulty, one of them showing a dogged determination to seat himself in the gutter.

Mr Dempster had done as much justice to the punch as any of the party, and his friend Boots, though aware that the lawyer could 'carry his liquor like Old Nick', with whose social demeanour Boots seemed to be particularly well acquainted, nevertheless thought it might be as well to see so good a customer in safety to his own door, and walked quietly behind his elbow out of the inn yard. Dempster, however, soon became aware of him, stopped short, and, turning slowly round upon him, recognised the well-known drab waistcoat sleeves, conspicuous enough in the starlight.

'You twopenny scoundrel! What do you mean by dogging a professional man's footsteps in this way? I'll break every bone in your skin if you attempt to track me, like a beastly cur sniffing at one's pocket. Do you think a gentleman will make his way home any the better for having the scent of your blacking-bottle thrust up his nostrils?'

Boots slunk back, in more amusement than ill humour, thinking the lawyer's 'rum talk' was doubtless part and parcel of his professional ability, and Mr Dempster pursued his slow way alone.

His house lay in Orchard Street, which opened on the prettiest outskirt of the town – the church, the parsonage and a long stretch of green fields. It was an old-fashioned house, with an overhanging upper storey; outside, it had a face of rough stucco, and casement windows with green frames and shutters; inside, it was full of long passages, and rooms with low ceilings. There was a large heavy knocker on the green door, and though Mr Dempster carried a latch key, he sometimes chose to use the knocker. He chose to do so now. The thunder resounded through Orchard Street, and, after a single minute, there was a second clap louder than the first. Another minute, and still the door was not opened; where-upon Mr Dempster, muttering, took out his latch key, and, with less difficulty than might have been expected, thrust it into the door. When he opened the door the passage was dark.

'Janet!' in the loudest rasping tone, was the next sound that rang through the house.

'Janet!' again – before a slow step was heard on the stairs, and a distant light began to flicker on the wall of the passage.

'Curse you! you creeping idiot! Come faster, can't you?'

Yet a few seconds, and the figure of a tall woman, holding aslant a heavy-plated drawing-room candlestick, appeared at the turning of the passage that led to the broader entrance.

She had on a light dress which sat loosely about her figure, but did not disguise its liberal, graceful outline. A heavy mass of straight jet-black hair had escaped from its fastening, and hung over her shoulders. Her grandly cut features, pale with the natural paleness of a brunette, had premature lines about them, telling that the years had been lengthened by sorrow, and the delicately curved nostril, which seemed made to quiver with the proud consciousness of power and beauty, must have quivered to the heart-piercing griefs which had given that worn look to the corners of the mouth. Her wide open black eyes had a strangely fixed, sightless gaze, as she paused at the turning, and stood silent before her husband.

'I'll teach you to keep me waiting in the dark, you pale staring fool!' he said, advancing with his slow drunken step. 'What, you've been drinking again, have you? I'll beat you into your senses.'

He laid his hand with a firm grip on her shoulder, turned her round, and pushed her slowly before him along the passage and through the dining-room door, which stood open on their left hand.

There was a portrait of Janet's mother, a grey-haired, dark-eyed old woman, in a neatly fluted cap, hanging over the mantelpiece. Surely the aged eyes take on a look of anguish as they see Janet – not trembling, no! it would be better if she trembled – standing stupidly unmoved in her great beauty while the heavy arm is lifted to strike her. The blow falls – another – and another. Surely the mother hears that cry – 'Oh, Robert! pity! pity!'

Poor grey-haired woman! Was it for this you suffered a mother's pangs in your lone widowhood five-and-thirty years ago? Was it for this you kept the little worn morocco shoes Janet had first run in, and kissed them day by day when she was away from you, a tall girl at school? Was it for this you looked proudly at her when she came back to you in her rich pale beauty, like a tall white arum that has just unfolded its grand pure curves to the sun?

The mother lies sleepless and praying in her lonely house, weeping the difficult tears of age, because she dreads this may be a cruel night for her child.

She too has a picture over her mantelpiece, drawn in chalk by Janet long years ago. She looked at it before she went to bed. It is a head bowed beneath a cross, and wearing a crown of thorns.

5

It was half-past nine o'clock in the morning. The midsummer sun was already warm on the roofs and weathercocks of Milby. The church bells were ringing, and many families were conscious of Sunday sensations, chiefly referable to the fact that the daughters had come down to breakfast in their best frocks, and with their hair particularly well dressed. For it was not Sunday, but Wednesday, and though the Bishop was going to hold a confirmation, and to decide whether or not there should be a Sunday evening lecture in Milby, the sunbeams had the usual working-day look to the haymakers already long out in the fields, and to laggard weavers just 'setting up' their week's 'piece'. The notion of its being Sunday was the strongest in young ladies like Miss Phipps, who was going to accompany her younger sister to the confirmation, and to wear a 'sweetly pretty' transparent bonnet with marabout feathers on the interesting occasion, thus throwing into relief the suitable simplicity of her sister's attire, who was, of course, to appear in a new white frock; or in the pupils at Miss Townley's, who were absolved from all lessons, and were going to church to see the Bishop, and to hear the Honourable and Reverend Mr Prendergast, the rector, read prayers – a high intellectual treat, as Miss Townley assured them. It seemed only natural that a rector, who was honourable, should read better than old Mr Crewe, who was only a curate, and not honourable; and when little Clara Robins wondered why some clergymen were rectors and others not, Ellen Marriott assured her with great confidence that it was only the clever men who were made rectors. Ellen Marriott was going to be confirmed. She was a short, fair, plump girl, with blue eyes and sandy hair, which was this morning arranged in taller cannon curls than usual, for the reception of the episcopal bene-diction, and some of the young ladies thought her the prettiest girl in the school, but others gave the preference to her rival, Maria Gardner, who was much taller, and had a lovely 'crop' of dark brown ringlets, and who, being also about to take upon herself the vows made in her name at her baptism, had oiled and twisted her ringlets with especial care. As she seated herself at the breakfast table before Miss Townley's entrance to dispense the weak coffee, her crop excited so strong a sen-sation that Ellen Marriott was at length impelled to look at it, and to say with suppressed but bitter sarcasm, 'Is that Miss Gardner's head?' 'Yes,' said Maria, amiable and stuttering, and no match for Ellen in retort; 'th – th – this is my head.' 'Then I don't admire it at all!' was the crushing rejoinder of Ellen, followed by a murmur of approval among her friends. Young ladies, I suppose, exhaust their sac of venom in this way at school. That is the reason why they have such a harmless tooth for each other in after life.

The only other candidate for confirmation at Miss Townley's was Mary Dunn, a draper's daughter in Milby and a distant relation of the Miss Linnets. Her pale lanky hair could never be coaxed into permanent curl, and this morning the heat had brought it down to its natural condition of lankiness earlier than usual. But that was not what made her sit melancholy and apart at the lower end of the form. Her parents were admirers of Mr Tryan, and had been persuaded, by the Miss Linnets' influence, to insist that their daughter should be prepared for confirmation by him, over and above the preparation given to Miss Townley's pupils by Mr Crewe. Poor Mary Dunn! I am afraid she thought it too heavy a price to pay for these spiritual advantages, to be excluded from every game at ball, to be obliged to walk with none but little girls – in fact, to be the object of an aversion that nothing short of an incessant supply of plumcakes would have neutralised. And Mrs Dunn was of opinion that plumcake was unwholesome. The anti-Tryanite spirit, you perceive, was very strong at Miss Townley's, imported probably by day scholars, as well as encouraged by the fact that that clever woman was herself strongly opposed to innovation, and remarked every Sunday that Mr Crewe had preached an 'excellent discourse'. Poor Mary Dunn dreaded the moment when school hours would be over, for then she was sure to be the butt of those very explicit remarks which, in young ladies' as well as young gentlemen's seminaries, constitute the most subtle and delicate form of the innuendo. 'I'd never be a Tryanite, would you?' 'Oh, here comes the lady that knows so much more about religion than we do!' 'Some people think themselves so very pious!'

It is really surprising that young ladies should not be thought competent to the same curriculum as young gentlemen. I observe that their powers of sarcasm are quite equal, and if there had been a genteel academy for young gentlemen at Milby, I am inclined to think that, notwithstanding Euclid and the classics, the party spirit there would not have exhibited itself in more pungent irony, or more incisive satire, than was heard in Miss Townley's seminary. But there was no such academy, the existence of the grammar school under Mr Crewe's superintendence probably discouraging speculations of that kind, and the genteel youths of Milby were chiefly come home for the midsummer holidays from distant schools. Several of us had just assumed coat-tails, and the assumption of new responsibilities apparently following as a matter of course, we were among the candidates for confirmation. I wish I could say that the solemnity of our feelings was on a level with the solemnity of the occasion, but unimaginative boys find it difficult to recognise apostolical institutions in their developed form, and I fear our chief emotion concerning the ceremony was a sense of sheepishness, and our chief opinion, the speculative and heretical position, that it ought to be confined to the girls. It was a pity, you will say, but it is the way with us men in other crises, that come a long while after confirmation. The golden moments in the stream of life rush past us, and we see nothing but sand; the angels come to visit us, and we only know them when they are gone.

But, as I said, the morning was sunny, the bells were ringing, the ladies of Milby were dressed in their Sunday garments.

And who is this bright-looking woman walking with hasty step along Orchard Street so early, with a large nosegay in her hand? Can it be Janet Dempster, on whom we looked with such deep pity, one sad midnight, hardly a fortnight ago? Yes; no other woman in Milby has those searching black eyes, that tall graceful unconstrained figure, set off by her simple muslin dress and black lace shawl, that massy black hair now so neatly braided in glossy contrast with the white satin ribbons of her modest cap and bonnet. No other woman has that sweet speaking smile, with which she nods to Jonathan Lamb, the old parish clerk. And, ah! – now she comes nearer – there are those sad lines about the mouth and eyes on which that sweet smile plays like sunbeams on the storm-beaten beauty of the full and ripened corn.

She is turning out of Orchard Street, and making her way as fast as she can to her mother's house, a pleasant cottage facing a roadside meadow, from which the hay is being carried. Mrs Raynor has had her breakfast, and is seated in her armchair reading, when Janet opens the door, saying, in her most playful voice, 'Please, Mother, I'm come to show myself to you before I go to the Parsonage. Have I put on my pretty cap and bonnet to satisfy you?'

Mrs Raynor looked over her spectacles, and met her daughter's glance with eyes as dark and loving as her own. She was a much smaller woman than Janet, both in figure and feature, the chief resemblance lying in the eyes and the clear brunette complexion. The mother's hair had long been grey, and was gathered under the neatest of caps, made by her own clever fingers, as all Janet's caps and bonnets were too. They were well-practised fingers, for Mrs Raynor had supported herself in her widowhood by keeping a millinery establishment, and in this way had earned money enough to give her daughter what was then thought a first-rate education, as well as to save a sum which, eked out by her son-in-law, sufficed to support her in her solitary old age. Always the same clean, neat old lady, dressed in black silk, was Mrs Raynor: a patient, brave woman, who bowed with resignation under the burden of remembered sorrow, and bore with meek fortitude the new load that the new days brought with them.

'Your bonnet wants pulling a trifle forwarder, my child,' she said, smiling, and taking off her spectacles, while Janet at once knelt down before her, and waited to be 'set to rights', as she would have done when she was a child. 'You're going straight to Mrs Crewe's, I suppose? Are those flowers to garnish the dishes?'

'No, indeed, Mother. This is a nosegay for the middle of the table. I've sent up the dinner service and the ham we had cooked at our house yesterday, and Betty is coming directly with the garnish and the plate. We shall get our good Mrs Crewe through her troubles famously. Dear tiny woman! You should have seen her lift up her hands yesterday, and pray Heaven to take her before ever she should have another collation to get ready for the Bishop. She said, "It's bad enough to have the Archdeacon, though he doesn't want half so many jelly glasses. I wouldn't mind, Janet, if it was to feed all the old hungry cripples in Milby, but so much trouble and expense for people who eat too much every day of their lives!" We had such a cleaning and furbishing up of the sitting room yesterday! Nothing will ever do away with the smell of Mr Crewe's pipes, you know, but we have thrown it into the background, with yellow soap and dry lavender. And now I must run away. You will come to church, Mother?'

'Yes, my dear, I wouldn't lose such a pretty sight. It does my old eyes good to see so many fresh young faces. Is your husband going?'

'Yes, Robert will be there. I've made him as neat as a new pin this morning, and he says the Bishop will think him too buckish by half. I took him into Mammy Dempster's room to show himself. We hear Tryan is making sure of the Bishop's support, but we shall see. I would give my crooked guinea, and all the luck it will ever bring me, to have him beaten, for I can't endure the sight of the man coming to harass dear old Mr and Mrs Crewe in their last days. Preaching the Gospel indeed!

That is the best Gospel that makes everybody happy and comfortable, isn't it, Mother?'

'Ah, child, I'm afraid there's no Gospel will do that here below.'

'Well, I can do something to comfort Mrs Crewe, at least, so give me a kiss, and goodbye till church time.'

The mother leaned back in her chair when Janet was gone, and sank into a painful reverie. When our life is a continuous trial, the moments of respite seem only to substitute the heaviness of dread for the heaviness of actual suffering: the curtain of cloud seems parted an instant only that we may measure all its horror as it hangs low, black and imminent, in contrast with the transient brightness; the water drops that visit the parched lips in the desert bear with them only the keen imagination of thirst. Janet looked glad and tender now – but what scene of misery was coming next? She was too like the cistus flowers in the little garden before the window, that, with the shades of evening, might lie with the delicate white and glossy dark of their petals trampled in the roadside dust. When the sun had sunk, and the twilight was deepening, Janet might be sitting there, heated, maddened, sobbing out her griefs with selfish passion, and wildly wishing herself dead.

Mrs Raynor had been reading about the lost sheep, and the joy there is in heaven over the sinner that repenteth. Surely the eternal love she believed in through all the sadness of her lot, would not leave her child to wander further and further into the wilderness till here was no turning – the child so lovely, so pitiful to others, so good – till she was goaded into sin by woman's bitterest sorrows! Mrs Raynor had her faith and her spiritual comforts, though she was not in the least Evangelical and knew nothing of doctrinal zeal. I fear most of Mr Tryan's hearers would have considered her destitute of saving knowledge, and I am quite sure she had no well-defined views on justification. Nevertheless, she read her Bible a great deal, and thought she found divine lessons there – how to bear the cross meekly, and be merciful. Let us hope that there is a saving ignorance, and that Mrs Raynor was justified without knowing exactly how.

She tried to have hope and trust, though it was hard to believe that the future would be anything else than the harvest of the seed that was being sown before her eyes. But always there is seed being sown silently and unseen, and everywhere there come sweet flowers without our foresight or labour. We reap what we sow, but Nature has love over and above that justice, and gives us shadow and blossom and fruit that spring from no planting of ours.

6

Most people must have agreed with Mrs Raynor that the confirmation that day was a pretty sight, at least when those slight girlish forms and fair young faces moved in a white rivulet along the aisles, and flowed into kneeling semicircles under the light of the great chancel window, softened by patches of dark old painted glass; and one would think that to look on while a pair of venerable hands pressed such young heads, and a venerable face looked upward for a blessing on them, would be very likely to make the heart swell gently, and to moisten the eyes. Yet I remember the eyes seemed very dry in Milby Church that day, notwithstanding that the Bishop was an old man, and probably venerable (for though he was not an eminent Grecian, he was the brother of a Whig lord); and I think the eyes must have remained dry, because he had small delicate womanish hands adorned with ruffles, and, instead of laying them on the girls' heads, just let them hover over each in quick succession, as if it were not etiquette to touch them, and as if the laying on of hands were like the theatrical embrace – part of the play, and not to be really believed in. To be sure there were a great many heads, and the Bishop's time was limited. Moreover, a wig can, under no circumstances, be affecting, except in rare cases of illusion, and copious lawn sleeves cannot be expected to go directly to any heart except a washerwoman's.

I know Ned Phipps, who knelt against me, and I am sure made me behave much worse than I should have done without him, whispered that he thought the Bishop was a 'guy', and I certainly remember thinking that Mr Prendergast looked much more dignified with his plain white surplice and black hair. He was a tall commanding man, and read the Liturgy in a strikingly sonorous and uniform voice, which I tried to imitate the next Sunday at home, until my little sister began to cry, and said I was 'yoaring at her'.

Mr Tryan sat in a pew near the pulpit with several other clergymen. He looked pale, and rubbed his hand over his face and pushed back his hair oftener than usual. Standing in the aisle close to him, and repeating the responses with edifying loudness, was Mr Budd, churchwarden and delegate, with a white staff in his hand and a backward bend of his small head and person, such as, I suppose, he considered suitable to a friend of sound religion. Conspicuous in the gallery, too, was the tall figure of Mr Dempster, whose professional avocations rarely allowed him to occupy his place at church.

'There's Dempster,' said Mrs Linnet to her daughter Mary, 'looking more respectable than usual, I declare. He's got a fine speech by heart to make to the Bishop, I'll answer for it. But he'll be pretty well sprinkled with snuff before service is over, and the Bishop won't be able to listen to him for sneezing, that's one comfort.'

At length the last stage in the long ceremony was over, the large assembly streamed warm and weary into the open afternoon sunshine, and the Bishop retired to the Parsonage, where, after honouring Mrs Crewe's collation, he was to give audience to the delegates and Mr Tryan on the great question of the evening lecture.

Between five and six o'clock the Parsonage was once more as quiet as usual under the shadow of its tall elms, and the only traces of the Bishop's recent presence there were the wheel marks on the gravel, and the long table with its garnished dishes awry, its damask sprinkled with crumbs, and its decanters without their stoppers. Mr Crewe was already calmly smoking his pipe in the opposite sitting room, and Janet was agreeing with Mrs Crewe that some of the blancmange would be a nice thing to take to Sally Martin, while the little old lady herself had a spoon in her hand ready to gather the crumbs into a plate, that she might scatter them on the gravel for the little birds.

Before that time, the Bishop's carriage had been seen driving through the High Street on its way to Lord Trufford's, where he was to dine. The question of the lecture was decided, then?

The nature of the decision may be gathered from the following conversation which took place in the bar of the Red Lion that evening.

'So you're done, eh, Dempster?' was Mr Pilgrim's observation, uttered with some gusto. He was not glad Mr Tryan had gained his point, but he was not sorry Dempster was disappointed.

'Done, sir? Not at all. It is what I anticipated. I knew we had nothing else to expect in these days, when the Church is infested by a set of men who are only fit to give out hymns from an empty cask, to tunes set by a journeyman cobbler. But I was not the less to exert myself in the cause of sound churchmanship for the good of the town. Any coward can fight a battle when he's sure of winning, but give me the man who has pluck to fight when he's sure of losing. That's my way, sir, and there are many victories worse than a defeat, as Mr Tryan shall learn to his cost.'

'He must be a poor shuperannyated sort of a bishop, that's my opinion,' said Mr Tomlinson, 'to go along with a sneaking Methodist like Tryan. And, for my part, I think we should be as well wi'out bishops, if they're no wiser than that. Where's the use o' havin' thousands a-year an' livin' in a pallis, if they don't stick to the Church?'

'No. There you're going out of your depth, Tomlinson,' said Mr Dempster. 'No one shall hear me say a word against episcopacy – it is a safeguard of the Church; we must have ranks and dignities there as well as everywhere else. No, sir! Episcopacy is a good thing; but it may happen that a bishop is not a good thing. Just as brandy is a good thing, though this particular brandy is British, and tastes like sugared rainwater caught down the chimney. Here, Ratcliffe, let me have something to drink, a little less like a decoction of sugar and soot.'

'*I* said nothing again' episcopacy,' returned Mr Tomlinson. 'I only said I thought we should do as well wi'out bishops; an' I'll say it again for the matter o' that. Bishops never brought any grist to my mill.'

'Do you know when the lectures are to begin?' said Mr Pilgrim.

'They are to *begin* on Sunday next,' said Mr Dempster, in a significant tone, 'but I think it will not take a long-sighted prophet to foresee the end of them. It strikes me Mr Tryan will be looking out for another curacy shortly.'

'He'll not get many Milby people to go and hear his lectures after a while, I'll bet a guinea,' observed Mr Budd. 'I know I'll not keep a single workman on my ground who either goes to the lecture himself or lets anybody belonging to him go.'

'Nor me nayther,' said Mr Tomlinson. 'No Tryanite shall touch a sack or drive a waggon o' mine, that you may depend on. An' I know more besides me as are o' the same mind.'

'Tryan has a good many friends in the town, though, and friends that are likely to stand by him too,' said Mr Pilgrim. 'I should say it would be as well to let him and his lectures alone. If he goes on preaching as he does, with such a constitution as his, he'll get a relaxed throat by-and-by, and you'll be rid of him without any trouble.'

'We'll not allow him to do himself that injury,' said Mr Dempster. 'Since his health is not good, we'll persuade him to try change of air. Depend upon it, he'll find the climate of Milby too hot for him.'

7

Mr Dempster did not stay long at the Red Lion that evening. He was summoned home to meet Mr Armstrong, a wealthy client, and as he was kept in consultation till a late hour, it happened that this was one of the nights on which Mr Dempster went to bed tolerably sober. Thus the day, which had been one of Janet's happiest, because it had been spent by her in helping her dear old friend Mrs Crewe, ended for her with unusual quietude; and as a bright sunset promises a fair morning, so a calm lying down is a good augury for a calm waking. Mr Dempster, on the Thursday morning, was in one of his best humours, and though perhaps some of the good humour might result from the prospect of a lucrative and exciting bit of business in Mr Armstrong's probable lawsuit, the greater part of it was doubtless due to those stirrings of the more kindly, healthy sap of human feeling, by which goodness tries to get the upper hand in us whenever it seems to have the slightest chance – on Sunday mornings, perhaps, when we are set free from the grinding hurry of the week, and take the little three-year-old on our knee at breakfast to share our egg and muffin; in moments of trouble, when death visits our roof or illness makes us dependent on the tending hand of a slighted wife; in quiet talks with an aged mother, of the days when we stood at her knee with our first picture-book, or wrote her loving letters from school. In the man whose childhood has known caresses there is always a fibre of memory that can be touched to gentle issues, and Mr Dempster, whom you have hitherto seen only as the orator of the Red Lion, and the drunken tyrant of a dreary midnight home, was the first-born darling son of a fair little mother. That mother was living still, and her own large black easy chair, where she sat knitting through the livelong day, was now set ready for her at the breakfast table, by her son's side, a sleek tortoiseshell cat acting as provisional incumbent.

'Good morning, Mamsey! why, you're looking as fresh as a daisy this morning. You're getting young again,' said Mr Dempster, looking up from his newspaper when the little old lady entered. A very little old lady she was, with a pale, scarcely wrinkled face, hair of that peculiar white which tells that the locks have once been blond, a natty pure white cap on her head, and a white shawl pinned over her shoulders. You saw at a glance that she had been a mignonne blonde, strangely unlike her tall, ugly, dingy-complexioned son; unlike her daughter-in-law, too, whose large-featured brunette beauty seemed always thrown into higher relief by the white presence of little Mamsey. The unlikeness between Janet and her mother-in-law went deeper than outline and complexion, and indeed there was little sympathy between them, for old Mrs Dempster had not yet learned to believe that her son, Robert, would have gone wrong if he had married the right woman – a meek woman like herself, who would have borne him children, and been a deft, orderly housekeeper. In spite of Janet's tenderness and attention to her, she had had little love for her daughter-in-law from the first, and had witnessed the sad growth of home misery through long years, always with a disposition to lay the blame on the wife rather than on the husband, and to reproach Mrs Raynor for encouraging her daughter's faults by a too exclusive sympathy. But old Mrs Dempster had that rare gift of silence and passivity which often supplies the absence of mental strength, and, whatever were her thoughts, she said no word to aggravate the domestic discord. Patient and mute, she sat at her knitting through many a scene of quarrel and anguish; resolutely she appeared unconscious of the sounds that reached her ears, and the facts she divined after she had retired to her bed; mutely she witnessed poor Janet's faults, only registering them as a balance of excuse on the side of her son. The hard, astute, domineering attorney was still that little old woman's pet, as he had been when she watched with triumphant pride his first tumbling effort to march alone across the nursery floor. 'See what a good son he is to me!' she often thought. 'Never gave me a harsh word. And so he might have been a good husband.'

Oh, it is piteous – that sorrow of aged women! In early youth, perhaps, they said to themselves, 'I shall be happy when I have a husband to love me best of all'; then, when the husband was too careless, 'My child will comfort me'; then, through the mother's watching and toil, 'My child will repay me all when it grows up'; and at last, after the long journey of years has been wearily travelled through, the mother's heart is weighed down by a heavier burthen, and no hope remains but the grave.

But this morning old Mrs Dempster sat down in her easy chair without any painful, suppressed remembrance of the preceding night.

'I declare Mammy looks younger than Mrs Crewe, who is only sixty-five,' said Janet. 'Mrs Crewe will come to see you today, Mammy, and tell you all about her troubles with the Bishop and the collation. She'll bring her knitting, and you'll have a regular gossip together.'

'The gossip will be all on one side, then, for Mrs Crewe gets so very deaf, I can't make her hear a word. And if I motion to her, she always understands me wrong.'

'Oh, she will have so much to tell you today, you will not want to speak yourself. You, who have patience to knit those wonderful counterpanes, Mammy, must not be impatient with dear Mrs Crewe. Good old lady! I can't bear her to think she's ever tiresome to people, and you know she's very ready to fancy herself in the way. I think she would like to shrink up to the size of a mouse, that she might run about and do people good without their noticing her.'

'It isn't patience I want, God knows; it's lungs to speak loud enough. But you'll be at home yourself, I suppose, this morning; and you can talk to her for me.'

'No, Mammy; I promised poor Mrs Lowme to go and sit with her. She's confined to her room, and both the Miss

Lowmes are out, so I'm going to read the newspaper to her and amuse her.'

'Couldn't you go another morning? As Mr Armstrong and that other gentleman are coming to dinner, I should think it would be better to stay at home. Can you trust Betty to see to everything? She's new to the place.'

'Oh, I couldn't disappoint Mrs Lowme; I promised her. Betty will do very well, no fear.'

Old Mrs Dempster was silent after this, and began to sip her tea. The breakfast went on without further conversation for some time, Mr Dempster being absorbed in the papers. At length, when he was running over the advertisements, his eye seemed to be caught by something that suggested a new thought to him. He presently thumped the table with an air of exultation, and said, turning to Janet, 'I've a capital idea, Gypsy!' (that was his name for his dark-eyed wife when he was in an extraordinarily good humour,) 'and you shall help me. It's just what you're up to.'

'What is it?' said Janet, her face beaming at the sound of the pet name, now heard so seldom. 'Anything to do with conveyancing?'

'It's a bit of fun worth a dozen fees – a plan for raising a laugh against Tryan and his gang of hypocrites.'

'What is it? Nothing that wants a needle and thread, I hope, else I must go and tease mother.'

'No, nothing sharper than your wit – except mine. I'll tell you what it is. We'll get up a programme of the Sunday evening lecture, like a playbill, you know – "Grand Performance of the celebrated Mountebank", and so on. We'll bring in the Tryanites – old Landor and the rest – in appropriate characters. Proctor shall print it, and we'll circulate it in the town. It will be a capital hit.'

'Bravo!' said Janet, clapping her hands. She would just then have pretended to like almost anything, in her pleasure at being appealed to by her husband, and she really did like to laugh at the Tryanites. 'We'll set about it directly, and sketch it out before you go to the office. I've got Tryan's sermons upstairs, but I don't think there's anything in them we can use. I've only just looked into them; they're not at all what I expected – dull, stupid things – nothing of the roaring fire-and-brimstone sort that I expected.'

'Roaring? No, Tryan's as soft as a sucking dove – one of your honey-mouthed hypocrites. Plenty of devil and malice in him, though, I could see that, while he was talking to the Bishop; but as smooth as a snake outside. He's beginning a single-handed fight with me, I can see – persuading my clients away from me. We shall see who will be the first to cry *peccavi*.[25] Milby will do better without Mr Tryan than without Robert Dempster, I fancy! and Milby shall never be flooded with cant as long as I can raise a breakwater against it. But now, get the breakfast things cleared away, and let us set about the playbill. Come, Mamsey, come and have a walk with me round the garden, and let us see how the cucumbers are getting on. I've never taken you round the garden for an age. Come, you don't want a bonnet. It's like walking in a greenhouse this morning.'

'But she will want a parasol,' said Janet. 'There's one on the stand against the garden door, Robert.'

The little old lady took her son's arm with placid pleasure. She could barely reach it so as to rest upon it, but he inclined a little towards her, and accommodated his heavy long-limbed steps to her feeble pace. The cat chose to sun herself too, and walked close beside them, with tail erect, rubbing her sleek sides against their legs, too well fed to be excited by the twittering birds. The garden was of the grassy, shady kind, often seen attached to old houses in provincial towns; the apple trees had had time to spread their branches very wide, the shrubs and hardy perennial plants had grown into a luxuriance that required constant trimming to prevent them from intruding on the space for walking. But the further end, which united with green fields, was open and sunny.

It was rather sad, and yet pretty, to see that little group passing out of the shadow into the sunshine, and out of the sunshine into the shadow again: sad, because this tenderness of the son for the mother was hardly more than a nucleus of healthy life in an organ hardening by disease, because the man who was linked in this way with an innocent past, had become callous in worldliness, fevered by sensuality, enslaved by chance impulses; pretty, because it showed how hard it is to kill the deep-down fibrous roots of human love and goodness – how the man from whom we make it our pride to shrink, has yet a close brotherhood with us through some of our most sacred feelings.

As they were returning to the house, Janet met them, and said, 'Now, Robert, the writing things are ready. I shall be clerk, and Mat Paine can copy it out after.'

Mammy once more deposited in her armchair, with her knitting in her hand, and the cat purring at her elbow, Janet seated herself at the table, while Mr Dempster placed himself near her, took out his snuffbox, and plentifully suffusing himself with the inspiring powder, began to dictate.

What he dictated, we shall see by-and-by.

The next day, Friday, at five o'clock by the sundial, the large bow-window of Mrs Jerome's parlour was open, and that lady herself was seated within its ample semicircle, having a table before her on which her best tea tray, her best china and her best urn rug had already been standing in readiness for half an hour. Mrs Jerome's best tea service was of delicate white fluted china, with gold sprigs upon it – as pretty a tea service as you need wish to see, and quite good enough for chimney ornaments; indeed, as the cups were without handles, most visitors who had the distinction of taking tea out of them, wished that such charming china had already been promoted to that honorary position. Mrs Jerome was like her china, handsome and old-fashioned. She was a buxom lady of sixty, in an elaborate lace cap fastened by a frill under her chin, a dark, well-curled front concealing her forehead, a snowy neckerchief exhibiting its ample folds as far as her waist, and a stiff grey silk gown. She had a clean damask napkin pinned before her to guard her dress during the process of tea making; her favourite geraniums in the bow-window were looking as healthy as she could desire; her own handsome portrait, painted when she was twenty years younger, was smiling down on her with agreeable flattery; and altogether she seemed to be in as peaceful and pleasant a position as a buxom, well-dressed elderly lady need desire. But, as in so many other cases, appearances were deceptive. Her mind was greatly perturbed and her temper ruffled by the fact that it was more than a quarter past five even by the losing timepiece, that it was half-past by her large gold watch, which she held in her hand as if she were counting the pulse of the afternoon, and that, by the kitchen clock, which she felt sure was not an hour too fast,

it had already struck six. The lapse of time was rendered the more unendurable to Mrs Jerome by her wonder that Mr Jerome could stay out in the garden with Lizzie in that thoughtless way, taking it so easily that teatime was long past, and that, after all the trouble of getting down the best tea things, Mr Tryan would not come.

This honour had been shown to Mr Tryan, not at all because Mrs Jerome had any high appreciation of his doctrine or of his exemplary activity as a pastor, but simply because he was a 'Church clergyman', and as such was regarded by her with the same sort of exceptional respect that a white woman who had married a native of the Society Islands might be supposed to feel towards a white-skinned visitor from the land of her youth. For Mrs Jerome had been reared a churchwoman, and having attained the age of thirty before she was married, had felt the greatest repugnance in the first instance to renouncing the religious forms in which she had been brought up. 'You know,' she said in confidence to her Church acquaintances, 'I wouldn't give no ear at all to Mr Jerome at fust, but after all, I begun to think as there was a many things worse nor goin' to chapel, an' you'd better do that nor not pay your way. Mr Jerome had a very pleasant manner with him, an' there was niver another as kept a gig, an' 'ud make a settlement on me like him, chapel or no chapel. It seemed very odd to me for a long while, the preachin' without book, an' the stannin' up to one long prayer, istid o' changin' your postur. But la! there's nothin' as you mayn't get used to i' time; you can al'ys sit down, you know, before the prayer's done. The ministers say pretty nigh the same things as the Church parsons, by what I could iver make out, an' we're out o' chapel i' the mornin' a deal sooner nor they're out o' church. An' as for pews, ourn's is a deal comfortabler nor any i' Milby Church.'

Mrs Jerome, you perceive, had not a keen susceptibility to shades of doctrine, and it is probable that, after listening to Dissenting eloquence for thirty years, she might safely have re-entered the Establishment without performing any spiritual quarantine. Her mind, apparently, was of that non-porous flinty character which is not in the least danger from surrounding damp. But on the question of getting start of the sun on the day's business, and clearing her conscience of the necessary sum of meals and the consequent 'washing up' as soon as possible, so that the family might be well in bed at nine, Mrs Jerome *was* susceptible; and the present lingering pace of things, united with Mr Jerome's unaccountable obliviousness, was not to be borne any longer. So she rang the bell for Sally.

'Goodness me, Sally! go into the garden an' see after your master. Tell him it's goin' on for six, an' Mr Tryan 'ull niver think o' comin' now, an' it's time we got tea over. An' he's lettin' Lizzie stain her frock, I expect, among them strawberry beds. Mek her come in this minute.'

No wonder Mr Jerome was tempted to linger in the garden, for though the house was pretty and well deserved its name, 'the White House', the tall damask roses that clustered over the porch being thrown into relief by rough stucco of the most brilliant white, yet the garden and orchards were Mr Jerome's glory, as well they might be, and there was nothing in which he had a more innocent pride – peace to a good man's memory! all his pride was innocent – than in conducting a hitherto uninitiated visitor over his grounds, and making him in some degree aware of the incomparable advantages possessed by the inhabitants of the White House in the matter of red-streaked apples, russets, northern greens (excellent for baking), swan-egg pears and early vegetables, to say nothing of flowering 'srubs', pink hawthorns, lavender bushes more than ever Mrs Jerome could use, and, in short, a superabundance of everything that a person retired from business could desire to possess himself or to share with his friends. The garden was one of those old-fashioned paradises which hardly exist any longer except as memories of our childhood: no finical separation between flower and kitchen garden there; no monotony of enjoyment for one sense to the exclusion of another, but a charming paradisiacal mingling of all that was pleasant to the eyes and good for food. The rich flower border running along every walk, with its endless succession of spring flowers, anemones, auriculas, wallflowers, sweet williams, campanulas, snapdragons and tigerlilies, had its taller beauties, such as moss and Provence roses, varied with espalier apple trees; the crimson of a carnation was carried out in the lurking crimson of the neighbouring strawberry beds; you gathered a moss rose one moment and a bunch of currants the next; you were in a delicious fluctuation between the scent of jasmine and the juice of gooseberries. Then what a high wall at one end, flanked by a summer house so lofty, that after ascending its long flight of steps you could see perfectly well there was no view worth looking at; what alcoves and garden seats in all directions; and along one side, what a hedge, tall, and firm, and unbroken, like a green wall!

It was near this hedge that Mr Jerome was standing when Sally found him. He had set down the basket of strawberries on the gravel, and had lifted up little Lizzie in his arms to look at a bird's nest. Lizzie peeped, and then looked at her grandpa with round blue eyes, and then peeped again.

'D'ye see it, Lizzie?' he whispered.

'Yes,' she whispered in return, putting her lips very near grandpa's face. At this moment Sally appeared.

'Eh, eh, Sally, what's the matter? Is Mr Tryan come?'

'No, sir, an' Missis says she's sure he won't come now, an' she wants you to come in an' hev tea. Dear heart, Miss Lizzie, you've stained your pinafore, an' I shouldn't wonder if it's gone through to your frock. There'll be fine work! Come alonk wi' me, do.'

'Nay, nay, nay, we've done no harm, we've done no harm, hev we, Lizzie? The washtub'll make all right again.'

Sally, regarding the washtub from a different point of view, looked sourly serious, and hurried away with Lizzie, who trotted submissively along, her little head in eclipse under a large nankin bonnet, while Mr Jerome followed leisurely with his full broad shoulders in rather a stooping posture, and his large good-natured features and white locks shaded by a broad-brimmed hat.

'Mr Jerome, I wonder at you,' said Mrs Jerome, in a tone of indignant remonstrance, evidently sustained by a deep sense of injury, as her husband opened the parlour door. 'When will you leave off invitin' people to meals an' not lettin' 'em know the time? I'll answer for't, you niver said a word to Mr Tryan as we should take tea at five o'clock. It's just like you!'

'Nay, nay, Susan,' answered the husband in a soothing tone, 'there's nothin' amiss. I told Mr Tryan as we took tea at five punctial; mayhap summat's a detainin' on him. He's a deal to do, an' to think on, remember.'

'Why, it's struck six i' the kitchen a'ready. It's nonsense to look for him comin' now. So you may's well ring for th' urn. Now Sally's got th' heater in the fire, we may's well hev th' urn in, though he doesn't come. I niver see'd the like o' you, Mr Jerome, for axin' people an' givin' me the trouble o' gettin' things down an' hevin' crumpets made, an' after all they don't come. I shall hev to wash every one o' these tea things myself, for there's no trustin' Sally – she'd break a fortin i' crockery i' no time!'

'But why will you give yourself sich trouble, Susan? Our everyday tea things would ha' done as well for Mr Tryan, an' they're a deal convenenter to hold.'

'Yes, that's just your way, Mr Jerome, you're al'ys a-findin' faut wi' my chany, because I bought it myself afore I was married. But let me tell you, I knowed how to choose chany if I didn't know how to choose a husband. An' where's Lizzie? You've niver left her i' the garden by herself, with her white frock on an' clean stockins?'

'Be easy, my dear Susan, be easy; Lizzie's come in wi' Sally. She's hevin' her pinafore took off, I'll be bound. Ah! there's Mr Tryan a-comin' through the gate.'

Mrs Jerome began hastily to adjust her damask napkin and the expression of her countenance for the reception of the clergyman, and Mr Jerome went out to meet his guest, whom he greeted outside the door.

'Mr Tryan, how do you do, Mr Tryan? Welcome to the White House! I'm glad to see you, sir – I'm glad to see you.'

If you had heard the tone of mingled good will, veneration, and condolence in which this greeting was uttered, even without seeing the face that completely harmonised with it, you would have no difficulty in inferring the ground notes of Mr Jerome's character. To a fine ear that tone said as plainly as possible, 'Whatever recommends itself to me, Thomas Jerome, as piety and goodness, shall have my love and honour. Ah, friends, this pleasant world is a sad one, too, isn't it? Let us help one another, let us help one another.' And it was entirely owing to this basis of character, not at all from any clear and precise doctrinal discrimination, that Mr Jerome had very early in life become a Dissenter. In his boyish days he had been thrown where Dissent seemed to have the balance of piety, purity and good works on its side, and to become a Dissenter seemed to him identical with choosing God instead of mammon. That race of Dissenters is extinct in these days, when opinion has got far ahead of feeling, and every chapel-going youth can fill our ears with the advantages of the Voluntary system,[26] the corruptions of a State Church, and the Scriptural evidence that the first Christians were Congregationalists. Mr Jerome knew nothing of this theoretic basis for Dissent, and in the utmost extent of his polemical discussion he had not gone further than to question whether a Christian man was bound in conscience to distinguish Christmas and Easter by any peculiar observance beyond the eating of mince pies and cheesecakes. It seemed to him that all seasons were alike good for thanking God, departing from evil and doing well, whereas it might be desirable to restrict the period for indulging in unwholesome forms of pastry. Mr Jerome's Dissent being of this simple, non-polemical kind, it is easy to understand that the report he heard of Mr Tryan as a good man and a powerful preacher, who was stirring the hearts of the people, had been enough to attract him to the Paddiford church, and that having felt himself more edified there than he had of late been under Mr Stickney's discourses at Salem, he had driven thither repeatedly in the Sunday afternoons, and had sought an opportunity of making Mr Tryan's acquaintance. The evening lecture was a subject of warm interest with him, and the opposition Mr Tryan met with gave that interest a strong tinge of partisanship, for there was a store of irascibility in Mr Jerome's nature which must find a vent somewhere, and in so kindly and upright a man could only find it in indignation against those whom he held to be enemies of truth and goodness. Mr Tryan had not hitherto been to the White House, but yesterday, meeting Mr Jerome in the street, he had at once accepted the invitation to tea, saying there was something he wished to talk about. He appeared worn and fatigued now, and after shaking hands with Mrs Jerome, threw himself into a chair and looked out on the pretty garden with an air of relief.

'What a nice place you have here, Mr Jerome! I've not seen anything so quiet and pretty since I came to Milby. On Paddiford Common, where I live, you know, the bushes are all sprinkled with soot, and there's never any quiet except in the dead of night.'

'Dear heart! dear heart! That's very bad – and for you, too, as hev to study. Wouldn't it be better for you to be somewhere more out i' the country like?'

'Oh no! I should lose so much time in going to and fro, and besides I like to be *among* the people. I've no face to go and preach resignation to those poor things in their smoky air and comfortless homes, when I come straight from every luxury myself. There are many things quite lawful for other men, which a clergyman must forego if he would do any good in a manufacturing population like this.'

Here the preparations for tea were crowned by the simultaneous appearance of Lizzie and the crumpet. It is a pretty surprise, when one visits an elderly couple, to see a little figure enter in a white frock with a blond head as smooth as satin, round blue eyes, and a cheek like an apple blossom. A toddling little girl is a centre of common feeling which makes the most dissimilar people understand each other, and Mr Tryan looked at Lizzie with that quiet pleasure which is always genuine.

'Here we are, here we are!' said proud Grandpapa. 'You didn't think we'd got such a little gell as this, did you, Mr

Tryan? Why, it seems but th' other day since her mother was just such another. This is our little Lizzie, this is. Come an' shake hands wi' Mr Tryan, Lizzie; come.'

Lizzie advanced without hesitation, and put out one hand, while she fingered her coral necklace with the other, and looked up into Mr Tryan's face with a reconnoitring gaze. He stroked the satin head, and said in his gentlest voice, 'How do you do, Lizzie? will you give me a kiss?' She put up her little bud of a mouth, and then retreating a little and glancing down at her frock, said, 'Dit id my noo fock. I put it on 'tod you wad toming. Tally taid you wouldn't 'ook at it.'

'Hush, hush, Lizzie, little gells must be seen and not heard,' said Mrs Jerome; while Grandpapa, winking significantly, and looking radiant with delight at Lizzie's extraordinary promise of cleverness, set her up on her high cane chair by the side of Grandma, who lost no time in shielding the beauties of the new frock with a napkin.

'Well now, Mr Tryan,' said Mr Jerome, in a very serious tone, when tea had been distributed, 'let me hear how you're a-goin' on about the lectur. When I was i' the town yisterday, I heared as there was pessecutin' schemes a-bein' laid again' you. I fear me those raskills 'll mek things very onpleasant to you.'

'I've no doubt they will attempt it; indeed, I quite expect there will be a regular mob got up on Sunday evening, as there was when the delegates returned, on purpose to annoy me and the congregation on our way to church.'

'Ah, they're capible o' anything, such men as Dempster an' Budd, an' Tomlinson backs 'em wi' money, though he can't wi' brains. Howiver, Dempster's lost one client by his wicked doins, an' I'm deceived if he won't lose more nor one. I little thought, Mr Tryan, when I put my affairs into his hands

twenty 'ear ago this Michaelmas, as he was to turn out a pes-
secutor o' religion. I niver lighted on a cliverer, promisiner
young man nor he was then. They talked of his bein' fond of a
extry glass now an' then, but niver nothin' like what he's come
to since. An' it's headpiece you must look for in a lawyer, Mr
Tryan, it's headpiece. His wife, too, was al'ys an uncommon
favourite o' mine – poor thing! I hear sad stories about her
now. But she's druv to it, she's druv to it, Mr Tryan. A tender-
hearted woman to the poor, she is, as iver lived, an' as pretty-
spoken a woman as you need wish to talk to. Yes! I'd al'ys a
likin' for Dempster an' his wife, spite o' iverything. But as soon
as iver I heared o' that dilegate business, I says, says I, that man
shall hev no more to do wi' my affairs. It may put me t' inconvenience, but I'll encourage no man as pessecutes religion.'

'He is evidently the brain and hand of the persecution,'
said Mr Tryan. 'There may be a strong feeling against me in
a large number of the inhabitants – it must be so from the
great ignorance of spiritual things in this place. But I fancy
there would have been no formal opposition to the lecture,
if Dempster had not planned it. I am not myself the least
alarmed at anything he can do; he will find I am not to be
cowed or driven away by insult or personal danger. God has
sent me to this place, and, by His blessing, I'll not shrink from
anything I may have to encounter in doing His work among
the people. But I feel it right to call on all those who know the
value of the Gospel, to stand by me publicly. I think – and Mr
Landor agrees with me – that it will be well for my friends to
proceed with me in a body to the church on Sunday evening.
Dempster, you know, has pretended that almost all the
respectable inhabitants are opposed to the lecture. Now, I wish
that falsehood to be visibly contradicted. What do you think
of the plan? I have today been to see several of my friends,

who will make a point of being there to accompany me, and will communicate with others on the subject.'

'I'll mek one, Mr Tryan, I'll mek one. You shall not be wantin' in any support as I can give. Before you come to it, sir, Milby was a dead an' dark place; you are the fust man i' the Church to my knowledge as has brought the word o' God home to the people, an' I'll stan' by you, sir, I'll stan' by you. I'm a Dissenter, Mr Tryan; I've been a Dissenter ever sin' I was fifteen 'ear old; but show me good i' the Church, an' I'm a churchman too. When I was a boy I lived at Tilston; you mayn't know the place; the best part o' the land there belonged to Squire Sandeman; he'd a club foot, had Squire Sandeman – lost a deal o' money by canal shares. Well, sir, as I was sayin', I lived at Tilston, an' the rector there was a terrible drinkin', fox-huntin' man; you niver see'd such a parish i' your time for wickedness; Milby's nothin' to it. Well, sir, my father was a workin' man, an' couldn't afford to gi' me ony eddication, so I went to a night school as was kep by a Dissenter, one Jacob Wright, an' it was from that man, sir, as I got my little schoolin' an' my knowledge o' religion. I went to chapel wi' Jacob – he was a good man was Jacob – an' to chapel I've been iver since. But I'm no enemy o' the Church, sir, when the Church brings light to the ignorant and the sinful, an' that's what you're a-doin', Mr Tryan. Yes, sir, I'll stan' by you. I'll go to church wi' you o' Sunday evenin'.'

'You'd far better stay at home, Mr Jerome, if I may give my opinion,' interposed Mrs Jerome. 'It's not as I hevn't ivery respect for you, Mr Tryan, but Mr Jerome 'ull do you no good by his interferin'. Dissenters are not at all looked on i' Milby, an' he's as nervous as iver he can be; he'll come back as ill as ill, an' niver let me hev a wink o' sleep all night.'

Mrs Jerome had been frightened at the mention of a mob, and her retrospective regard for the religious communion of her youth by no means inspired her with the temper of a martyr. Her husband looked at her with an expression of tender and grieved remonstrance, which might have been that of the patient patriarch on the memorable occasion when he rebuked his wife.

'Susan, Susan, let me beg on you not to oppose me, and put stumblin'-blocks i' the way o' doing' what's right. I can't give up my conscience, let me give up what else I may.'

'Perhaps,' said Mr Tryan, feeling slightly uncomfortable, 'since you are not very strong, my dear sir, it will be well, as Mrs Jerome suggests, that you should not run the risk of any excitement.'

'Say no more, Mr Tryan. I'll stan' by you, sir. It's my duty. It's the cause o' God, sir; it's the cause o' God.'

Mr Tryan obeyed his impulse of admiration and gratitude, and put out his hand to the white-haired old man, saying, 'Thank you, Mr Jerome, thank you.'

Mr Jerome grasped the proffered hand in silence, and then threw himself back in his chair, casting a regretful look at his wife, which seemed to say, 'Why don't you feel with me, Susan?'

The sympathy of this simple-minded old man was more precious to Mr Tryan than any mere onlooker could have imagined. To persons possessing a great deal of that facile psychology which prejudges individuals by means of formulae, and casts them, without further trouble, into duly lettered pigeonholes, the Evangelical curate might seem to be doing simply what all other men like to do – carrying out objects which were identified not only with his theory, which is but a kind of secondary egoism, but also with the primary egoism of his feelings. Opposition may become sweet to a man when he has christened it persecution: a self-obtrusive, over-hasty reformer complacently disclaiming all merit, while his friends call him a martyr, has not in reality a career the most arduous to the fleshly mind. But Mr Tryan was not cast in the mould of the gratuitous martyr. With a power of persistence which had been often blamed as obstinacy, he had an acute sensibility to the very hatred or ridicule he did not flinch from provoking. Every form of disapproval jarred him painfully; and, though he fronted his opponents manfully, and often with considerable warmth of temper, he had no pugnacious pleasure in the contest. It was one of the weaknesses of his nature to be too keenly alive to every harsh wind of opinion; to wince under the frowns of the foolish; to be irritated by the injustice of those who could not possibly have the elements indispensable for judging him rightly; and with all this acute sensibility to blame, this dependence on sympathy, he had for years been constrained into a position of antagonism. No wonder, then, that good old Mr Jerome's cordial words were balm to him. He had often been thankful to an old woman for saying 'God bless you'; to a little child for smiling at him; to a dog for submitting to be patted by him.

Tea being over by this time, Mr Tryan proposed a walk in the garden as a means of dissipating all recollection of the recent conjugal dissidence. Little Lizzie's appeal, 'Me go, Gandpa!' could not be rejected, so she was duly bonneted and pinafored, and then they turned out into the evening sunshine. Not Mrs Jerome, however; she had a deeply meditated plan of retiring *ad interim* to the kitchen and washing up the best tea things, as a mode of getting forward with the sadly retarded business of the day.

'This way, Mr Tryan, this way,' said the old gentleman; 'I must take you to my pastur fust, an' show you our cow – the best milker i' the county. An' see here at these backbuildins, how convenent the dairy is; I planned it ivery bit myself. An' here I've got my little carpenter's shop an' my blacksmith's shop; I do no end o' jobs here myself. I niver could bear to be idle, Mr Tryan; I must al'ys be at somethin' or other. It was time for me to lay by business an mek room for younger folks. I'd got money enough, wi' only one daughter to leave it to, an' I says to myself, says I, it's time to leave off moitherin' myself wi' this world so much, an' give more time to thinkin' of another. But there's a many hours atween getting up an' lyin' down, an' thoughts are no cumber; you can move about wi' a good many on 'em in your head. See, here's the pastur.'

A very pretty pasture it was, where the large-spotted short-horned cow quietly chewed the cud as she lay and looked sleepily at her admirers – a daintily trimmed hedge all round, dotted here and there with a mountain ash or a cherry tree.

'I've a good bit more land besides this, worth your while to look at, but mayhap it's further nor you'd like to walk now. Bless you! I've welly an' acre o' potato-ground yonders; I've a good big family to supply, you know.' (Here Mr Jerome winked and smiled significantly.) 'An' that puts me i' mind, Mr Tryan, o' summat I wanted to say to you. Clergymen like you, I know, see a deal more poverty an' that, than other folks, an' hev a many claims on 'em more nor they can well meet, an' if you'll mek use o' my purse any time, or let me know where I can be o' any help, I'll tek it very kind on you.'

'Thank you, Mr Jerome, I will do so, I promise you. I saw a sad case yesterday; a collier – a fine broad-chested fellow about thirty – was killed by the falling of a wall in the Paddiford colliery. I was in one of the cottages near, when they brought him home on a door, and the shriek of the wife has been ringing in my ears ever since. There are three little children. Happily the woman has her loom, so she will be able to keep out of the workhouse, but she looks very delicate.'

'Give me her name, Mr Tryan,' said Mr Jerome, drawing out his pocketbook. 'I'll call an' see her.'

Deep was the fountain of pity in the good old man's heart! He often ate his dinner stintingly, oppressed by the thought that there were men, women and children with no dinner to sit down to, and would relieve his mind by going out in the afternoon to look for some need that he could supply, some honest struggle in which he could lend a helping hand. That any living being should want, was his chief sorrow; that any rational being should waste, was the next. Sally, indeed, having been scolded by master for a too lavish use of sticks in lighting the kitchen fire, and various instances of recklessness with regard to candle ends, considered him 'as mean as anythink', but he had as kindly a warmth as the morning sunlight, and, like the sunlight, his goodness shone on all that came in his way, from the saucy rosy-cheeked lad whom he delighted to make happy with a Christmas box, to the pallid sufferers up dim entries, languishing under the tardy death of want and misery.

It was very pleasant to Mr Tryan to listen to the simple chat of the old man – to walk in the shade of the incomparable orchard, and hear the story of the crops yielded by the red-streaked apple tree, and the quite embarrassing plentifulness of the summer pears – to drink in the sweet evening breath of the garden, as they sat in the alcove – and so, for a short interval, to feel the strain of his pastoral task relaxed.

Perhaps he felt the return to that task through the dusty roads all the more painfully, perhaps something in that quiet shady home had reminded him of the time before he had taken on him the yoke of self-denial. The strongest heart will faint sometimes under the feeling that enemies are bitter, and that friends only know half its sorrows. The most resolute soul will now and then cast back a yearning look in treading the rough mountain path, away from the greensward and laughing voices of the valley. However it was, in the nine o'clock twilight that evening, when Mr Tryan had entered his small study and turned the key in the door, he threw himself into the chair before his writing table, and, heedless of the papers there, leaned his face low on his hand, and moaned heavily.

It is apt to be so in this life, I think. While we are coldly discussing a man's career, sneering at his mistakes, blaming his rashness and labelling his opinions – 'he is Evangelical and narrow', or 'Latitudinarian and Pantheistic'[27] or 'Anglican and supercilious' – that man, in his solitude, is perhaps shedding hot tears because his sacrifice is a hard one, because strength and patience are failing him to speak the difficult word, and do the difficult deed.

9

Mr Tryan showed no such symptoms of weakness on the critical Sunday. He unhesitatingly rejected the suggestion that he should be taken to church in Mr Landor's carriage – a proposition which that gentleman made as an amendment on the original plan, when the rumours of meditated insult became alarming. Mr Tryan declared he would have no precautions taken, but would simply trust in God and his good cause. Some of his more timid friends thought this conduct rather defiant than wise, and reflecting that a mob has great talents for impromptu, and that legal redress is imperfect satisfaction for having one's head broken with a brickbat, were beginning to question their consciences very closely as to whether it was not a duty they owed to their families to stay at home on Sunday evening. These timorous persons, however, were in a small minority, and the generality of Mr Tryan's friends and hearers rather exulted in an opportunity of braving insult for the sake of a preacher to whom they were attached on personal as well as doctrinal grounds. Miss Pratt spoke of Cranmer, Ridley and Latimer,[28] and observed that the present crisis afforded an occasion for emulating their heroism even in these degenerate times, while less highly instructed persons, whose memories were not well stored with precedents, simply expressed their determination, as Mr Jerome had done, to 'stan' by' the preacher and his cause, believing it to be the 'cause of God'.

On Sunday evening, then, at a quarter past six, Mr Tryan, setting out from Mr Landor's with a party of his friends who had assembled there, was soon joined by two other groups from Mr Pratt's and Mr Dunn's, and stray persons on their way to church naturally falling into rank behind this leading file, by the time they reached the entrance of Orchard Street, Mr Tryan's friends formed a considerable procession, walking three or four abreast. It was in Orchard Street, and towards the church gates, that the chief crowd was collected, and at Mr Dempster's drawing-room window, on the upper floor, a more select assembly of anti-Tryanites were gathered to witness the entertaining spectacle of the Tryanites walking to church amidst the jeers and hootings of the crowd.

To prompt the popular wit with appropriate sobriquets, numerous copies of Mr Dempster's playbill were posted on the walls, in suitably large and emphatic type. As it is possible that the most industrious collector of mural literature may not have been fortunate enough to possess himself of this production, which ought by all means to be preserved amongst the materials of our provincial religious history, I subjoin a faithful copy.

GRAND ENTERTAINMENT!!!
To be given at Milby on Sunday evening next, by the
FAMOUS COMEDIAN, TRY-IT-ON!
And his first-rate company, including not only an
UNPARALLELED CAST FOR COMEDY!
But a Large Collection of *reclaimed and converted Animals*:
Among the rest
A Bear, who used to *dance!*
A Parrot, once given to swearing!!
A Polygamous Pig!!!
and
A Monkey who used to *catch fleas on a Sunday!!!!*
Together with a
Pair of *regenerated* LINNETS!
With an entirely new song, and *plumage*.
MR TRY-IT-ON
Will first pass through the streets, in procession, with his
unrivalled Company warranted to have their *eyes turned up higher*,
and the *corners of their mouths turned down lower*, than any other
company of Mountebanks in this circuit!
AFTER WHICH
The Theatre will be opened, and the entertainment will
commence at HALF-PAST SIX
When will be presented
A piece, never before performed on any stage, entitled
THE WOLF IN SHEEP'S CLOTHING;

or

The Methodist in a Mask

Mr Boanerges Soft Sawder....................Mr Try-it-on.
Old Ten-per-cent Godly.........................Mr Gander.
Dr Feedemup.......................................Mr Tonic.
Mr Lime-Twig Lady-winner..................Mr Try-it-on.
Miss Piety Bait-the-hook........................Miss Tonic.
Angelica............................Miss Seraphina Tonic.

After which
A miscellaneous Musical Interlude, commencing with
The *Lamentations of Jerom-iah!*
In nasal recitative.
To be followed by
The favourite Cackling Quartette,
by Two Hen-birds who are *no chickens!*
The well-known counter-tenor, Mr Done, and a *Gander*,
lineally descended from the Goose that laid golden eggs!
To conclude with a
Grand Chorus by the
Entire Orchestra of Converted Animals!!
But owing to the unavoidable absence (from illness) of the
Bulldog, who has left off fighting, Mr Tonic has kindly
undertaken, at a moment's notice, to supply the '*bark!*'
The whole to conclude with a
Screaming Farce of
THE PULPIT SNATCHER

Mr Saintly Smooth-face........................Mr Try-it-on!
Mr Worming Sneaker..........................Mr Try-it-on!!
Mr All-grace No-works.......................Mr Try-it-on!!!
Mr Elect-and-Chosen Apewell.............Mr Try-it-on!!!!
Mr Malevolent Prayerful...................Mr Try-it-on!!!!!

Mr Foist-himself Everywhere............Mʀ Tʀʏ-ɪᴛ-ᴏɴ!!!!!!
Mr Flout-the-aged Upstart...............Mʀ Tʀʏ-ɪᴛ-ᴏɴ!!!!!!!
Admission Free. *A Collection* will be made at the Doors.
Vivat Rex![29]

This satire, though it presents the keenest edge of Milby wit, does not strike you as lacerating, I imagine. But hatred is like fire – it makes even light rubbish deadly. And Mr Dempster's sarcasms were not merely visible on the walls, they were re-flected in the derisive glances, and audible in the jeering voices of the crowd. Through this pelting shower of nicknames and bad puns, with an *ad libitum* accompaniment of groans, howls, hisses and hee-haws, but of no heavier missiles, Mr Tryan walked pale and composed, giving his arm to old Mr Landor, whose step was feeble. On the other side of him was Mr Jerome, who still walked firmly, though his shoulders were slightly bowed.

Outwardly Mr Tryan was composed, but inwardly he was suffering acutely from these tones of hatred and scorn. How-ever strong his consciousness of right, he found it no stronger armour against such weapons as derisive glances and virulent words, than against stones and clubs: his conscience was in repose, but his sensibility was bruised.

Once more only did the Evangelical curate pass up Orchard Street followed by a train of friends; once more only was there a crowd assembled to witness his entrance through the church gates. But that second time no voice was heard above a whisper, and the whispers were words of sorrow and blessing. That second time, Janet Dempster was not looking on in scorn and merriment; her eyes were worn with grief and watching, and she was following her beloved friend and pastor to the grave.

10

History, we know, is apt to repeat herself, and to foist very old incidents upon us with only a slight change of costume. From the time of Xerxes downwards, we have seen generals playing the braggadocio at the outset of their campaigns, and conquering the enemy with the greatest ease in after-dinner speeches. But events are apt to be in disgusting discrepancy with the anticipations of the most ingenious tacticians; the difficulties of the expedition are ridiculously at variance with able calculations; the enemy has the impudence not to fall into confusion as had been reasonably expected of him; the mind of the gallant general begins to be distracted by news of intrigues against him at home, and, notwithstanding the handsome compliments he paid to Providence as his undoubted patron before setting out, there seems every probability that the *Te Deums* will be all on the other side.

So it fell out with Mr Dempster in his memorable campaign against the Tryanites. After all the premature triumph of the return from Elmstoke, the battle of the Evening Lecture had been lost, the enemy was in possession of the field, and the utmost hope remaining was, that by a harassing guerilla warfare he might be driven to evacuate the country.

For some time this sort of warfare was kept up with considerable spirit. The shafts of Milby ridicule were made more formidable by being poisoned with calumny, and very ugly stories, narrated with circumstantial minuteness, were soon in circulation concerning Mr Tryan and his hearers, from which stories it was plainly deducible that Evangelicalism led by a necessary consequence to hypocritical indulgence in vice. Some old friendships were broken asunder, and there were near relations who felt that religious differences, unmitigated by any prospect of a legacy, were a sufficient ground for exhibiting their family antipathy. Mr Budd harangued his workmen, and threatened them with dismissal if they or their families were known to attend the evening lecture, and Mr Tomlinson, on discovering that his foreman was a rank Tryanite, blustered to a great extent, and would have cashiered that valuable functionary on the spot, if such a retributive procedure had not been inconvenient.

On the whole, however, at the end of a few months, the balance of substantial loss was on the side of the anti-Tryanites. Mr Pratt, indeed, had lost a patient or two besides Mr Dempster's family, but as it was evident that Evangelicalism had not dried up the stream of his anecdote, or in the least altered his view of any lady's constitution, it is probable that a change accompanied by so few outward and visible signs, was rather the pretext than the ground of his dismissal in those additional cases. Mr Dunn was threatened with the loss of several good customers, Mrs Phipps and Mrs Lowme having set the example of ordering him to send in his bill; and the draper began to look forward to his next stocktaking with an anxiety which was but slightly mitigated by the parallel his wife suggested between his own case and that of Shadrach, Meshech and Abednego,[30] who were thrust into a burning fiery furnace. For, as he observed to her the next morning, with that perspicacity which belongs to the period of shaving, whereas their deliverance consisted in the fact that their linen and woollen goods were not consumed, his own deliverance lay in precisely the opposite result. But convenience, that admirable branch system from the main line of self-interest, makes us all fellow helpers in spite of adverse resolutions. It is probable that no speculative or theological hatred would be ultimately strong enough to resist the persuasive power of convenience: that a Latitudinarian baker, whose bread was honourably free from alum, would command the custom of any dyspeptic Puseyite; that an Arminian with the toothache would prefer a skilful Calvinistic dentist to a bungler staunch against the doctrines of Election and Final Perseverance, who would be likely to break the tooth in his head; and that a Plymouth Brother, who had a well-furnished grocery shop in a favourable vicinage, would occasionally have the pleasure of furnishing sugar or vinegar to orthodox families that found themselves unexpectedly 'out of' those indispensable commodities.[31] In this persuasive power of convenience lay Mr Dunn's ultimate security from martyrdom. His drapery was the best in Milby; the comfortable use and wont of procuring satisfactory articles at a moment's notice proved too strong for anti-Tryanite zeal; and the draper could soon look forward to his next stocktaking without the support of a Scriptural parallel.

On the other hand, Mr Dempster had lost his excellent client, Mr Jerome – a loss which galled him out of proportion to the mere monetary deficit it represented. The attorney loved money, but he loved power still better. He had always been proud of having early won the confidence of a conventicle-goer, and of being able to 'turn the prop of Salem round his thumb'. Like most other men, too, he had a certain kindness towards those who had employed him when he was only starting in life, and just as we do not like to part with an old weather-glass from our study, or a two-feet ruler that we have carried in our pocket ever since we began business, so Mr Dempster did not like having to erase his old client's name from the accustomed drawer in the bureau. Our habitual life is like a wall hung with pictures, which has been shone on by the suns of many years: take one of the pictures away, and it leaves a definite blank space, to which our eyes can never turn without a sensation of discomfort. Nay, the involuntary loss of any familiar object almost always brings a chill as from an evil omen; it seems to be the first finger-shadow of advancing death.

From all these causes combined, Mr Dempster could never think of his lost client without strong irritation, and the very sight of Mr Jerome passing in the street was wormwood to him.

One day, when the old gentleman was coming up Orchard Street on his roan mare, shaking the bridle, and tickling her flank with the whip as usual, though there was a perfect mutual understanding that she was not to quicken her pace, Janet happened to be on her own doorstep, and he could not resist the temptation of stopping to speak to that 'nice little woman', as he always called her, though she was taller than all the rest of his feminine acquaintances. Janet, in spite of her disposition to take her husband's part in all public matters, could bear no malice against her old friend; so they shook hands.

'Well, Mrs Dempster, I'm sorry to my heart not to see you sometimes, that I am,' said Mr Jerome, in a plaintive tone. 'But if you've got any poor people as wants help, and you know's deservin', send 'em to me, send 'em to me, just the same.'

'Thank you, Mr Jerome, that I will. Goodbye.'

Janet made the interview as short as she could, but it was not short enough to escape the observation of her husband, who, as she feared, was on his midday return from his office at the other end of the street, and this offence of hers, in speaking to Mr Jerome, was the frequently recurring theme of Mr Dempster's objurgatory domestic eloquence.

Associating the loss of his old client with Mr Tryan's influence, Dempster began to know more distinctly why he hated the obnoxious curate. But a passionate hate, as well as a passionate love, demands some leisure and mental freedom. Persecution and revenge, like courtship and toadyism, will not prosper without a considerable expenditure of time and ingenuity, and these are not to spare with a man whose law business and liver are both beginning to show unpleasant symptoms. Such was the disagreeable turn affairs were taking with Mr Dempster, and, like the general distracted by home intrigues, he was too much harassed himself to lay ingenious plans for harassing the enemy.

Meanwhile, the evening lecture drew larger and larger congregations; not perhaps attracting many from that select aristocratic circle in which the Lowmes and Pittmans were predominant, but winning the larger proportion of Mr Crewe's morning and afternoon hearers, and thinning Mr Stickney's evening audiences at Salem. Evangelicalism was making its way in Milby, and gradually diffusing its subtle odour into chambers that were bolted and barred against it. The movement, like all other religious 'revivals', had a mixed effect. Religious ideas have the fate of melodies, which, once set afloat in the world, are taken up by all sorts of instruments, some of them woefully coarse, feeble, or out of tune, until people are in danger of crying out that the melody itself is detestable. It may be that some of Mr Tryan's hearers had gained a religious vocabulary rather than religious experience; that here and there a weaver's wife, who, a few months before, had been simply a silly slattern, was converted into that more complex nuisance, a silly and sanctimonious slattern; that the old Adam, with the pertinacity of middle age, continued to tell fibs behind the counter, notwithstanding the new Adam's addiction to Bible reading and family prayer; that the children in the Paddiford Sunday school had their memories crammed with phrases about the blood of cleansing, imputed righteousness and justification by faith alone, which an experience lying principally in chuck-farthing, hopscotch, parental slappings, and longings after unattainable lollipop, served rather to darken than to illustrate; and that at Milby, in those distant days, as in all other times and places where the mental atmosphere is changing, and men are inhaling the stimulus of new ideas, folly often mistook itself for wisdom, ignorance gave itself airs of knowledge, and selfishness, turning its eyes upward, called itself religion.

Nevertheless, Evangelicalism had brought into palpable existence and operation in Milby society that idea of duty, that recognition of something to be lived for beyond the mere satisfaction of self, which is to the moral life what the addition of a great central ganglion is to animal life. No man can begin to mould himself on a faith or an idea without rising to a higher order of experience: a principle of subordination, of self-mastery, has been introduced into his nature; he is no longer a mere bundle of impressions, desires and impulses. Whatever might be the weaknesses of the ladies who pruned the luxuriance of their lace and ribbons, cut out garments for the poor, distributed tracts, quoted Scripture and defined the true Gospel, they had learned this – that there was a divine work to be done in life, a rule of goodness higher than the opinion of their neighbours, and if the notion of a heaven in reserve for themselves was a little too prominent, yet the theory of fitness for that heaven consisted in purity of heart, in Christ-like compassion, in the subduing of selfish desires. They might give the name of piety to much that was only puritanic egoism; they might call many things sin that were not sin; but they had at least the feeling that sin was to be avoided and resisted, and colour-blindness, which may mistake drab for scarlet, is better than total blindness, which sees no distinction of colour at all. Miss Rebecca Linnet, in quiet attire, with a somewhat excessive solemnity of countenance, teaching at the Sunday school, visiting the poor and striving after a standard of purity and goodness, had surely more moral loveliness than in those flaunting peony-days, when she had no other model than the costumes of the heroines in the circulating library. Miss Eliza Pratt, listening in rapt attention to Mr Tryan's evening lecture, no doubt found Evangelical channels for vanity and egoism, but she was clearly in moral advance of Miss Phipps giggling under her feathers at old Mr Crewe's peculiarities of enunciation. And even elderly fathers and mothers, with minds, like Mrs Linnet's, too tough to imbibe much doctrine, were the better for having their hearts inclined towards the new preacher as a messenger from God. They became ashamed, perhaps, of their evil tempers, ashamed of their worldliness, ashamed of their trivial, futile past. The first condition of human goodness is something to love; the second, something to reverence. And this latter precious gift was brought to Milby by Mr Tryan and Evangelicalism.

Yes, the movement was good, though it had that mixture of folly and evil which often makes what is good an offence to feeble and fastidious minds, who want human actions and characters riddled through the sieve of their own ideas, before they can accord their sympathy or admiration. Such minds, I daresay, would have found Mr Tryan's character very much in need of that riddling process. The blessed work of helping the world forward, happily does not wait to be done by perfect men; and I should imagine that neither Luther nor John Bunyan, for example, would have satisfied the modern demand for an ideal hero, who believes nothing but what is true, feels nothing but what is exalted, and does nothing but what is graceful. The real heroes, of God's making, are quite different: they have their natural heritage of love and conscience which they drew in with their mother's milk; they know one or two of those deep spiritual truths which are only to be won by long wrestling with their own sins and their own sorrows; they have earned faith and strength so far as they have done genuine work; but the rest is dry barren theory, blank prejudice, vague hearsay. Their insight is blended with mere opinion; their sympathy is perhaps confined in narrow conduits of doctrine, instead of flowing forth with the freedom of a stream that blesses every weed in its course; obstinacy or self-assertion will often interfuse itself with their grandest impulses; and their very deeds of self-sacrifice are sometimes only the rebound of a passionate egoism. So it was with Mr Tryan: and any one looking at him with the bird's-eye glance of a critic might perhaps say that he made the mistake of identifying Christianity with a too narrow doctrinal system; that he saw God's work too exclusively in antagonism to the world, the flesh and the devil; that his intellectual culture was too limited – and so on, making Mr Tryan the text for a wise discourse on the characteristics of the Evangelical school in his day.

But I am not poised at that lofty height. I am on the level and in the press with him, as he struggles his way along the stony road, through the crowd of unloving fellow men. He is stumbling, perhaps; his heart now beats fast with dread, now heavily with anguish; his eyes are sometimes dim with tears, which he makes haste to dash away; he pushes manfully on, with fluctuating faith and courage, with a sensitive failing body; at last he falls, the struggle is ended, and the crowd closes over the space he has left.

'One of the Evangelical clergy, a disciple of Venn,'[32] says the critic from his bird's-eye station. 'Not a remarkable specimen;

the anatomy and habits of his species have been determined long ago.'

Yet surely, surely the only true knowledge of our fellow man is that which enables us to feel with him – which gives us a fine ear for the heart-pulses that are beating under the mere clothes of circumstance and opinion. Our subtlest analysis of schools and sects must miss the essential truth, unless it be lit up by the love that sees in all forms of human thought and work, the life and death struggles of separate human beings.

11

Mr Tryan's most unfriendly observers were obliged to admit that he gave himself no rest. Three sermons on Sunday, a nightschool for young men on Tuesday, a cottage lecture on Thursday, addresses to schoolteachers, and catechising of schoolchildren, with pastoral visits, multiplying as his influence extended beyond his own district of Paddiford Common, would have been enough to tax severely the powers of a much stronger man. Mr Pratt remonstrated with him on his imprudence, but could not prevail on him so far to economise time and strength as to keep a horse. On some ground or other, which his friends found difficult to explain to themselves, Mr Tryan seemed bent on wearing himself out. His enemies were at no loss to account for such a course. The Evangelical curate's selfishness was clearly of too bad a kind to exhibit itself after the ordinary manner of a sound, respectable selfishness. 'He wants to get the reputation of a saint,' said one; 'He's eaten up with spiritual pride,' said another; 'He's got his eye on some fine living, and wants to creep up the Bishop's sleeve,' said a third.

Mr Stickney, of Salem, who considered all voluntary discomfort as a remnant of the legal spirit, pronounced a severe condemnation on this self-neglect, and expressed his fear that Mr Tryan was still far from having attained true Christian liberty. Good Mr Jerome eagerly seized this doctrinal view of the subject as a means of enforcing the suggestions of his own benevolence, and one cloudy afternoon, in the end of November, he mounted his roan mare with the determination of riding to Paddiford and 'arguying' the point with Mr Tryan.

The old gentleman's face looked very mournful as he rode along the dismal Paddiford lanes, between rows of grimy houses, darkened with handlooms, while the black dust was whirled about him by the cold November wind. He was thinking of the object which had brought him on this afternoon ride, and his thoughts, according to his habit when alone, found vent every now and then in audible speech. It seemed to him, as his eyes rested on this scene of Mr Tryan's labours, that he could understand the clergyman's self-privation without resorting to Mr Stickney's theory of defective spiritual enlightenment. Do not philosophic doctors tell us that we are unable to discern so much as a tree, except by an unconscious cunning which combines many past and separate sensations; that no one sense is independent of another, so that in the dark we can hardly taste a fricassee, or tell whether our pipe is alight or not, and the most intelligent boy, if accommodated with claws or hoofs instead of fingers, would be likely to remain on the lowest form? If so, it is easy to understand that our discernment of men's motives must depend on the completeness of the elements we can bring from our own susceptibility and our own experience. See to it, friend, before you pronounce a too-hasty judgement, that your own moral sensibilities are not of a hoofed or clawed character. The keenest eye will not serve, unless you have the delicate fingers, with their subtle nerve filaments, which elude scientific lenses, and lose themselves in the invisible world of human sensations.

As for Mr Jerome, he drew the elements of his moral vision from the depths of his veneration and pity. If he himself felt so much for these poor things to whom life was so dim and meagre, what must the clergyman feel who had undertaken before God to be their shepherd?

'Ah!' he whispered, interruptedly, 'it's too big a load for his conscience, poor man! He wants to mek himself their brother, like; can't abide to preach to the fastin' on a full stomach. Ah! he's better nor we are, that's it – he's a deal better nor we are.'

Here Mr Jerome shook his bridle violently, and looked up with an air of moral courage, as if Mr Stickney had been present, and liable to take offence at this conclusion. A few minutes more brought him in front of Mrs Wagstaff's, where Mr Tryan lodged. He had often been here before, so that the contrast between this ugly square brick house, with its shabby bit of grass-plot, stared at all round by cottage windows, and his own pretty white home, set in a paradise of orchard and garden and pasture was not new to him, but he felt it with fresh force today, as he slowly fastened his roan by the bridle to the wooden paling, and knocked at the door. Mr Tryan was at home, and sent to request that Mr Jerome would walk up into his study, as the fire was out in the parlour below.

At the mention of a clergyman's study, perhaps, your too-active imagination conjures up a perfect snuggery, where the general air of comfort is rescued from a secular character by strong ecclesiastical suggestions in the shape of the furniture, the pattern of the carpet, and the prints on the wall; where, if a nap is taken, it is an easy chair with a Gothic back, and the very feet rest on a warm and velvety simulation of church windows; where the pure art of rigorous English Protestantism smiles above the mantelpiece in the portrait of an eminent bishop, or a refined Anglican taste is indicated by a German print from Overbeck;[33] where the walls are lined with choice divinity in sombre binding, and the light is softened by a screen of boughs with a grey church in the background.

But I must beg you to dismiss all such scenic prettiness, suitable as they may be to a clergyman's character and complexion, for I have to confess that Mr Tryan's study was a very ugly little room indeed, with an ugly slapdash pattern on the walls, an ugly carpet on the floor, and an ugly view of cottage roofs and cabbage gardens from the window. His own person, his writing table and his bookcase, were the only objects in the room that had the slightest air of refinement, and the sole provision for comfort was a clumsy straight-backed armchair covered with faded chintz. The man who could live in such a room, unconstrained by poverty, must either have his vision fed from within by an intense passion, or he must have chosen that least attractive form of self-mortification which wears no haircloth and has no meagre days, but accepts the vulgar, the commonplace, and the ugly, whenever the highest duty seems to lie among them.

'Mr Tryan, I hope you'll excuse me disturbin' on you,' said Mr Jerome. 'But I'd summat partickler to say.'

'You don't disturb me at all, Mr Jerome; I'm very glad to have a visit from you,' said Mr Tryan, shaking him heartily by the hand, and offering him the chintz-covered 'easy' chair. 'It is some time since I've had an opportunity of seeing you, except on a Sunday.'

'Ah, sir! your time's so taken up, I'm well aware o' that; it's not only what you hev to do, but it's goin' about from place to place; an' you don't keep a hoss, Mr Tryan. You don't take care enough o' yourself – you don't indeed, an' that's what I come to talk to y' about.'

'That's very good of you, Mr Jerome, but I assure you I think walking does me no harm. It is rather a relief to me after speaking or writing. You know I have no great circuit to make. The furthest distance I have to walk is to Milby Church, and if ever I want a horse on a Sunday, I hire Radley's, who lives not many hundred yards from me.'

'Well, but now! the winter's comin' on, an' you'll get wet i' your feet, an' Pratt tells me as your constitution's dillicate, as anybody may see, for the matter o' that, wi'out bein' a doctor. An' this is the light I look at it in, Mr Tryan: who's to fill up your place, if you was to be disabled, as I may say? Consider what a valyable life yours is. You've begun a great work i' Milby, and so you might carry it on, if you'd your health and strength. The more care you take o' yourself, the longer you'll live, belike, God willing, to do good to your fellow creaturs.'

'Why, my dear Mr Jerome, I think I should not be a long-lived man in any case, and if I were to take care of myself under the pretext of doing more good, I should very likely die and leave nothing done after all.'

'Well! but keepin' a hoss wouldn't hinder you from workin'. It 'ud help you to do more, though Pratt says as it's usin' your voice so constant as does you the most harm. Now, isn't it – I'm no scholard, Mr Tryan, an' I'm not a-goin' to dictate to you – but isn't it a'most a-killin' o' yourself, to go on a' that way beyond your strength? We mustn't fling ower lives away.'

'No, not fling them away lightly, but we are permitted to lay down our lives in a right cause. There are many duties, as you know, Mr Jerome, which stand before taking care of our own lives.'

'Ah! I can't arguy wi' you, Mr Tryan, but what I wanted to say's this – There's my little chacenut hoss; I should take it quite a kindness if you'd hev him through the winter an' ride him. I've thought o' sellin' him a many times, for Mrs Jerome can't abide him, and what do I want wi' two nags? But I'm fond o' the little chacenut, an' I shouldn't like to sell him. So if you'll only ride him for me, you'll do me a kindness – you will, indeed, Mr Tryan.'

'Thank you, Mr Jerome. I promise you to ask for him, when I feel that I want a nag. There is no man I would more gladly be indebted to than you, but at present I would rather not have a horse. I should ride him very little, and it would be an inconvenience to me to keep him rather than otherwise.'

Mr Jerome looked troubled and hesitating, as if he had something on his mind that would not readily shape itself into words. At last he said, 'You'll excuse me, Mr Tryan, I wouldn't be takin' a liberty, but I know what great claims you hev on you as a clergyman. Is it th' expense, Mr Tryan? is it the money?'

'No, my dear sir. I have much more than a single man needs. My way of living is quite of my own choosing, and I am doing nothing but what I feel bound to do, quite apart from money considerations. We cannot judge for one another, you know; we have each our peculiar weaknesses and temptations. I quite admit that it might be right for another man to allow himself more luxuries, and I assure you I think it no superiority in myself to do without them. On the contrary, if my heart were less rebellious, and if I were less liable to temptation, I should not need that sort of self-denial. But,' added Mr Tryan, holding out his hand to Mr Jerome, 'I understand your kindness, and bless you for it. If I want a horse, I shall ask for the chestnut.'

Mr Jerome was obliged to rest contented with this promise, and rode home sorrowfully, reproaching himself with not having said one thing he meant to say when setting out, and with having 'clean forgot' the arguments he had intended to quote from Mr Stickney.

Mr Jerome's was not the only mind that was seriously disturbed by the idea that the curate was over-working himself. There were tender women's hearts in which anxiety about the state of his affections was beginning to be merged in anxiety about the state of his health. Miss Eliza Pratt had at one time passed through much sleepless cogitation on the possibility of Mr Tryan's being attached to some lady at a distance – at Laxeter, perhaps, where he had formerly held a curacy, and her fine eyes kept close watch lest any symptom of engaged affections on his part should escape her. It seemed an alarming fact that his handkerchiefs were beautifully marked with hair, until she reflected that he had an unmarried sister of whom he spoke with much affection as his father's companion and comforter. Besides, Mr Tryan had never paid any distant visit, except one for a few days to his father, and no hint escaped him of his intending to take a house, or change his mode of living. No! he could not be engaged, though he might have been disappointed. But this latter misfortune is one from which a devoted clergyman has been known to recover, by the aid of a fine pair of grey eyes that beam on him with affectionate reverence. Before Christmas, however, her cogitations began to take another turn. She heard her father say very confidently that 'Tryan was consumptive, and if he didn't take more care of himself, his life would not be worth a year's purchase'; and shame at having speculated on suppositions that were likely to prove so false, sent poor Miss Eliza's feelings with all the stronger impetus into the one channel of sorrowful alarm at the prospect of losing the pastor who had opened to her a new life of piety and self-subjection. It is a sad weakness in us, after all, that the thought of a man's death hallows him anew to us, as if life were not sacred too – as if it were comparatively a light thing to fail in love and reverence to the brother who has to climb the whole toilsome steep with us, and all our tears and tenderness were due to the one who is spared that hard journey.

The Miss Linnets, too, were beginning to take a new view of the future, entirely uncoloured by jealousy of Miss Eliza Pratt.

'Did you notice,' said Mary, one afternoon when Mrs Pettifer was taking tea with them, 'did you notice that short dry cough of Mr Tryan's yesterday? I think he looks worse and worse every week, and I only wish I knew his sister; I would write to her about him. I'm sure something should be done to make him give up part of his work, and he will listen to no one here.'

'Ah,' said Mrs Pettifer, 'it's a thousand pities his father and sister can't come and live with him, if he isn't to marry. But I wish with all my heart he could have taken to some nice woman as would have made a comfortable home for him. I used to think he might take to Eliza Pratt; she's a good girl, and very pretty; but I see no likelihood of it now.'

'No, indeed,' said Rebecca, with some emphasis, 'Mr Tryan's heart is not for any woman to win; it is all given to his work, and I could never wish to see him with a young inexperienced wife who would be a drag on him instead of a helpmate.'

'He'd need have somebody, young or old,' observed Mrs Linnet, 'to see as he wears a flannel wescoat, an' changes his stockins when he comes in. It's my opinion he's got that cough wi' sittin i' wet shoes and stockins, an' that Mrs Wagstaff's a poor addle-headed thing; she doesn't half tek care on him.'

'Oh, Mother!' said Rebecca, 'she's a very pious woman. And I'm sure she thinks it too great a privilege to have Mr

Tryan with her, not to do the best she can to make him comfortable. She can't help her rooms being shabby.'

'I've nothing to say again' her piety, my dear, but I know very well I shouldn't like her to cook my victual. When a man comes in hungry an' tired, piety won't feed him, I reckon. Hard carrots 'ull lie heavy on his stomach, piety or no piety. I called in one day when she was dishin' up Mr Tryan's dinner, an' I could see the potatoes was as watery as watery. It's right enough to be speritial – I'm no enemy to that, but I like my potatoes mealy. I don't see as anybody 'ull go to heaven the sooner for not digestin' their dinner – providin' they don't die sooner, as mayhap Mr Tryan will, poor dear man!'

'It will be a heavy day for us all when that comes to pass,' said Mrs Pettifer. 'We shall never get anybody to fill up *that* gap. There's the new clergyman that's just come to Shepperton – Mr Parry; I saw him the other day at Mrs Bond's. He may be a very good man, and a fine preacher; they say he is, but I thought to myself, What a difference between him and Mr Tryan! He's a sharp-sort-of-looking man, and hasn't that feeling way with him that Mr Tryan has. What is so wonderful to me in Mr Tryan is the way he puts himself on a level with one, and talks to one like a brother. I'm never afraid of telling him anything. He never seems to look down on anybody. He knows how to lift up those that are cast down, if ever man did.'

'Yes,' said Mary. 'And when I see all the faces turned up to him in Paddiford Church, I often think how hard it would be for any clergyman who had to come after him; he has made the people love him so.'

12

In her occasional visits to her near neighbour Mrs Pettifer, too old a friend to be shunned because she was a Tryanite, Janet was obliged sometimes to hear allusions to Mr Tryan, and even to listen to his praises, which she usually met with playful incredulity.

'Ah, well,' she answered one day, 'I like dear old Mr Crewe and his pipes a great deal better than your Mr Tryan and his Gospel. When I was a little toddle, Mr and Mrs Crewe used to let me play about in their garden, and have a swing between the great elm trees, because mother had no garden. I like people who are kind; kindness is my religion; and that's the reason I like you, dear Mrs Pettifer, though you are a Tryanite.'

'But that's Mr Tryan's religion too – at least partly. There's nobody can give himself up more to doing good amongst the poor, and he thinks of their bodies too, as well as their souls.'

'Oh yes, yes, but then he talks about faith and grace, and all that, making people believe they are better than others, and that God loves them more than He does the rest of the world. I know he has put a great deal of that into Sally Martin's head, and it has done her no good at all. She was as nice, honest, patient a girl as need be before, and now she fancies she has new light and new wisdom. I don't like those notions.'

'You mistake him, indeed you do, my dear Mrs Dempster; I wish you'd go and hear him preach.'

'Hear him preach! Why, you wicked woman, you would persuade me to disobey my husband, would you? Oh, shocking! I shall run away from you. Goodbye.'

A few days after this conversation, however, Janet went to Sally Martin's about three o'clock in the afternoon. The pudding that had been sent in for herself and 'Mammy' struck her as just the sort of delicate morsel the poor consumptive girl would be likely to fancy, and in her usual impulsive way she had started up from the dinner table at once, put on her bonnet, and set off with a covered plateful to the neighbouring street. When she entered the house there was no one to be seen, but in the little side-room where Sally lay, Janet heard a voice. It was one she had not heard before, but she immediately guessed it to be Mr Tryan's. Her first impulse was to set down her plate and go away, but Mrs Martin might not be in, and then there would be no one to give Sally that delicious bit of pudding. So she stood still, and was obliged to hear what Mr Tryan was saying. He was interrupted by one of the invalid's violent fits of coughing.

'It is very hard to bear, is it not?' he said when she was still again. 'Yet God seems to support you under it wonderfully. Pray for me, Sally, that I may have strength too when the hour of great suffering comes. It is one of my worst weaknesses to shrink from bodily pain, and I think the time is perhaps not far off when I shall have to bear what you are bearing. But now I have tired you. We have talked enough. Goodbye.'

Janet was surprised, and forgot her wish not to encounter Mr Tryan: the tone and the words were so unlike what she had expected to hear. There was none of the self-satisfied unction of the teacher, quoting, or exhorting, or expounding, for the benefit of the hearer, but a simple appeal for help, a confession of weakness. Mr Tryan had his deeply felt troubles, then? Mr Tryan, too, like herself, knew what it was to tremble at a foreseen trial – to shudder at an impending burthen, heavier than he felt able to bear?

The most brilliant deed of virtue could not have inclined Janet's good will towards Mr Tryan so much as this fellowship in suffering, and the softening thought was in her eyes when he appeared in the doorway, pale, weary and depressed. The sight of Janet standing there with the entire absence of self-consciousness which belongs to a new and vivid impression, made him start and pause a little. Their eyes met, and they looked at each other gravely for a few moments. Then they bowed, and Mr Tryan passed out.

There is a power in the direct glance of a sincere and loving human soul, which will do more to dissipate prejudice and kindle charity than the most elaborate arguments. The fullest exposition of Mr Tryan's doctrine might not have sufficed to convince Janet that he had not an odious self-complacency in believing himself a peculiar child of God, but one direct, pathetic look of his had dissociated him with that conception for ever.

This happened late in the autumn, not long before Sally Martin died. Janet mentioned her new impression to no one, for she was afraid of arriving at a still more complete contradiction of her former ideas. We have all of us considerable regard for our past self, and are not fond of casting reflections on that respected individual by a total negation of his opinions. Janet could no longer think of Mr Tryan without sympathy, but she still shrank from the idea of becoming his hearer and admirer. That was a reversal of the past which was as little accordant with her inclination as her circumstances.

And indeed this interview with Mr Tryan was soon thrust into the background of poor Janet's memory by the daily thickening miseries of her life.

13

The loss of Mr Jerome as a client proved only the beginning of annoyances to Dempster. That old gentleman had in him the vigorous remnant of an energy and perseverance which had created his own fortune, and being, as I have hinted, given to chewing the cud of a righteous indignation with considerable relish, he was determined to carry on his retributive war against the persecuting attorney. Having some influence with Mr Pryme, who was one of the most substantial rate-payers in the neighbouring parish of Dingley, and who had himself a complex and long-standing private account with Dempster, Mr Jerome stirred up this gentleman to an investigation of some suspicious points in the attorney's conduct of the parish affairs. The natural consequence was a personal quarrel between Dempster and Mr Pryme; the client demanded his account, and then followed the old story of an exorbitant lawyer's bill, with the unpleasant anticlimax of taxing.

These disagreeables, extending over many months, ran along side by side with the pressing business of Mr Armstrong's lawsuit, which was threatening to take a turn rather depreciatory of Dempster's professional prevision, and it is not surprising that, being thus kept in a constant state of irritated excitement about his own affairs, he had little time for the further exhibition of his public spirit, or for rallying the forlorn hope of sound churchmanship against cant and hypocrisy. Not a few persons who had a grudge against him began to remark, with satisfaction, that 'Dempster's luck was forsaking him', particularly Mrs Linnet, who thought she saw distinctly the gradual ripening of a providential scheme, whereby a just retribution would be wrought on the man who had deprived her of Pye's Croft. On the other hand, Dempster's well-satisfied clients, who were of opinion that the punishment of his wickedness might conveniently be deferred to another world, noticed with some concern that he was drinking more than ever, and that both his temper and his driving were becoming more furious. Unhappily those additional glasses of brandy, that exasperation of loud-tongued abuse, had other effects than any that entered into the contemplation of anxious clients: they were the little super-added symbols that were perpetually raising the sum of home misery.

Poor Janet! how heavily the months rolled on for her, laden with fresh sorrows as the summer passed into autumn, the autumn into winter, and the winter into spring again. Every feverish morning, with its blank listlessness and despair, seemed more hateful than the last; every coming night more impossible to brave without arming herself in leaden stupor. The morning light brought no gladness to her: it seemed only to throw its glare on what had happened in the dim candlelight – on the cruel man seated immovable in drunken obstinacy by the dead fire and dying lights in the dining room, rating her in harsh tones, reiterating old reproaches – or on a hideous blank of something unremembered, something that must have made that dark bruise on her shoulder, which ached as she dressed herself.

Do you wonder how it was that things had come to this pass – what offence Janet had committed in the early years of marriage to rouse the brutal hatred of this man? The seeds of things are very small: the hours that lie between sunrise and the gloom of midnight are travelled through by tiniest markings of the clock, and Janet, looking back along the fifteen years of her married life, hardly knew how or where this total misery began; hardly knew when the sweet wedded love and hope that had set for ever had ceased to make a twilight of memory and relenting, before the oncoming of the utter dark.

Old Mrs Dempster thought she saw the true beginning of it all in Janet's want of housekeeping skill and exactness. 'Janet,' she said to herself, 'was always running about doing things for other people, and neglecting her own house. That provokes a man: what use is it for a woman to be loving, and making a fuss with her husband, if she doesn't take care and keep his home just as he likes it; if she isn't at hand when he wants anything done; if she doesn't attend to all his wishes, let them be as small as they may? That was what I did when I was a wife, though I didn't make half so much fuss about loving my husband. Then, Janet had no children.' ...Ah! there Mammy Dempster had touched a true spring, not perhaps of her son's cruelty, but of half Janet's misery. If she had had babes to rock to sleep – little ones to kneel in their nightdress and say their prayers at her knees – sweet boys and girls to put their young arms round her neck and kiss away her tears, her poor hungry heart would have been fed with strong love, and might never have needed that fiery poison to still its cravings. Mighty is the force of motherhood! says the great tragic poet to us across the ages, finding, as usual, the simplest words for the sublimest fact *deinon to tiktein estin*.[34] It transforms all things by its vital heat: it turns timidity into fierce courage, and dreadless defiance into tremulous submission; it turns thoughtlessness into foresight, and yet stills all anxiety into calm content; it makes selfishness become self-denial, and gives even to hard vanity the glance of admiring love. Yes! if Janet had been a mother, she might have been saved from much sin, and therefore from much of her sorrow.

But do not believe that it was anything either present or wanting in poor Janet that formed the motive of her husband's cruelty. Cruelty, like every other vice, requires no motive outside itself – it only requires opportunity. You do not suppose Dempster had any motive for drinking beyond the craving for drink; the presence of brandy was the only necessary condition. And an unloving, tyrannous, brutal man needs no motive to prompt his cruelty; he needs only the perpetual presence of a woman he can call his own. A whole park full of tame or timid-eyed animals to torment at his will would not serve him so well to glut his lust of torture; they could not feel as one woman does; they could not throw out the keen retort which whets the edge of hatred.

Janet's bitterness would overflow in ready words; she was not to be made meek by cruelty; she would repent of nothing in the face of injustice, though she was subdued in a moment by a word or a look that recalled the old days of fondness, and in times of comparative calm would often recover her sweet woman's habit of caressing playful affection. But such days were become rare, and poor Janet's soul was kept like a vexed sea, tossed by a new storm before the old waves have fallen. Proud, angry resistance and sullen endurance were now almost the only alternations she knew. She would bear it all proudly to the world, but proudly towards him too; her woman's weakness might shriek a cry for pity under a heavy blow, but voluntarily she would do nothing to mollify him, unless he first relented. What had she ever done to him but love him too well – but believe in him too foolishly? He had no pity on her tender flesh; he could strike the soft neck he had once asked to kiss. Yet she would not admit her wretchedness; she had married him blindly, and she would bear it out to the terrible end, whatever that might be. Better this misery than the blank that lay for her outside her married home.

But there was one person who heard all the plaints and all the outbursts of bitterness and despair which Janet was never tempted to pour into any other ear, and alas! in her worst moments, Janet would throw out wild reproaches against that patient listener. For the wrong that rouses our angry passions finds only a medium in us; it passes through us like a vibration, and we inflict what we have suffered.

Mrs Raynor saw too clearly all through the winter that things were getting worse in Orchard Street. She had evidence enough of it in Janet's visits to her; and, though her own visits to her daughter were so timed that she saw little of Dempster personally, she noticed many indications not only that he was drinking to greater excess, but that he was beginning to lose that physical power of supporting excess which had long been the admiration of such fine spirits as Mr Tomlinson. It seemed as if Dempster had some consciousness of this – some new distrust of himself, for, before winter was over, it was observed that he had renounced his habit of driving out alone, and was never seen in his gig without a servant by his side.

Nemesis is lame, but she is of colossal stature, like the gods, and sometimes, while her sword is not yet unsheathed, she stretches out her huge left arm and grasps her victim. The mighty hand is invisible, but the victim totters under the dire clutch.

The various symptoms that things were getting worse with the Dempsters afforded Milby gossip something new to say on an old subject. Mrs Dempster, everyone remarked, looked more miserable than ever, though she kept up the old pretence of being happy and satisfied. She was scarcely ever seen, as she used to be, going about on her good-natured errands, and even old Mrs Crewe, who had always been wilfully blind to anything wrong in her favourite Janet, was obliged to admit that she had not seemed like herself lately. 'The poor thing's out of health,' said the kind little old lady, in answer to all gossip about Janet. 'Her headaches always were bad, and

I know what headaches are; why, they make one quite deliri-
ous sometimes.' Mrs Phipps, for her part, declared she would
never accept an invitation to Dempster's again; it was getting
so very disagreeable to go there, Mrs Dempster was often 'so
strange'. To be sure, there were dreadful stories about the way
Dempster used his wife, but in Mrs Phipps's opinion, it was
six of one and half a dozen of the other. Mrs Dempster had
never been like other women; she had always a flighty way
with her, carrying parcels of snuff to old Mrs Tooke, and going
to drink tea with Mrs Brinley, the carpenter's wife, and then
never taking care of her clothes, always wearing the same
things weekday or Sunday. A man has a poor lookout with a
wife of that sort. Mr Phipps, amiable and laconic, wondered
how it was women were so fond of running each other down.

Mr Pratt having been called in provisionally to a patient of
Mr Pilgrim's in a case of compound fracture, observed in a
friendly colloquy with his brother surgeon the next day, 'So
Dempster has left off driving himself, I see; he won't end with
a broken neck after all. You'll have a case of meningitis and
delirium tremens instead.'

'Ah,' said Mr Pilgrim, 'he can hardly stand it much longer
at the rate he's going on, one would think. He's been con-
foundedly cut up about that business of Armstrong's, I fancy.
It may do him some harm, perhaps, but Dempster must have
feathered his nest pretty well; he can afford to lose a little
business.'

'His business will outlast him, that's pretty clear,' said Pratt.
'He'll run down like a watch with a broken spring one of these
days.'

Another prognostic of evil to Dempster came at the beginning of March. For then little 'Mamsey' died – died suddenly.
The housemaid found her seated motionless in her armchair,

her knitting fallen down, and the tortoiseshell cat reposing on it unreproved. The little white old woman had ended her wintry age of patient sorrow, believing to the last that 'Robert might have been a good husband as he had been a good son'.

When the earth was thrown on Mamsey's coffin, and the son, in crape scarf and hatband, turned away homeward, his good angel, lingering with outstretched wing on the edge of the grave, cast one despairing look after him, and took flight for ever.

14

The last week in March – three weeks after old Mrs Dempster died – occurred the unpleasant winding-up of affairs between Dempster and Mr Pryme, and under this additional source of irritation the attorney's diurnal drunkenness had taken on its most ill-tempered and brutal phase. On the Friday morning, before setting out for Rotherby, he told his wife that he had invited 'four men' to dinner at half-past six that evening. The previous night had been a terrible one for Janet, and when her husband broke his grim morning silence to say these few words, she was looking so blank and listless that he added in a loud sharp key, 'Do you hear what I say? or must I tell the cook?' She started, and said, 'Yes, I hear.'

'Then mind and have a dinner provided, and don't go mooning about like crazy Jane.'

Half an hour afterwards Mrs Raynor, quietly busy in her kitchen with her household labours – for she had only a little twelve-year-old girl as a servant – heard with trembling the rattling of the garden gate and the opening of the outer door. She knew the step, and in one short moment she lived beforehand through the coming scene. She hurried out of the kitchen, and there in the passage, as she had felt, stood Janet, her eyes worn as if by night-long watching, her dress careless, her step languid. No cheerful morning greeting to her mother – no kiss. She turned into the parlour, and, seating herself on the sofa opposite her mother's chair, looked vacantly at the walls and furniture until the corners of her mouth began to tremble, and her dark eyes filled with tears that fell unwiped down her cheeks. The mother sat silently opposite to her, afraid to speak. She felt sure there was nothing new the matter – sure that the torrent of words would come sooner or later.

'Mother! why don't you speak to me?' Janet burst out at last. 'You don't care about my suffering; you are blaming me because I feel – because I am miserable.'

'My child, I am not blaming you – my heart is bleeding for you. Your head is bad this morning – you have had a bad night. Let me make you a cup of tea now. Perhaps you didn't like your breakfast.'

'Yes, that is what you always think, Mother. It is the old story, you think. You don't ask me what it is I have had to bear. You are tired of hearing me. You are cruel, like the rest; everyone is cruel in this world. Nothing but blame – blame – blame; never any pity. God is cruel to have sent me into the world to bear all this misery.'

'Janet, Janet, don't say so. It is not for us to judge; we must submit; we must be thankful for the gift of life.'

'Thankful for life! Why should I be thankful? God has made me with a heart to feel, and He has sent me nothing but misery. How could I help it? How could I know what would come? Why didn't you tell me, Mother? – why did you let me marry? You knew what brutes men could be, and there's no help for me – no hope. I can't kill myself, I've tried, but I can't leave this world and go to another. There may be no pity for me there, as there is none here.'

'Janet, my child, there *is* pity. Have I ever done anything but love you? And there is pity in God. Hasn't He put pity into your heart for many a poor sufferer? Where did it come from, if not from Him?'

Janet's nervous irritation now broke out into sobs instead of complainings, and her mother was thankful, for after that crisis there would very likely come relenting, and tenderness, and comparative calm. She went out to make some tea, and when she returned with the tray in her hands, Janet had dried her eyes and now turned them towards her mother with a faint attempt to smile, but the poor face, in its sad blurred beauty, looked all the more piteous.

'Mother will insist upon her tea,' she said, 'and I really think I can drink a cup. But I must go home directly, for there are people coming to dinner. Could you go with me and help me, Mother?'

Mrs Raynor was always ready to do that. She went to Orchard Street with Janet, and remained with her through the day – comforted, as evening approached, to see her become more cheerful and willing to attend to her toilette. At half-past five everything was in order: Janet was dressed, and when the mother had kissed her and said goodbye, she could not help pausing a moment in sorrowful admiration at the tall rich figure, looking all the grander for the plainness of the deep mourning dress, and the noble face with its massy folds of black hair, made matronly by a simple white cap. Janet had that enduring beauty which belongs to pure majestic outline and depth of tint. Sorrow and neglect leave their traces on such beauty, but it thrills us to the last, like a glorious Greek temple, which, for all the loss it has suffered from time and barbarous hands, has gained a solemn history, and fills our imagination the more because it is incomplete to the sense.

It was six o'clock before Dempster returned from Rotherby. He had evidently drunk a great deal, and was in an angry humour, but Janet, who had gathered some little courage and forbearance from the consciousness that she had done her best today, was determined to speak pleasantly to him.

'Robert,' she said gently, as she saw him seat himself in the dining room in his dusty snuffy clothes, and take some documents out of his pocket, 'will you not wash and change your dress? It will refresh you.'

'Leave me alone, will you?' said Dempster, in his most brutal tone.

'Do change your coat and waistcoat, they are so dusty. I've laid all your things out ready.'

'Oh, you have, have you?' After a few minutes he rose very deliberately and walked upstairs into his bedroom. Janet had often been scolded before for not laying out his clothes, and she thought now, not without some wonder, that this attention of hers had brought him to compliance.

Presently he called out, 'Janet!' and she went upstairs.

'Here! Take that!' he said, as soon as she reached the door, flinging at her the coat she had laid out. 'Another time, leave me to do as I please, will you?'

The coat, flung with great force, only brushed her shoulder, and fell some distance within the drawing room, the door of which stood open just opposite. She hastily retreated as she saw the waistcoat coming, and one by one the clothes she had laid out were all flung into the drawing room.

Janet's face flushed with anger, and for the first time in her life her resentment overcame the long cherished pride that made her hide her griefs from the world. There are moments

117

when by some strange impulse we contradict our past selves – fatal moments, when a fit of passion, like a lava stream, lays low the work of half our lives. Janet thought, 'I will not pick up the clothes; they shall lie there until the visitors come, and he shall be ashamed of himself.'

There was a knock at the door, and she made haste to seat herself in the drawing room, lest the servant should enter and remove the clothes, which were lying half on the table and half on the ground. Mr Lowme entered with a less familiar visitor, a client of Dempster's, and the next moment Dempster himself came in.

His eye fell at once on the clothes, and then turned for an instant with a devilish glance of concentrated hatred on Janet, who, still flushed and excited, affected unconsciousness. After shaking hands with his visitors he immediately rang the bell.

'Take those clothes away,' he said to the servant, not looking at Janet again.

During dinner, she kept up her assumed air of indifference, and tried to seem in high spirits, laughing and talking more than usual. In reality, she felt as if she had defied a wild beast within the four walls of his den, and he was crouching backward in preparation for his deadly spring. Dempster affected to take no notice of her, talked obstreperously, and drank steadily.

About eleven the party dispersed, with the exception of Mr Budd, who had joined them after dinner, and appeared disposed to stay drinking a little longer. Janet began to hope that he would stay long enough for Dempster to become heavy and stupid, and so to fall asleep downstairs, which was a rare but occasional ending of his nights. She told the servants to sit up no longer, and she herself undressed and went to bed, trying to cheat her imagination into the belief that the day was ended

118

for her. But when she lay down, she became more intensely awake than ever. Everything she had taken this evening seemed only to stimulate her senses and her apprehensions to new vividness. Her heart beat violently, and she heard every sound in the house.

At last, when it was twelve, she heard Mr Budd go out; she heard the door slam. Dempster had not moved. Was he asleep? Would he forget? The minute seemed long, while, with a quickening pulse, she was on the stretch to catch every sound.

'Janet!' The loud jarring voice seemed to strike her like a hurled weapon.

'Janet!' he called again, moving out of the dining room to the foot of the stairs.

There was a pause of a minute.

'If you don't come, I'll kill you.'

Another pause, and she heard him turn back into the dining room. He was gone for a light – perhaps for a weapon. Perhaps he would kill her. Let him. Life was as hideous as death. For years she had been rushing on to some unknown but certain horror, and now she was close upon it. She was almost glad. She was in a state of flushed feverish defiance that neutralised her woman's terrors.

She heard his heavy step on the stairs; she saw the slowly advancing light. Then she saw the tall massive figure, and the heavy face, now fierce with drunken rage. He had nothing but the candle in his hand. He set it down on the table, and advanced close to the bed.

'So you think you'll defy me, do you? We'll see how long that will last. Get up, madam; out of bed this instant!'

In the close presence of the dreadful man – of this huge crushing force, armed with savage will – poor Janet's desperate defiance all forsook her, and her terrors came back. Trembling, she got up, and stood helpless in her nightdress before her husband.

He seized her with his heavy grasp by the shoulder, and pushed her before him.

'I'll cool your hot spirit for you! I'll teach you to brave me!'

Slowly he pushed her along before him, downstairs and through the passage, where a small oil lamp was still flickering. What was he going to do to her? She thought every moment he was going to dash her before him on the ground. But she gave no scream – she only trembled.

He pushed her on to the entrance, and held her firmly in his grasp while he lifted the latch of the door. Then he opened the door a little way, thrust her out and slammed it behind her.

For a short space, it seemed like a deliverance to Janet. The harsh north-east wind, that blew through her thin nightdress, and sent her long heavy black hair streaming, seemed like the breath of pity after the grasp of that threatening monster. But soon the sense of release from an overpowering terror gave way before the sense of the fate that had really come upon her.

This, then, was what she had been travelling towards through her long years of misery! Not yet death. Oh! if she had been brave enough for it, death would have been better. The servants slept at the back of the house; it was impossible to make them hear, so that they might let her in again quietly, without her husband's knowledge. And she would not have tried. He had thrust her out, and it should be for ever.

There would have been dead silence in Orchard Street but for the whistling of the wind and the swirling of the March dust on the pavement. Thick clouds covered the sky; every door was closed; every window was dark. No ray of light fell on the tall white figure that stood in lonely misery on the doorstep; no eye rested on Janet as she sank down on the cold stone, and looked into the dismal night. She seemed to be looking into her own blank future.

15

The stony street, the bitter north-east wind and darkness – and in the midst of them a tender woman thrust out from her husband's home in her thin nightdress, the harsh wind cutting her naked feet, and driving her long hair away from her half-clad bosom, where the poor heart is crushed with anguish and despair.

The drowning man, urged by the supreme agony, lives in an instant through all his happy and unhappy past: when the dark flood has fallen like a curtain, memory, in a single moment, sees the drama acted over again. And even in those earlier crises, which are but types of death – when we are cut off abruptly from the life we have known, when we can no longer expect tomorrow to resemble yesterday, and find ourselves by some sudden shock on the confines of the unknown – there is often the same sort of lightning-flash through the dark and unfrequented chambers of memory.

When Janet sat down shivering on the doorstone, with the door shut upon her past life, and the future black and unshapen before her as the night, the scenes of her childhood, her youth and her painful womanhood, rushed back upon her consciousness, and made one picture with her present desolation. The petted child taking her newest toy to bed with her – the young girl, proud in strength and beauty, dreaming that life was an easy thing, and that it was pitiful weakness to be unhappy – the bride, passing with trembling joy from the

121

outer court to the inner sanctuary of woman's life – the wife, beginning her initiation into sorrow, wounded, resenting, yet still hoping and forgiving –the poor bruised woman, seeking through weary years the one refuge of despair, oblivion – Janet seemed to herself all these in the same moment that she was conscious of being seated on the cold stone under the shock of a new misery. All her early gladness, all her bright hopes and illusions, all her gifts of beauty and affection, served only to darken the riddle of her life; they were the betraying promises of a cruel destiny which had brought out those sweet blossoms only that the winds and storms might have a greater work of desolation, which had nursed her like a pet fawn into tenderness and fond expectation, only that she might feel a keener terror in the clutch of the panther. Her mother had sometimes said that troubles were sent to make us better and draw us nearer to God. What mockery that seemed to Janet! Her troubles had been sinking her lower from year to year, pressing upon her like heavy fever-laden vapours, and perverting the very plenitude of her nature into a deeper source of disease. Her wretchedness had been a perpetually tightening instrument of torture, which had gradually absorbed all the other sensibilities of her nature into the sense of pain and the maddened craving for relief. Oh, if some ray of hope, of pity, of consolation, would pierce through the horrible gloom, she might believe then in a divine love – in a heavenly Father who cared for His children! But now she had no faith, no trust. There was nothing she could lean on in the wide world, for her mother was only a fellow sufferer in her own lot. The poor patient woman could do little more than mourn with her daughter: she had humble resignation enough to sustain her own soul, but she could no more give comfort and fortitude to Janet, than the withered ivy-covered trunk can bear up its strong, full-boughed offspring crashing down under an Alpine storm. Janet felt she was alone: no human soul had measured her anguish, had understood her self-despair, had entered into her sorrows and her sins with that deep-sighted sympathy which is wiser than all blame, more potent than all reproof – such sympathy as had swelled her own heart for many a sufferer. And if there was any divine pity, she could not feel it; it kept aloof from her, it poured no balm into her wounds, it stretched out no hand to bear up her weak resolve, to fortify her fainting courage.

Now, in her utmost loneliness, she shed no tear; she sat staring fixedly into the darkness, while inwardly she gazed at her own past, almost losing the sense that it was her own, or that she was anything more than a spectator at a strange and dreadful play.

The loud sound of the church clock, striking one, startled her. She had not been there more than half an hour, then? And it seemed to her as if she had been there half the night. She was getting benumbed with cold. With that strong instinctive dread of pain and death which had made her recoil from suicide, she started up, and the disagreeable sensation of resting on her benumbed feet helped to recall her completely to the sense of the present. The wind was beginning to make rents in the clouds, and there came every now and then a dim light of stars that frightened her more than the darkness; it was like a cruel finger pointing her out in her wretchedness and humiliation; it made her shudder at the thought of the morning twilight. What could she do? Not go to her mother – not rouse her in the dead of night to tell her this. Her mother would think she was a spectre; it would be enough to kill her with horror. And the way there was so long… if she should meet someone… yet she must seek some shelter, somewhere to hide herself. Five doors off there was Mrs Pettifer's; that kind woman would take her in. It was of no use now to be proud and mind about the world's knowing: she had nothing to wish for, nothing to care about; only she could not help shuddering at the thought of braving the morning light, there in the street – she was frightened at the thought of spending long hours in the cold. Life might mean anguish, might mean despair, but oh, she must clutch it, though with bleeding fingers; her feet must cling to the firm earth that the sunlight would revisit, not slip into the untried abyss, where she might long even for familiar pains.

Janet trod slowly with her naked feet on the rough pavement, trembling at the fitful gleams of starlight, and supporting herself by the wall, as the gusts of wind drove right against her. The very wind was cruel: it tried to push her back from the door where she wanted to go and knock and ask for pity.

Mrs Pettifer's house did not look into Orchard Street: it stood a little way up a wide passage which opened into the street through an archway. Janet turned up the archway, and saw a faint light coming from Mrs Pettifer's bedroom window. The glimmer of a rushlight from a room where a friend was lying, was like a ray of mercy to Janet, after that long, long time of darkness and loneliness; it would not be so dreadful to awake Mrs Pettifer as she had thought. Yet she lingered some minutes at the door before she gathered courage to knock; she felt as if the sound must betray her to others besides Mrs Pettifer, though there was no other dwelling that opened into the passage – only warehouses and outbuildings. There was no gravel for her to throw up at the window, nothing but heavy pavement, there was no doorbell, she must knock. Her first rap was very timid – one feeble fall of the knocker, and then she stood still again for many minutes, but presently she rallied her courage and knocked several times together, not loudly, but rapidly, so that Mrs Pettifer, if she only heard the sound, could not mistake it. And she had heard it, for by and by the casement of her window was opened, and Janet perceived that she was bending out to try and discern who it was at the door.

'It is I, Mrs Pettifer; it is Janet Dempster. Take me in, for pity's sake.'

'Merciful God! what has happened?'

'Robert has turned me out. I have been in the cold a long while.'

Mrs Pettifer said no more, but hurried away from the window, and was soon at the door with a light in her hand.

'Come in, my poor dear, come in,' said the good woman in a tremulous voice, drawing Janet within the door. 'Come into my warm bed, and may God in heaven save and comfort you.'

The pitying eyes, the tender voice, the warm touch, caused a rush of new feeling in Janet. Her heart swelled, and she burst out suddenly, like a child, into loud passionate sobs. Mrs Pettifer could not help crying with her, but she said, 'Come upstairs, my dear, come. Don't linger in the cold.'

She drew the poor sobbing thing gently upstairs, and persuaded her to get into the warm bed. But it was long before Janet could lie down. She sat leaning her head on her knees, convulsed by sobs, while the motherly woman covered her with clothes and held her arms round her to comfort her with warmth. At last the hysterical passion had exhausted itself, and she fell back on the pillow, but her throat was still agitated by piteous after-sobs, such as shake a little child even when it has found a refuge from its alarms on its mother's lap.

Now Janet was getting quieter, Mrs Pettifer determined to go down and make a cup of tea, the first thing a kind old woman thinks of as a solace and restorative under all calamities. Happily there was no danger of awaking her servant, a heavy girl of sixteen, who was snoring blissfully in the attic, and might be kept ignorant of the way in which Mrs Dempster had come in. So Mrs Pettifer busied herself with rousing the kitchen fire, which was kept in under a huge 'raker' – a possibility by which the coal of the midland counties atones for all its slowness and white ashes.

When she carried up the tea, Janet was lying quite still; the spasmodic agitation had ceased, and she seemed lost in thought; her eyes were fixed vacantly on the rushlight shade, and all the lines of sorrow were deepened in her face.

'Now, my dear,' said Mrs Pettifer, 'let me persuade you to drink a cup of tea; you'll find it warm you and soothe you very much. Why, dear heart, your feet are like ice still. Now, do drink this tea, and I'll wrap 'em up in flannel, and then they'll get warm.'

Janet turned her dark eyes on her old friend and stretched out her arms. She was too much oppressed to say anything; her suffering lay like a heavy weight on her power of speech; but she wanted to kiss the good kind woman. Mrs Pettifer, setting down the cup, bent towards the sad beautiful face, and Janet kissed her with earnest sacramental kisses – such kisses as seal a new and closer bond between the helper and the helped.

She drank the tea obediently. 'It does warm me,' she said. 'But now you will get into bed. I shall lie still now.'

Mrs Pettifer felt it was the best thing she could do to lie down quietly and say no more. She hoped Janet might go to sleep. As for herself, with that tendency to wakefulness common to advanced years, she found it impossible to compose herself to sleep again after this agitating surprise. She lay listening to the clock, wondering what had led to this new outrage of Dempster's, praying for the poor thing at her side, and pitying the mother who would have to hear it all tomorrow.

16

Janet lay still, as she had promised, but the tea, which had warmed her and given her a sense of greater bodily ease, had only heightened the previous excitement of her brain. Her ideas had a new vividness, which made her feel as if she had only seen life through a dim haze before; her thoughts, instead of springing from the action of her own mind, were external existences that thrust themselves imperiously upon her like haunting visions. The future took shape after shape of misery before her, always ending in her being dragged back again to her old life of terror, and stupor, and fevered despair. Her husband had so long overshadowed her life that her imagination could not keep hold of a condition in which that great dread was absent, and even his absence – what was it? only a dreary vacant flat, where there was nothing to strive after, nothing to long for.

At last, the light of morning quenched the rushlight, and Janet's thoughts became more and more fragmentary and confused. She was every moment slipping off the level on which she lay thinking, down, down into some depth from which she tried to rise again with a start. Slumber was stealing over her weary brain: that uneasy slumber which is only better than wretched waking, because the life we seemed to live in it determines no wretched future, because the things we do and suffer in it are but hateful shadows, and leave no impress that petrifies into an irrevocable past.

She had scarcely been asleep an hour when her movements became more violent, her mutterings more frequent and agitated, till at last she started up with a smothered cry, and looked wildly round her, shaking with terror.

'Don't be frightened, dear Mrs Dempster,' said Mrs Pettifer, who was up and dressing, 'you are with me, your old friend, Mrs Pettifer. Nothing will harm you.'

Janet sank back again on her pillow, still trembling. After lying silent a little while, she said, 'It was a horrible dream. Dear Mrs Pettifer, don't let anyone know I am here. Keep it a secret. If he finds out, he will come and drag me back again.'

'No, my dear, depend on me. I've just thought I shall send the servant home on a holiday – I've promised her a good while. I'll send her away as soon as she's had her breakfast, and she'll have no occasion to know you're here. There's no holding servants' tongues, if you let 'em know anything. What they don't know, they won't tell; you may trust 'em so far. But shouldn't you like me to go and fetch your mother?'

'No, not yet, not yet. I can't bear to see her yet.'

'Well, it shall be just as you like. Now try and get to sleep again. I shall leave you for an hour or two, and send off Phoebe, and then bring you some breakfast. I'll lock the door behind me, so that the girl mayn't come in by chance.'

The daylight changes the aspect of misery to us, as of everything else. In the night it presses on our imagination – the forms it takes are false, fitful, exaggerated; in broad day it sickens our sense with the dreary persistence of definite measurable reality. The man who looks with ghastly horror on all his property aflame in the dead of night, has not half the sense of destitution he will have in the morning, when he walks over the ruins lying blackened in the pitiless sunshine. That moment of intensest depression was come to Janet, when the daylight which showed her the walls and chairs and tables, and all the commonplace reality that surrounded her, seemed to lay bare the future too, and bring out into oppressive distinctness all the details of a weary life to be lived from day to day, with no hope to strengthen her against that evil habit, which she loathed in retrospect and yet was powerless to resist. Her husband would never consent to her living away from him: she was become necessary to his tyranny; he would never willingly loosen his grasp on her. She had a vague notion of some protection the law might give her, if she could prove her life in danger from him, but she shrank utterly, as she had always done, from any active, public resistance or vengeance; she felt too crushed, too faulty, too liable to reproach, to have the courage, even if she had had the wish to put herself openly in the position of a wronged woman seeking redress. She had no strength to sustain her in a course of self-defence and independence: there was a darker shadow over her life than the dread of her husband – it was the shadow of self-despair. The easiest thing would be to go away and hide herself from him. But then there was her mother: Robert had all her little property in his hands, and that little was scarcely enough to keep her in comfort without his aid. If Janet went away alone he would be sure to persecute her mother, and if she did go away – what then? She must work to maintain herself, she must exert herself, weary and hopeless as she was, to begin life afresh. How hard that seemed to her! Janet's nature did not belie her grand face and form: there was energy, there was strength in it, but it was the strength of the vine, which must have its broad leaves and rich clusters borne up by a firm stay. And now she had nothing to rest on – no faith, no love. If her mother had been very feeble, aged or sickly, Janet's deep pity and tenderness might have made a daughter's duties an interest and a solace, but Mrs Raynor had never needed tendance; she had always been giving help to her daughter; she had always been a sort of humble ministering spirit, and it was one of Janet's pangs of memory, that instead of being her mother's comfort, she had been her mother's trial. Everywhere the same sadness! Her life was a sun-dried, barren tract, where there was no shadow, and where all the waters were bitter.

No! She suddenly thought – and the thought was like an electric shock – there was one spot in her memory which seemed to promise her an untried spring, where the waters might be sweet. That short interview with Mr Tryan had come back upon her – his voice, his words, his look, which told her that he knew sorrow. His words have implied that he thought his death was near, yet he had a faith which enabled him to labour – enabled him to give comfort to others. That look of his came back on her with a vividness greater than it had had for her in reality: surely he knew more of the secrets of sorrow than other men; perhaps he had some message of comfort, different from the feeble words she had been used to hear from others. She was tired, she was sick of that barren exhortation – Do right, and keep a clear conscience, and God will reward you, and your troubles will be easier to bear. She wanted strength to do right – she wanted something to rely on besides her own resolutions, for was not the path behind her all strewn with broken resolutions? How could she trust in new ones? She had often heard Mr Tryan laughed at for being fond of great sinners. She began to see a new meaning in those words; he would perhaps understand her helplessness, her wants. If she could pour out her heart to him! if she could for the first time in her life unlock all the chambers of her soul!

The impulse to confession almost always requires the presence of a fresh ear and a fresh heart; and in our moments of spiritual need, the man to whom we have no tie but our common nature, seems nearer to us than mother, brother or friend. Our daily familiar life is but a hiding of ourselves from each other behind a screen of trivial words and deeds, and those who sit with us at the same hearth are often the furthest off from the deep human soul within us, full of unspoken evil and unacted good.

When Mrs Pettifer came back to her, turning the key and opening the door very gently, Janet, instead of being asleep, as her good friend had hoped, was intensely occupied with her new thought. She longed to ask Mrs Pettifer if she could see Mr Tryan, but she was arrested by doubts and timidity. He might not feel for her – he might be shocked at her confession – he might talk to her of doctrines she could not understand or believe. She could not make up her mind yet, but she was too restless under this mental struggle to remain in bed.

'Mrs Pettifer,' she said, 'I can't lie here any longer; I must get up. Will you lend me some clothes?'

Wrapped in such drapery as Mrs Pettifer could find for her tall figure, Janet went down into the little parlour, and tried to take some of the breakfast her friend had prepared for her. But her effort was not a successful one; her cup of tea and bit of toast were only half finished. The leaden weight of discouragement pressed upon her more and more heavily. The wind had fallen, and a drizzling rain had come on; there was no prospect from Mrs Pettifer's parlour but a blank wall, and as Janet looked out at the window, the rain and the smoke-blackened bricks seemed to blend themselves in sickening identity with her desolation of spirit and the headachy weariness of her body.

Mrs Pettifer got through her household work as soon as she could, and sat down with her sewing, hoping that Janet would perhaps be able to talk a little of what had passed, and find some relief by unbosoming herself in that way. But Janet could not speak to her; she was importuned with the longing to see Mr Tryan, and yet hesitating to express it.

Two hours passed in this way. The rain went on drizzling, and Janet sat still, leaning her aching head on her hand, and looking alternately at the fire and out of the window. She felt this could not last – this motionless, vacant misery. She must determine on something, she must take some step, and yet everything was so difficult.

It was one o'clock, and Mrs Pettifer rose from her seat, saying, 'I must go and see about dinner.'

The movement and the sound startled Janet from her reverie. It seemed as if an opportunity were escaping her, and she said hastily, 'Is Mr Tryan in the town today, do you think?'

'No, I should think not, being Saturday, you know,' said Mrs Pettifer, her face lighting up with pleasure, 'but he would come, if he was sent for. I can send Jesson's boy with a note to him any time. Should you like to see him?'

'Yes, I think I should.'

'Then I'll send for him this instant.'

17

When Dempster awoke in the morning, he was at no loss to account to himself for the fact that Janet was not by his side. His hours of drunkenness were not cut off from his other hours by any blank wall of oblivion; he remembered what Janet had done to offend him the evening before, he remembered what he had done to her at midnight, just as he would have remembered if he had been consulted about a right of road.

The remembrance gave him a definite ground for the extra ill humour which had attended his waking every morning this week, but he would not admit to himself that it cost him any anxiety. 'Pooh,' he said inwardly, 'she would go straight to her mother's. She's as timid as a hare, and she'll never let anybody know about it. She'll be back again before night.'

But it would be as well for the servants not to know anything of the affair, so he collected the clothes she had taken off the night before, and threw them into a fire-proof closet of which he always kept the key in his pocket. When he went downstairs he said to the housemaid, 'Mrs Dempster is gone to her mother's; bring in the breakfast.'

The servants, accustomed to hear domestic broils, and to see their mistress put on her bonnet hastily and go to her mother's, thought it only something a little worse than usual that she should have gone thither in consequence of a violent quarrel, either at midnight, or in the early morning before they were up. The housemaid told the cook what she supposed had happened; the cook shook her head and said, 'Eh, dear, dear!' but they both expected to see their mistress back again in an hour or two.

Dempster, on his return home the evening before, had ordered his man, who lived away from the house, to bring up his horse and gig from the stables at ten. After breakfast he said to the housemaid, 'No one need sit up for me tonight; I shall not be at home till tomorrow evening,' and then he walked to the office to give some orders, expecting, as he returned, to see the man waiting with his gig. But though the church clock had struck ten, no gig was there. In Dempster's mood this was more than enough to exasperate him. He went in to take his accustomed glass of brandy before setting out, promising himself the satisfaction of presently thundering at Dawes for being a few minutes behind his time. An outbreak of temper towards his man was not common with him, for Dempster, like most tyrannous people, had that dastardly kind of self-restraint which enabled him to control his temper where it suited his own convenience to do so, and feeling the value of Dawes, a steady punctual fellow, he not only gave him high wages, but usually treated him with exceptional civility. This morning, however, ill humour got the better of prudence, and Dempster was determined to rate him soundly, a resolution for which Dawes gave him much better ground than he expected. Five minutes, ten minutes, a quarter of an hour, had passed, and Dempster was setting off to the stables in a back street to see what was the cause of the delay, when Dawes appeared with the gig.

'What the devil do you keep me here for?' thundered Dempster, 'kicking my heels like a beggarly tailor waiting for a carrier's cart? I ordered you to be here at ten. We might have driven to Whitlow by this time.'

'Why, one o' the traces was welly i' two, an' I had to take it to Brady's to be mended, an' he didn't get it done i' time.'

'Then why didn't you take it to him last night? Because of your damned laziness, I suppose. Do you think I give you wages for you to choose your own hours, and come dawdling up a quarter of an hour after my time?'

'Come, give me good words, will yer?' said Dawes, sulkily. 'I'm not lazy, nor no man shall call me lazy. I know well anuff what you gi' me wages for, it's for doin' what yer won't find many men as 'ull do.'

'What, you impudent scoundrel,' said Dempster, getting into the gig, 'you think you're necessary to me, do you? As if a beastly bucket-carrying idiot like you wasn't to be got any day. Look out for a new master, then, who'll pay you for not doing as you're bid.'

Dawes' blood was now fairly up. 'I'll look out for a master as has got a better charicter nor a lyin', bletherin' drunkard, an' I shouldn't hev to go fur.'

Dempster, furious, snatched the whip from the socket, and gave Dawes a cut which he meant to fall across his shoulders saying, 'Take that, sir, and go to hell with you!'

Dawes was in the act of turning with the reins in his hand when the lash fell, and the cut went across his face. With white lips, he said, 'I'll have the law on yer for that, lawyer as y'are,' and threw the reins on the horse's back.

Dempster leaned forward, seized the reins, and drove off.

'Why, there's your friend Dempster driving out without his man again,' said Mr Luke Byles, who was chatting with Mr Budd in the Bridge Way. 'What a fool he is to drive that two-wheeled thing! he'll get pitched on his head one of these days.'

'Not he,' said Mr Budd, nodding to Dempster as he passed, 'he's got nine lives, Dempster has.'

18

It was dusk, and the candles were lighted before Mr Tryan knocked at Mrs Pettifer's door. Her messenger had brought back word that he was not at home, and all afternoon Janet had been agitated by the fear that he would not come, but as soon as that anxiety was removed by the knock at the door, she felt a sudden rush of doubt and timidity: she trembled and turned cold.

Mrs Pettifer went to open the door, and told Mr Tryan, in as few words as possible, what had happened in the night. As he laid down his hat and prepared to enter the parlour, she said, 'I won't go in with you, for I think perhaps she would rather see you go in alone.'

Janet, wrapped up in a large white shawl which threw her dark face into startling relief, was seated with her eyes turned anxiously towards the door when Mr Tryan entered. He had not seen her since their interview at Sally Martin's long months ago, and he felt a strong movement of compassion at the sight of the pain-stricken face which seemed to bear written on it the signs of all Janet's intervening misery. Her heart gave a great leap, as her eyes met his once more. No! she had not deceived herself: there was all the sincerity, all the sadness, all the deep pity in them her memory had told her of; more than it had told her, for in proportion as his face had become thinner and more worn, his eyes appeared to have gathered intensity.

He came forward, and, putting out his hand, said, 'I am so glad you sent for me – I am so thankful you thought I could be any comfort to you.' Janet took his hand in silence. She was unable to utter any words of mere politeness, or even of gratitude; her heart was too full of other words that had welled up the moment she met his pitying glance, and felt her doubts fall away.

They sat down opposite each other, and she said in a low voice, while slow difficult tears gathered in her aching eyes, 'I want to tell you how unhappy I am – how weak and wicked. I feel no strength to live or die. I thought you could tell me something that would help me.' She paused.

'Perhaps I can,' Mr Tryan said, 'for in speaking to me you are speaking to a fellow sinner who has needed just the comfort and help you are needing.'

'And you did find it?'

'Yes, and I trust you will find it.'

'Oh, I should like to be good and to do right,' Janet burst forth, 'but indeed, indeed, my lot has been a very hard one.

I loved my husband very dearly when we were married, and I meant to make him happy – I wanted nothing else. But he began to be angry with me for little things and… I don't want to accuse him… but he drank and got more and more unkind to me, and then very cruel, and he beat me. And that cut me to the heart. It made me almost mad sometimes to think all our love had come to that… I couldn't bear up against it. I had never been used to drink anything but water. I hated wine and spirits because Robert drank them so, but one day when I was very wretched, and the wine was standing on the table, I suddenly… I can hardly remember how I came to do it… I poured some wine into a large glass and drank it. It blunted my feelings, and made me more indifferent. After that, the temptation was always coming, and it got stronger and stronger. I was ashamed, and I hated what I did, but almost while the thought was passing through my mind that I would never do it again, I did it. It seemed as if there was a demon in me always making me rush to do what I longed not to do. And I thought all the more that God was cruel, for if He had not sent me that dreadful trial, so much worse than other women have to bear, I should not have done wrong in that way. I suppose it is wicked to think so… I feel as if there must be goodness and right above us, but I can't see it, I can't trust in it. And I have gone on in that way for years and years. At one time it used to be better now and then, but everything has got worse lately. I felt sure it must soon end somehow. And last night he turned me out of doors… I don't know what to do. I will never go back to that life again if I can help it, and yet everything else seems so miserable. I feel sure that demon will always be urging me to satisfy the craving that comes upon me, and the days will go on as they have done through all those miserable years. I shall always be doing wrong, and hating myself after –

sinking lower and lower, and knowing that I am sinking. Oh, can you tell me any way of getting strength? Have you ever known anyone like me that got peace of mind and power to do right? Can you give me any comfort – any hope?'

While Janet was speaking, she had forgotten everything but her misery and her yearning for comfort. Her voice had risen from the low tone of timid distress to an intense pitch of imploring anguish. She clasped her hands tightly, and looked at Mr Tryan with eager questioning eyes, with parted, trembling lips, with the deep horizontal lines of overmastering pain on her brow. In this artificial life of ours, it is not often we see a human face with all a heart's agony in it, uncontrolled by self-consciousness; when we do see it, it startles us as if we had suddenly waked into the real world of which this everyday one is but a puppet-show copy. For some moments Mr Tryan was too deeply moved to speak.

'Yes, dear Mrs Dempster,' he said at last, 'there is comfort, there is hope for you. Believe me there is, for I speak from my own deep and hard experience.' He paused, as if he had not made up his mind to utter the words that were urging themselves to his lips. Presently he continued, 'Ten years ago, I felt as wretched as you do. I think my wretchedness was even worse than yours, for I had a heavier sin on my conscience. I had suffered no wrong from others as you have, and I had injured another irreparably in body and soul. The image of the wrong I had done pursued me everywhere, and I seemed on the brink of madness. I hated my life, for I thought, just as you do, that I should go on falling into temptation and doing more harm in the world, and I dreaded death, for with that sense of guilt on my soul, I felt that whatever state I entered on must be one of misery. But a dear friend to whom I opened my mind showed me it was just such as I – the helpless who feel themselves helpless – that God specially invites to come to Him, and offers all the riches of His salvation: not forgiveness only, forgiveness would be worth little if it left us under the powers of our evil passions, but strength – that strength which enables us to conquer sin.'

'But,' said Janet, 'I can feel no trust in God. He seems always to have left me to myself. I have sometimes prayed to Him to help me, and yet everything has been just the same as before. If you felt like me, how did you come to have hope and trust?'

'Do not believe that God has left you to yourself. How can you tell but that the hardest trials you have known have been only the road by which He was leading you to that complete sense of your own sin and helplessness, without which you would never have renounced all other hopes, and trusted in His love alone? I know, dear Mrs Dempster, I know it is hard to bear. I would not speak lightly of your sorrows. I feel that the mystery of our life is great, and at one time it seemed as dark to me as it does to you.' Mr Tryan hesitated again. He saw that the first thing Janet needed was to be assured of sympathy. She must be made to feel that her anguish was not strange to him, that he entered into the only half-expressed secrets of her spiritual weakness, before any other message of consolation could find its way to her heart. The tale of the Divine Pity was never yet believed from lips that were not felt to be moved by human pity. And Janet's anguish was not strange to Mr Tryan. He had never been in the presence of a sorrow and a self-despair that had sent so strong a thrill through all the recesses of his saddest experience, and it is because sympathy is but a living again through our own past in a new form, that confession often prompts a response of confession. Mr Tryan felt this prompting, and his judgement, too, told him that in obeying it he would be taking the best means of administering comfort to Janet. Yet he hesitated, as we tremble to let in the daylight on a chamber of relics which we have never visited except in curtained silence. But the first impulse triumphed, and he went on, 'I had lived all my life at a distance from God. My youth was spent in thoughtless self-indulgence, and all my hopes were of a vain worldly kind. I had no thought of entering the Church; I looked forward to a political career, for my father was private secretary to a man high in the Whig Ministry, and had been promised strong interest in my behalf. At college I lived in intimacy with the gayest men, even adopting follies and vices for which I had no taste, out of mere pliancy and the love of standing well with my companions. You see, I was more guilty even then than you have been, for I threw away all the rich blessings of untroubled youth and health; I had no excuse in my outward lot. But while I was at college that event in my life occurred, which in the end brought on the state of mind I have mentioned to you – the state of self-reproach and despair, which enables me to understand to the full what you are suffering, and I tell you the facts, because I want you to be assured that I am not uttering mere vague words when I say that I have been raised from as low a depth of sin and sorrow as that in which you feel yourself to be. At college I had an attachment to a lovely girl of seventeen; she was very much below my own station in life, and I never contemplated marrying her, but I induced her to leave her father's house. I did not mean to forsake her when I left college, and I quieted all scruples of conscience by promising myself that I would always take care of poor Lucy. But on my return from a vacation spent in travelling, I found that Lucy was gone – gone away with a gentleman, her neighbours said. I was a good deal distressed, but I tried to persuade myself that no harm would come to her. Soon afterwards I had an illness which left my health delicate, and made all dissipation distasteful to me. Life seemed very wearisome and empty, and I looked with envy on everyone who had some great and absorbing object – even on my cousin who was preparing to go out as a missionary, and whom I had been used to think a dismal, tedious person, because he was constantly urging religious subjects upon me. We were living in London then; it was three years since I had lost sight of Lucy, and one summer evening, about nine o'clock, as I was walking along Gower Street, I saw a knot of people on the causeway before me. As I came up to them, I heard one woman say, "I tell you, she is dead." This awakened my interest, and I pushed my way within the circle. The body of a woman, dressed in fine clothes, was lying against a doorstep. Her head was bent on one side, and the long curls had fallen over her cheek. A tremor seized me when I saw the hair: it was light chestnut – the colour of Lucy's. I knelt down and turned aside the hair; it was Lucy – dead – with paint on her cheeks. I found out afterwards that she had taken poison – that she was in the power of a wicked woman – that the very clothes on her back were not her own. It was then that my past life burst upon me in all its hideousness. I wished I had never been born. I couldn't look into the future. Lucy's dead painted face would follow me there, as it did when I looked back into the past – as it did when I sat down to table with my friends, when I lay down in my bed, and when I rose up. There was only one thing that could make life tolerable to me: that was, to spend all the rest of it in trying to save others from the ruin I had brought on one. But how was that possible for me? I had no comfort, no strength, no wisdom in my own soul; how could I give them to others? My mind was dark, rebellious, at war with itself and with God.'

Mr Tryan had been looking away from Janet. His face was towards the fire, and he was absorbed in the images his memory was recalling. But now he turned his eyes on her, and they met hers, fixed on him with the look of rapt expectation, with which one clinging to a slippery summit of a rock, while the waves are rising higher and higher, watches the boat that has put from shore to his rescue.

'You see, Mrs Dempster, how deep my need was. I went on in this way for months. I was convinced that if I ever got health and comfort, it must be from religion. I went to hear celebrated preachers, and I read religious books. But I found nothing that fitted my own need. The faith which puts the sinner in possession of salvation seemed, as I understood it, to be quite out of my reach. I had no faith; I only felt utterly wretched, under the power of habits and dispositions which had wrought hideous evil. At last, as I told you, I found a friend to whom I opened all my feelings – to whom I confessed everything. He was a man who had gone through very deep experience, and could understand the different wants of different minds. He made it clear to me that the only preparation for coming to Christ and partaking of His salvation, was that very sense of guilt and helplessness which was weighing me down. He said, You are weary and heavy-laden; well, it is you Christ invites to come to Him and find rest. He asks you to cling to Him, to lean on Him; He does not command you to walk alone without stumbling. He does not tell you, as your fellow men do, that you must first merit His love; He neither condemns nor reproaches you for the past, He only bids you come to Him that you may have life; He bids you stretch out your hands, and take of the fullness of His love. You have only to rest on Him as a child rests on its mother's arms, and you will be upborne by His divine strength. That is what is meant by faith. Your evil habits, you feel, are too strong for you; you are unable to wrestle with them; you know beforehand you shall fall. But when once we feel our helplessness in that way, and go to the Saviour, desiring to be freed from the power as well as the punishment of sin, we are no longer left to our own strength. As long as we live in rebellion against God, desiring to have our own will, seeking happiness in the things of this world, it is as if we shut ourselves up in a crowded stifling room, where we breathe only poisoned air, but we have only to walk out under the infinite heavens, and we breathe the pure free air that gives us health, and strength, and gladness. It is just so with God's spirit: as soon as we submit ourselves to His will, as soon as we desire to be united to Him, and made pure and holy, it is as if the walls had fallen down that shut us out from God, and we are fed with His spirit, which gives us new strength.'

'That is what I want,' said Janet; 'I have left off minding about pleasure. I think I could be contented in the midst of hardship, if I felt that God cared for me, and would give me strength to lead a pure life. But tell me, did you soon find peace and strength?'

'Not perfect peace for a long while, but hope and trust, which is strength. No sense of pardon for myself could do away with the pain I had in thinking what I had helped to bring on another. My friend used to urge upon me that my sin against God was greater than my sin against her, but – it may be from want of deeper spiritual feeling – that has remained to this hour the sin which causes me the bitterest pang. I could never rescue Lucy, but by God's blessing I might rescue other weak and falling souls, and that was why I entered the Church. I asked for nothing through the rest of my life but that I might be devoted to God's work, without swerving in search of pleasure either to the right hand or to the left. It has been often a hard struggle – but God has been with me – and perhaps it may not last much longer.'

Mr Tryan paused. For a moment he had forgotten Janet, and for a moment she had forgotten her own sorrows. When she recurred to herself, it was with a new feeling.

'Ah, what a difference between our lives! you have been choosing pain, and working, and denying yourself, and I have been thinking only of myself. I was only angry and discontented because I had pain to bear. You never had that wicked feeling that I have had so often, did you? that God was cruel to send me trials and temptations worse than others have.'

'Yes, I had; I had very blasphemous thoughts, and I know that spirit of rebellion must have made the worst part of your lot. You did not feel how impossible it is for us to judge rightly of God's dealings, and you opposed yourself to His will. But what do we know? We cannot foretell the working of the smallest event in our own lot; how can we presume to judge of things that are so much too high for us? There is nothing that becomes us but entire submission, perfect resignation. As long as we set up our own will and our own wisdom against God's, we make that wall between us and His love which I have spoken of just now. But as soon as we lay ourselves entirely at His feet, we have enough light given us to guide our own steps; as the foot-soldier who hears nothing of the councils that determine the course of the great battle he is in, hears plainly enough the word of command which he must himself obey. I know, dear Mrs Dempster, I know it is hard – the hardest thing of all, perhaps – to flesh and blood. But carry that difficulty to the Saviour along with all your other sins and weaknesses, and ask Him to pour into you a spirit of submission. He enters into your struggles; He has drunk the cup of our suffering to the dregs; He knows the hard wrestling it costs us to say, "Not my will, but Thine be done."'

'Pray with me,' said Janet, 'pray now that I may have light and strength.'

19

Before leaving Janet, Mr Tryan urged her strongly to send for her mother.

'Do not wound her,' he said, 'by shutting her out any longer from your troubles. It is right that you should be with her.'

'Yes, I will send for her,' said Janet. 'But I would rather not go to my mother's yet, because my husband is sure to think I am there, and he might come and fetch me. I can't go back to him… at least, not yet. Ought I to go back to him?'

'No, certainly not, at present. Something should be done to secure you from violence. Your mother, I think, should consult some confidential friend, some man of character and experience, who might mediate between you and your husband.'

'Yes, I will send for my mother directly. But I will stay here, with Mrs Pettifer, till something has been done. I want no one to know where I am, except you. You will come again, will you not? you will not leave me to myself?'

'You will not be left to yourself. God is with you. If I have been able to give you any comfort, it is because His power and love have been present with us. But I am very thankful that He has chosen to work through me. I shall see you again tomorrow – not before evening, for it will be Sunday, you know; but after the evening lecture I shall be at liberty. You will be in my prayers till then. In the meantime, dear Mrs Dempster, open your heart as much as you can to your mother and Mrs Pettifer. Cast away from you the pride that makes us shrink from acknowledging our weakness to our friends. Ask them to help you in guarding yourself from the least approach of the sin you most dread. Deprive yourself as far as possible of the very means and opportunity of committing it. Every effort of that kind made in humility and dependence is a prayer. Promise me you will do this.'

'Yes, I promise you. I know I have always been too proud; I could never bear to speak to anyone about myself. I have been proud towards my mother, even; it has always made me angry when she has seemed to take notice of my faults.'

'Ah, dear Mrs Dempster, you will never say again that life is blank, and that there is nothing to live for, will you? See what work there is to be done in life, both in our own souls and for others. Surely it matters little whether we have more or less of this world's comfort in these short years, when God is training us for the eternal enjoyment of His love. Keep that great end of life before you, and your troubles here will seem only the small hardships of a journey. Now I must go.'

Mr Tryan rose and held out his hand. Janet took it and said, 'God has been very good to me in sending you to me. I will trust in Him. I will try to do everything you tell me.'

Blessed influence of one true loving human soul on another! Not calculable by algebra, not deducible by logic, but mysterious, effectual, mighty as the hidden process by which the tiny seed is quickened, and bursts forth into tall stem and broad leaf, and glowing tasselled flower. Ideas are often poor ghosts; our sun-filled eyes cannot discern them; they pass athwart us in thin vapour, and cannot make themselves felt. But sometimes they are made flesh: they breathe upon us with warm breath, they touch us with soft responsive hands, they look at us with sad sincere eyes, and speak to us in appealing tones; they are clothed in a living human soul, with all its conflicts, its faith, and its love. Then their presence is a power, then they shake us like a passion, and we are drawn after them with gentle compulsion, as flame is drawn to flame.

Janet's dark grand face, still fatigued, had become quite calm, and looked up, as she sat, with a humble childlike expression at the thin blond face and slightly sunken grey eyes which now shone with hectic brightness. She might have been taken for an image of passionate strength beaten and worn with conflict, and he for an image of the self-renouncing faith which has soothed that conflict into rest. As he looked at the sweet submissive face, he remembered its look of despairing anguish, and his heart was very full as he turned away from her. 'Let me only live to see this work confirmed, and then…'

It was nearly ten o'clock when Mr Tryan left, but Janet was bent on sending for her mother; so Mrs Pettifer, as the readiest plan, put on her bonnet and went herself to fetch Mrs Raynor. The mother had been too long used to expect that every fresh week would be more painful than the last, for Mrs Pettifer's news to come upon her with the shock of a surprise. Quietly, without any show of distress, she made up a bundle of clothes, and, telling her little maid that she should not return home that night, accompanied Mrs Pettifer back in silence.

When they entered the parlour, Janet, wearied out, had sunk to sleep in the large chair, which stood with its back to the door. The noise of the opening door disturbed her, and she was looking round wonderingly when Mrs Raynor came up to her chair, and said, 'It's your mother, Janet.'

'Mother, dear Mother!' Janet cried, clasping her closely. 'I have not been a good tender child to you, but I will be – I will not grieve you any more.'

The calmness which had withstood a new sorrow was overcome by a new joy, and the mother burst into tears.

20

On Sunday morning the rain had ceased, and Janet, looking out of the bedroom window, saw, above the housetops, a shining mass of white cloud rolling under the faraway blue sky. It was going to be a lovely April day. The fresh sky, left clear and calm after the long vexation of wind and rain, mingled its mild influence with Janet's new thoughts and prospects. She felt a buoyant courage that surprised herself, after the cold crushing weight of despondency which had oppressed her the day before: she could think even of her husband's rage without the old overpowering dread. For a delicious hope – the hope of purification and inward peace – had entered into Janet's soul, and made it springtime there as well as in the outer world.

While her mother was brushing and coiling up her thick black hair – a favourite task, because it seemed to renew the days of her daughter's girlhood – Janet told how she came to send for Mr Tryan, how she had remembered their meeting at Sally Martin's in the autumn, and had felt an irresistible desire to see him, and tell him her sins and her troubles.

'I see God's goodness now, Mother, in ordering it so that we should meet in that way, to overcome my prejudice against him, and make me feel that he was good, and then bringing it back to my mind in the depth of my trouble. You know what foolish things I used to say about him, knowing nothing of him all the while. And yet he was the man who was to give me comfort and help when everything else failed me. It is wonderful how I feel able to speak to him as I never have done to anyone before, and how every word he says to me enters my heart and has a new meaning for me. I think it must be because he has felt life more deeply than others, and has a deeper faith.

I believe everything he says at once. His words come to me like rain on the parched ground. It has always seemed to me before as if I could see behind people's words, as one sees behind a screen; but in Mr Tryan it is his very soul that speaks.'

'Well, my dear child, I love and bless him for your sake, if he has given you any comfort. I never believed the harm people said of him, though I had no desire to go and hear him, for I am contented with old-fashioned ways. I find more good teaching than I can practise in reading my Bible at home, and hearing Mr Crewe at church. But your wants are different, my dear, and we are not all led by the same road. That was certainly good advice of Mr Tryan's you told me of last night – that we should consult someone that may interfere for you with your husband – and I have been turning it over in my mind while I've been lying awake in the night. I think nobody will do so well as Mr Benjamin Landor, for we must have a man that knows the law, and that Robert is rather afraid of. And perhaps he could bring about an agreement for you to live apart. Your husband's bound to maintain you, you know; and, if you liked, we could move away from Milby and live somewhere else.'

'Oh, Mother, we must do nothing yet; I must think about it a little longer. I have a different feeling this morning from what I had yesterday. Something seems to tell me that I must go back to Robert some time – after a little while. I loved him once better than all the world, and I have never had any children to love. There were things in me that were wrong, and I should like to make up for them if I can.'

'Well, my dear, I won't persuade you. Think of it a little longer. But something must be done soon.'

'How I wish I had my bonnet, and shawl, and black gown here!' said Janet, after a few minutes' silence. 'I should like to go to Paddiford Church and hear Mr Tryan. There would be no fear of my meeting Robert, for he never goes out on a Sunday morning.'

'I'm afraid it would not do for me to go to the house and fetch your clothes,' said Mrs Raynor.

'Oh no, no! I must stay quietly here while you two go to church. I will be Mrs Pettifer's maid, and get the dinner ready for her by the time she comes back. Dear good woman! She was so tender to me when she took me in, in the night, Mother, and all the next day, when I couldn't speak a word to her to thank her.'

21

The servants at Dempster's felt some surprise when the morning, noon and evening of Saturday had passed, and still their mistress did not reappear.

'It's very odd,' said Kitty, the housemaid, as she trimmed her next week's cap, while Betty, the middle-aged cook, looked on with folded arms. 'Do you think as Mrs Raynor was ill, and sent for the missis afore we was up?'

'Oh,' said Betty, 'if it had been that, she'd ha' been back'ards an' for'ards three or four times afore now; leastways, she'd ha' sent little Ann to let us know.'

'There's summat up more nor usual between her an' the master, that you may depend on,' said Kitty. 'I know those clothes as was lying i' the drawing room yesterday, when the company was come, meant summat. I shouldn't wonder if that was what they've had a fresh row about. She's p'raps gone away, an's made up her mind not to come back again.'

'An' i' the right on't, too,' said Betty. 'I'd ha' overrun him long afore now, if it had been me. I wouldn't stan' bein' mauled as she is by no husband, not if he was the biggest lord i' the land. It's poor work bein' a wife at that price; I'd sooner be a cook wi'out perkises, an' hev roast, an' boil, an' fry, an' bake, all to mind at once. She may well do as she does. I know I'm glad enough of a drop o' summat myself when I'm plagued. I feel very low, like, tonight; I think I shall put my beer i' the saucepan an' warm it.'

'What a one you are for warmin' your beer, Betty! I couldn't abide it – nasty bitter stuff!'

'It's fine talkin', if you was a cook you'd know what belongs to bein' a cook. It's none so nice to hev a sinkin' at your stomach, I can tell you. You wouldn't think so much o' fine ribbins i' your cap then.'

'Well, well, Betty, don't be grumpy. Liza Thomson, as is at Phipps's, said to me last Sunday, "I wonder you'll stay at Dempster's," she says, "such goins-on as there is." But I says, "There's things to put up wi' in ivery place, an' you may change, an' change, an' not better yourself when all's said an' done." Lors! why, Liza told me herself as Mrs Phipps was as skinny as skinny i' the kitchen, for all they keep so much company; and as for follyers, she's as cross as a turkeycock if she finds 'em out. There's nothin' o' that sort i' the missis. How pretty she come an' spoke to Job last Sunday! There isn't a good-natur'der woman i' the world, that's my belief – an' hansome too. I al'ys think there's nobody looks half so well as the missis when she's got her 'air done nice. Lors! I wish I'd got long 'air like her – my 'air's a-comin' off dreadful.'

'There'll be fine work tomorrow, I expect,' said Betty, 'when the master comes home, an' Dawes a-swearin' as he'll niver do a stroke o' work for him again. It'll be good fun if he sets the justice on him for cuttin' him wi' the whip; the master'll p'raps get his comb cut for once in his life!'

'Why, he was in a temper like a fiend this morning,' said Kitty. 'I daresay it was along o' what had happened wi' the missis. We shall hev a pretty house wi' him if she doesn't come back – he'll want to be leatherin' us, I shouldn't wonder. He must hev somethin' t' ill-use when he's in a passion.'

'I'd tek care he didn't leather me – no, not if he was my husban' ten times o'er; I'd pour hot drippin' on him sooner. But the missis hasn't a sperrit like me. He'll mek her come back, you'll see; he'll come round her somehow. There's no likelihood of her coming back tonight, though, so I should think we might fasten the doors and go to bed when we like.'

On Sunday morning, however, Kitty's mind became disturbed by more definite and alarming conjectures about her mistress. While Betty, encouraged by the prospect of unwonted leisure, was sitting down to continue a letter which had long lain unfinished between the leaves of her Bible, Kitty came running into the kitchen and said, 'Lor! Betty, I'm all of a tremble; you might knock me down wi' a feather. I've just looked into the missis's wardrobe, an' there's both her bonnets. She must ha' gone wi'out her bonnet. An' then I remember as her nightclothes wasn't on the bed yesterday mornin'; I thought she'd put 'em away to be washed, but she hedn't, for I've been lookin'. It's my belief he's murdered her, and shut her up i' that closet as he keeps locked al'ys. He's capible on't.'

'Lors-ha'-massy, why you'd better run to Mrs Raynor's an' see if she's there, arter all. It was p'raps all a lie.'

Mrs Raynor had returned home to give directions to her little maiden, when Kitty, with the elaborate manifestation of alarm which servants delight in, rushed in without knocking, and, holding her hands on her heart as if the consequences to that organ were likely to be very serious, said, 'If you please 'm, is the missis here?'

'No, Kitty; why are you come to ask?'

'Because 'm, she's niver been at home since yesterday mornin', since afore we was up, an' we thought somethin' must ha' happened to her.'

'No, don't be frightened, Kitty. Your mistress is quite safe; I know where she is. Is your master at home?'

'No 'm; he went out yesterday mornin', an' said he shouldn't be back afore tonight.'

'Well, Kitty, there's nothing the matter with your mistress. You needn't say anything to anyone about her being away from home. I shall call presently and fetch her gown and bonnet. She wants them to put on.'

Kitty, perceiving there was a mystery she was not to enquire into, returned to Orchard Street, really glad to know that her mistress was safe, but disappointed nevertheless at being told that she was not to be frightened. She was soon followed by Mrs Raynor in quest of the gown and bonnet. The good mother, on learning that Dempster was not at home, had at once thought that she could gratify Janet's wish to go to Paddiford Church.

'See, my dear,' she said, as she entered Mrs Pettifer's parlour, 'I've brought you your black clothes. Robert's not at home, and is not coming till this evening. I couldn't find your best black gown, but this will do. I wouldn't bring anything else, you know, but there can't be any objection to my fetching clothes to cover you. You can go to Paddiford Church, now, if you like, and I will go with you.'

'That's a dear mother! Then we'll all three go together. Come and help me to get ready. Good little Mrs Crewe! It will vex her sadly that I should go to hear Mr Tryan. But I must kiss her, and make it up with her.'

Many eyes were turned on Janet with a look of surprise as she walked up the aisle of Paddiford Church. She felt a little tremor at the notice she knew she was exciting, but it was a strong satisfaction to her that she had been able at once to take a step that would let her neighbours know her change of feeling towards Mr Tryan; she had left herself now no room for proud reluctance or weak hesitation. The walk through the sweet spring air had stimulated all her fresh hopes, all her yearning desires after purity, strength and peace. She thought she should find a new meaning in the prayers this morning; her full heart, like an overflowing river, wanted those ready-made channels to pour itself into, and then she should hear Mr Tryan again, and his words would fall on her like precious balm, as they had done last night. There was a liquid brightness in her eyes as they rested on the mere walls, the pews, the weavers and colliers in their Sunday clothes. The commonest things seemed to touch the spring of love within her, just as, when we are suddenly released from an acute absorbing bodily pain, our heart and senses leap out in new freedom; we think even the noise of streets harmonious, and are ready to hug the tradesman who is wrapping up our change. A door had been opened in Janet's cold dark prison of self-despair, and the golden light of morning was pouring in its slanting beams through the blessed opening. There was sunlight in the world; there was a divine love caring for her; it had given her an earnest of good things; it had been preparing comfort for her in the very moment when she had thought herself most forsaken.

Mr Tryan might well rejoice when his eye rested on her as he entered his desk, but he rejoiced with trembling. He could not look at the sweet hopeful face without remembering its yesterday's look of agony, and there was the possibility that that look might return.

Janet's appearance at church was greeted not only by wondering eyes, but by kind hearts, and after the service several of Mr Tryan's hearers with whom she had been on cold terms of late, contrived to come up to her and take her by the hand.

'Mother,' said Miss Linnet, 'do let us go and speak to Mrs Dempster. I'm sure there's a great change in her mind towards Mr Tryan. I noticed how eagerly she listened to the sermon, and she's come with Mrs Pettifer, you see. We ought to go and give her a welcome among us.'

'Why, my dear, we've never spoke friendly these five year. You know she's been as haughty as anything since I quarrelled with her husband. However, let bygones be bygones, I've no grudge again' the poor thing, more particular as she must ha' flew in her husband's face to come an' hear Mr Tryan. Yes, let us go an' speak to her.'

The friendly words and looks touched Janet a little too keenly, and Mrs Pettifer wisely hurried her home by the least-frequented road. When they reached home, a violent fit of weeping, followed by continuous lassitude, showed that the emotions of the morning had overstrained her nerves. She was suffering, too, from the absence of the long-accustomed stimulus which she had promised Mr Tryan not to touch again. The poor thing was conscious of this, and dreaded her own weakness, as the victim of intermittent insanity dreads the oncoming of the old illusion.

'Mother,' she whispered, when Mrs Raynor urged her to lie down and rest all the afternoon, that she might be the better prepared to see Mr Tryan in the evening, 'Mother, don't let me have anything if I ask for it.'

In the mother's mind there was the same anxiety, and in her it was mingled with another fear – the fear lest Janet, in her present excited state of mind, should take some premature step in relation to her husband, which might lead back to all the former troubles. The hint she had thrown out in the morning of her wish to return to him after a time, showed a new eagerness for difficult duties, that only made the long-saddened sober mother tremble. But as evening approached, Janet's morning heroism all forsook her: her imagination, influenced by physical depression as well as by mental habits, was haunted by the vision of her husband's return home, and she began to shudder with the yesterday's dread. She heard him calling her, she saw him going to her mother's to look for her, she felt sure he would find her out, and burst in upon her.

'Pray, pray, don't leave me, don't go to church,' she said to Mrs Pettifer. 'You and Mother both stay with me till Mr Tryan comes.'

At twenty minutes past six, the church bells were ringing for the evening service, and soon the congregation was streaming along Orchard Street in the mellow sunset. The street opened toward the west. The red half-sunken sun shed a solemn splendour on the everyday houses, and crimsoned the windows of Dempster's projecting upper storey.

Suddenly a loud murmur arose and spread along the stream of churchgoers, and one group after another paused and looked backward. At the far end of the street, men, accompanied by a miscellaneous group of onlookers, were slowly carrying something – a body stretched on a door. Slowly they passed along the middle of the street, lined all the way with awestruck faces, till they turned aside and paused in the red sunlight before Dempster's door.

It was Dempster's body. No one knew whether he was alive or dead.

22

It was probably a hard saying to the Pharisees, that 'there is more joy in heaven over one sinner that repenteth, than over ninety and nine just persons that need no repentance'.[35] And certain ingenious philosophers of our own day must surely take offence at a joy so entirely out of correspondence with arithmetical proportion. But a heart that has been taught by its own sore struggles to bleed for the woes of another – that has 'learned pity through suffering' – is likely to find very imperfect satisfaction in the 'balance of happiness', 'doctrine of compensations', and other short and easy methods of obtaining thorough complacency in the presence of pain, and for such a heart that saying will not be altogether dark. The emotions, I have observed, are but slightly influenced by arithmetical considerations: the mother, when her sweet lisping little ones have all been taken from her one after another, and she is hanging over her last dead babe, finds small consolation in the fact that the tiny dimpled corpse is but one of a necessary average, and that a thousand other babes brought into the world at the same time are doing well, and are likely to live; and if you stood beside that mother – if you knew her pang and shared it – it is probable you would be equally unable to see a ground of complacency in statistics.

Doubtless a complacency resting on that basis is highly rational, but emotion, I fear, is obstinately irrational: it insists on caring for individuals; it absolutely refuses to adopt the quantitative view of human anguish, and to admit that thirteen happy lives are a set-off against twelve miserable lives, which leaves a clear balance on the side of satisfaction. This is the inherent imbecility of feeling, and one must be a great philosopher to have got quite clear of all that, and to have emerged into the serene air of pure intellect, in which it is evident that individuals really exist for no other purpose than that abstractions may be drawn from them – abstractions that may rise from heaps of ruined lives like the sweet savour of a sacrifice in the nostrils of philosophers, and of a philosophic Deity. And so it comes to pass that for the man who knows sympathy because he has known sorrow, that old, old saying about the joy of angels over the repentant sinner outweighing their joy over the ninety-nine just, has a meaning which does not jar with the language of his own heart. It only tells him, that for angels, too, there is a transcendent value in human pain, which refuses to be settled by equations; that the eyes of angels, too, are turned away from the serene happiness of the righteous to bend with yearning pity on the poor erring soul wandering in the desert where no water is; that for angels, too, the misery of one casts so tremendous a shadow as to eclipse the bliss of ninety-nine.

Mr Tryan had gone through the initiation of suffering; it is no wonder, then, that Janet's restoration was the work that lay nearest his heart, and that, weary as he was in body when he entered the vestry after the evening service, he was impatient to fulfil the promise of seeing her. His experience enabled him to divine – what was the fact – that the hopefulness of the morning would be followed by a return of depression and discouragement, and his sense of the inward and outward difficulties in the way of her restoration was so keen, that he could only find relief from the foreboding it excited by lifting up his heart in prayer. There are unseen elements which often frustrate our wisest calculations – which raise up the sufferer from the edge of the grave, contradicting the prophecies of the clear-sighted physician, and fulfilling the blind clinging hopes of affection; such unseen elements Mr Tryan called the Divine

Will, and filled up the margin of ignorance which surrounds all our knowledge with the feelings of trust and resignation. Perhaps the profoundest philosophy could hardly fill it up better.

His mind was occupied in this way as he was absently taking off his gown, when Mr Landor startled him by entering the vestry and asking abruptly, 'Have you heard the news about Dempster?'

'No,' said Mr Tryan anxiously, 'what is it?'

'He has been thrown out of his gig in the Bridge Way, and he was taken up for dead. They were carrying him home as we were coming to church, and I stayed behind to see what I could do. I went in to speak to Mrs Dempster, and prepare her a little, but she was not at home. Dempster is not dead, however, he was stunned with the fall. Pilgrim came in a few minutes, and he says the right leg is broken in two places. It's likely to be a terrible case, with his state of body. It seems he was more drunk than usual, and they say he came along the Bridge Way flogging his horse like a madman, till at last it gave a sudden wheel, and he was pitched out. The servants said they didn't know where Mrs Dempster was: she had been away from home since yesterday morning, but Mrs Raynor knew.'

'I know where she is,' said Mr Tryan, 'but I think it will be better for her not to be told of this just yet.'

'Ah, that was what Pilgrim said, and so I didn't go round to Mrs Raynor's. He said it would be all the better if Mrs Dempster could be kept out of the house for the present. Do you know if anything new has happened between Dempster and his wife lately? I was surprised to hear of her being at Paddiford Church this morning.'

'Yes, something has happened, but I believe she is anxious that the particulars of his behaviour towards her should not be known. She is at Mrs Pettifer's – there is no reason for concealing that, since what has happened to her husband, and yesterday, when she was in very deep trouble, she sent for me. I was very thankful she did so: I believe a great change of feeling has begun in her. But she is at present in that excitable state of mind – she has been shaken by so many painful emotions during the last two days, that I think it would be better, for this evening at least, to guard her from a new shock, if possible. But I am going now to call upon her, and I shall see how she is.'

'Mr Tryan,' said Mr Jerome, who had entered during the dialogue, and had been standing by, listening with a distressed face, 'I shall take it as a favour if you'll let me know if iver there's anything I can do for Mrs Dempster. Eh, dear, what a world this is! I think I see 'em fifteen year ago – as happy a young couple as iver was; and now, what it's all come to! I was in a hurry, like, to punish Dempster for pessecutin', but there was a stronger hand at work nor mine.'

'Yes, Mr Jerome, but don't let us rejoice in punishment, even when the hand of God alone inflicts it. The best of us are but poor wretches just saved from shipwreck; can we feel anything but awe and pity when we see a fellow passenger swallowed by the waves?'

'Right, right, Mr Tryan. I'm over-hot and hasty, that I am. But I beg on you to tell Mrs Dempster – I mean, in course, when you've an opportunity – tell her she's a friend at the White House as she may send for any hour o' the day.'

'Yes, I shall have an opportunity, I dare say, and I will remember your wish. I think,' continued Mr Tryan, turning to Mr Landor, 'I had better see Mr Pilgrim on my way, and learn what is exactly the state of things by this time. What do you think?'

'By all means; if Mrs Dempster is to know, there's no one can break the news to her so well as you. I'll walk with you to Dempster's door. I dare say Pilgrim is there still. Come, Mr Jerome, you've got to go our way too, to fetch your horse.'

Mr Pilgrim was in the passage giving some directions to his assistant, when, to his surprise, he saw Mr Tryan enter. They shook hands, for Mr Pilgrim, never having joined the party of the anti-Tryanites, had no ground for resisting the growing conviction, that the Evangelical curate was really a good fellow, though he was a fool for not taking better care of himself.

'Why, I didn't expect to see you in your old enemy's quarters,' he said to Mr Tryan. 'However, it will be a good while before poor Dempster shows any fight again.'

'I came on Mrs Dempster's account,' said Mr Tryan. 'She is staying at Mrs Pettifer's; she has had a great shock from some severe domestic trouble lately, and I think it will be wiser to defer telling her of this dreadful event for a short time.'

'Why, what has been up, eh?' said Mr Pilgrim, whose curiosity was at once awakened. 'She used to be no friend of yours. Has there been some split between them? It's a new thing for her to turn round on him.'

'Oh, merely an exaggeration of scenes that must often have happened before. But the question now is, whether you think there is any immediate danger of her husband's death, for in that case, I think, from what I have observed of her feelings, she would be pained afterwards to have been kept in ignorance.'

'Well, there's no telling in these cases, you know. I don't apprehend speedy death, and it is not absolutely impossible that we may bring him round again. At present he's in a state of apoplectic stupor, but if that subsides, delirium is almost sure to supervene, and we shall have some painful scenes. It's one of those complicated cases in which the delirium is likely to be of the worst kind – meningitis and delirium tremens together – and we may have a good deal of trouble with him. If Mrs Dempster were told, I should say it would be desirable to persuade her to remain out of the house at present. She could do no good, you know. I've got nurses.'

'Thank you,' said Mr Tryan. 'That is what I wanted to know. Goodbye.'

When Mrs Pettifer opened the door for Mr Tryan, he told her in a few words what had happened, and begged her to take an opportunity of letting Mrs Raynor know, that they might, if possible, concur in preventing a premature or sudden disclosure of the event to Janet.

'Poor thing!' said Mrs Pettifer. 'She's not fit to hear any bad news; she's very low this evening – worn out with feeling, and she's not had anything to keep her up, as she's been used to. She seems frightened at the thought of being tempted to take it.'

'Thank God for it; that fear is her greatest security.'

When Mr Tryan entered the parlour this time, Janet was again awaiting him eagerly, and her pale sad face was lighted up with a smile as she rose to meet him. But the next moment she said, with a look of anxiety, 'How very ill and tired you look! You have been working so hard all day, and yet you are come to talk to me. Oh, you are wearing yourself out. I must go and ask Mrs Pettifer to come and make you have some supper. But this is my mother; you have not seen her before, I think.'

While Mr Tryan was speaking to Mrs Raynor, Janet hurried out, and he, seeing that this good-natured thoughtfulness on his behalf would help to counteract her depression, was not inclined to oppose her wish, but accepted the supper Mrs Pettifer offered him, quietly talking the while about a clothing club he was going to establish in Paddiford, and the want of provident habits among the poor.

Presently, however, Mrs Raynor said she must go home for an hour, to see how her little maiden was going on, and Mrs Pettifer left the room with her to take the opportunity of telling her what had happened to Dempster. When Janet was left alone with Mr Tryan, she said, 'I feel so uncertain what to do about my husband. I am so weak – my feelings change so from hour to hour. This morning, when I felt so hopeful and happy, I thought I should like to go back to him, and try to make up for what has been wrong in me. I thought, now God would help me, and I should have you to teach and advise me, and I could bear the troubles that would come. But since then – all this afternoon and evening – I have had the same feelings I used to have, the same dread of his anger and cruelty, and it seems to me as if I should never be able to bear it without falling into the same sins, and doing just what I did before. Yet, if it were settled that I should live apart from him, I know it would always be a load on my mind that I had shut myself out from going back to him. It seems a dreadful thing in life, when anyone has been so near to one as a husband for fifteen years, to part and be nothing to each other any more. Surely that is a very strong tie, and I feel as if my duty can never lie quite away from it. It is very difficult to know what to do; what ought I to do?'

'I think it will be well not to take any decisive step yet. Wait until your mind is calmer. You might remain with your mother for a little while; I think you have no real ground for fearing any annoyance from your husband at present; he has put himself too much in the wrong; he will very likely leave you unmolested for some time. Dismiss this difficult question from your mind just now, if you can. Every new day may bring you new grounds for decision, and what is most needful for your health of mind is repose from that haunting anxiety about the future which has been preying on you. Cast yourself on God, and trust that He will direct you; He will make your duty clear to you, if you wait submissively on Him.'

'Yes, I will wait a little, as you tell me. I will go to my mother's tomorrow, and pray to be guided rightly. You will pray for me, too.'

23

The next morning Janet was so much calmer, and at breakfast spoke so decidedly of going to her mother's, that Mrs Pettifer and Mrs Raynor agreed it would be wise to let her know by degrees what had befallen her husband, since as soon as she went out there would be danger of her meeting someone who would betray the fact. But Mrs Raynor thought it would be well first to call at Dempster's, and ascertain how he was, so she said to Janet, 'My dear, I'll go home first and see to things, and get your room ready. You needn't come yet, you know. I shall be back again in an hour or so, and we can go together.'

'Oh no,' said Mrs Pettifer. 'Stay with me till evening. I shall be lost without you. You needn't go till quite evening.'

Janet had dipped into the *Life of Henry Martyn*,[36] which Mrs Pettifer had from the Paddiford Lending Library, and her interest was so arrested by that pathetic missionary story that she readily acquiesced in both propositions, and Mrs Raynor set out.

She had been gone more than an hour, and it was nearly twelve o'clock, when Janet put down her book, and after sitting meditatively for some minutes with her eyes unconsciously fixed on the opposite wall, she rose, went to her bedroom, and, hastily putting on her bonnet and shawl, came down to Mrs Pettifer, who was busy in the kitchen.

'Mrs Pettifer,' she said, 'tell Mother, when she comes back, I'm gone to see what has become of those poor Lakins in Butchers Lane. I know they're half starving, and I've neglected them so, lately. And then, I think, I'll go on to Mrs Crewe. I want to see the dear little woman, and tell her myself about my going to hear Mr Tryan. She won't feel it half so much if I tell her myself.'

'Won't you wait till your mother comes, or put it off till tomorrow?' said Mrs Pettifer, alarmed. 'You'll hardly be back in time for dinner, if you get talking to Mrs Crewe. And you'll have to pass by your husband's, you know; and yesterday, you were so afraid of seeing him.'

'Oh, Robert will be shut up at the office now, if he's not gone out of the town. I must go – I feel I must be doing something for someone – not be a mere useless log any longer. I've been reading about that wonderful Henry Martyn; he's just like Mr Tryan – wearing himself out for other people, and I sit thinking of nothing but myself. I must go. Goodbye; I shall be back soon.'

She ran off before Mrs Pettifer could utter another word of dissuasion, leaving the good woman in considerable anxiety lest this new impulse of Janet's should frustrate all precautions to save her from a sudden shock.

Janet having paid her visit in Butcher Lane, turned again into Orchard Street on her way to Mrs Crewe's, and was thinking, rather sadly, that her mother's economical house-keeping would leave no abundant surplus to be sent to the hungry Lakins, when she saw Mr Pilgrim in advance of her on the other side of the street. He was walking at a rapid pace, and when he reached Dempster's door he turned and entered without knocking.

Janet was startled. Mr Pilgrim would never enter in that way unless there were someone very ill in the house. It was her husband, she felt certain of it at once. Something had happened to him. Without a moment's pause, she ran across the street, opened the door, and entered. There was no one in the passage. The dining room door was wide open no one was there. Mr Pilgrim, then, was already upstairs. She rushed up at once to Dempster's room – her own room. The door was open, and she paused in pale horror at the sight before her, which seemed to stand out only with the more appalling distinctness because the noonday light was darkened to twilight in the chamber.

Two strong nurses were using their utmost force to hold Dempster in bed, while the medical assistant was applying a sponge to his head, and Mr Pilgrim was busy adjusting some apparatus in the background. Dempster's face was purple and swollen, his eyes dilated and fixed with a look of dire terror on something he seemed to see approaching him from the iron closet. He trembled violently, and struggled as if to jump out of bed.

'Let me go, let me go,' he said in a loud, hoarse whisper, 'she's coming... she's cold... she's dead... she'll strangle me with her black hair. Ah!' he shrieked aloud, 'her hair is all serpents... they're black serpents... they hiss... they hiss... let me go... let me go... she wants to drag me with her cold arms... her arms are serpents... they are great white serpents... they'll twine round me... she wants to drag me into the cold water... her bosom is cold... it is black... it is all serpents...'

'No, Robert,' Janet cried, in tones of yearning pity, rushing to the side of the bed, and stretching out her arms towards him, 'no, here is Janet. She is not dead – she forgives you.'

Dempster's maddened senses seemed to receive some new impression from her appearance. The terror gave way to rage.

'Ha! you sneaking hypocrite!' he burst out in a grating voice, 'you threaten me... you mean to have your revenge on me, do you? Do your worst! I've got the law on my side... I know the law... I'll hunt you down like a hare... prove it... prove that I was tampered with... prove that I took the money... prove it... you can prove nothing... you damned psalm-singing maggots! I'll make a fire under you, and smoke off the whole pack of you... I'll sweep you up... I'll grind you to powder... small powder...' (here his voice dropped to a low tone of shuddering disgust) '...powder on the bedclothes... running about... black lice... they are coming in swarms... Janet! come and take them away... curse you! why don't you come? Janet!'

Poor Janet was kneeling by the bed with her face buried in her hands. She almost wished her worst moment back again rather than this. It seemed as if her husband was already imprisoned in misery, and she could not reach him – his ear deaf for ever to the sounds of love and forgiveness. His sins had made a hard crust round his soul; her pitying voice could not pierce it.

'Not there, isn't she?' he went on in a defiant tone. 'Why do you ask me where she is? I'll have every drop of yellow blood out of your veins if you come questioning me. Your blood is yellow... in your purse... running out of your purse... What! you're changing it into toads, are you? They're crawling... they're flying... they're flying about my head... the toads are flying about. Ostler! ostler! bring out my gig... bring it out, you lazy beast... ha! you'll follow me, will you?... you'll fly about my head... you've got fiery tongues... Ostler! curse you! why don't you come? Janet! come and take the toads away... Janet!'

This last time he uttered her name with such a shriek of terror, that Janet involuntarily started up from her knees, and stood as if petrified by the horrible vibration. Dempster stared wildly in silence for some moments, then he spoke again in a hoarse whisper: 'Dead... is she dead? She did it, then. She buried herself in the iron chest... she left her clothes out, though... she isn't dead... why do you pretend she's dead?... she's coming... she's coming out of the iron closet... there are the black serpents... stop her... let me go... stop her... she wants to drag me away into the cold black water... her bosom is black... it is all serpents... they are getting longer... the great white serpents are getting longer...'

Here Mr Pilgrim came forward with the apparatus to bind him, but Dempster's struggles became more and more violent. 'Ostler! ostler!' he shouted, 'bring out the gig... give me the whip!' and bursting loose from the strong hands that held him, he began to flog the bedclothes furiously with his right arm.

'Get along, you lame brute! – sc – sc – sc! that's it! there you go! They think they've outwitted me, do they? The sneaking idiots! I'll be up with them by-and-by. I'll make them say the Lord's Prayer backwards... I'll pepper them so that the devil shall eat them raw... sc – sc – sc – we shall see who'll be the winner yet... get along, you damned limping beast... I'll lay your back open... I'll...'

He raised himself with a stronger effort than ever to flog the bedclothes, and fell back in convulsions. Janet gave a scream, and sank on her knees again. She thought he was dead.

As soon as Mr Pilgrim was able to give her a moment's attention, he came to her, and, taking her by the arm, attempted to draw her gently out of the room.

'Now, my dear Mrs Dempster, let me persuade you not to remain in the room at present. We shall soon relieve these symptoms, I hope; it is nothing but the delirium that ordinarily attends such cases.'

'Oh, what is the matter? what brought it on?'

'He fell out of the gig; the right leg is broken. It is a terrible accident, and I don't disguise that there is considerable danger attending it, owing to the state of the brain. But Mr Dempster has a strong constitution, you know; in a few days these symptoms may be allayed, and he may do well. Let me beg of you to keep out of the room at present; you can do no good until Mr Dempster is better, and able to know you. But you ought not to be alone; let me advise you to have Mrs Raynor with you.'

'Yes, I will send for Mother. But you must not object to my being in the room. I shall be very quiet now, only just at first the shock was so great; I knew nothing about it. I can help the nurses a great deal; I can put the cold things to his head. He may be sensible for a moment and know me. Pray do not say any more against it; my heart is set on being with him.'

Mr Pilgrim gave way, and Janet, having sent for her mother and put off her bonnet and shawl, returned to take her place by the side of her husband's bed.

24

Day after day, with only short intervals of rest, Janet kept her place in that sad chamber. No wonder the sick-room and the lazaretto have so often been a refuge from the tossings of intellectual doubt – a place of repose for the worn and wounded spirit. Here is a duty about which all creeds and all philosophies are at one; here, at least, the conscience will not be dogged by doubt, the benign impulse will not be checked by adverse theory; here you may begin to act without settling one preliminary question. To moisten the sufferer's parched lips through the long night-watches, to bear up the drooping head, to lift the helpless limbs, to divine the want that can find no utterance beyond the feeble motion of the hand or beseeching glance of the eye – these are offices that demand no self-questionings, no casuistry, no assent to propositions, no weighing of consequences. Within the four walls where the stir and glare of the world are shut out, and every voice is subdued – where a human being lies prostrate, thrown on the tender mercies of his fellow, the moral relation of man to man is reduced to its utmost clearness and simplicity: bigotry cannot confuse it, theory cannot pervert it, passion, awed into quiescence, can neither pollute nor perturb it. As we bend over the sick-bed, all the forces of our nature rush towards the channels of pity, of patience and of love, and sweep down the miserable choking drift of our quarrels, our debates, our would-be wisdom, and our clamorous selfish desires. This blessing of serene freedom from the importunities of opinion lies in all simple direct acts of mercy, and is one source of that sweet calm which is often felt by the watcher in the sick-room, even when the duties there are of a hard and terrible kind.

Something of that benign result was felt by Janet during her tendance in her husband's chamber. When the first heart-piercing hours were over – when her horror at his delirium was no longer fresh, she began to be conscious of her relief from the burden of decision as to her future course. The question that agitated her, about returning to her husband, had been solved in a moment; and this illness, after all, might be the herald of another blessing, just as that dreadful midnight when she stood an outcast in cold and darkness had been followed by the dawn of a new hope. Robert would get better; this illness might alter him; he would be a long time feeble, needing help, walking with a crutch, perhaps. She would wait on him with such tenderness, such all-forgiving love, that the old harshness and cruelty must melt away for ever under the heart-sunshine she would pour around him. Her bosom heaved at the thought, and delicious tears fell. Janet's was a nature in which hatred and revenge could find no place; the long bitter years drew half their bitterness from her ever-living remembrance of the too short years of love that went before; and the thought that her husband would ever put her hand to his lips again, and recall the days when they sat on the grass together, and he laid scarlet poppies on her black hair, and called her his gypsy queen, seemed to send a tide of loving oblivion over all the harsh and stony space they had traversed since. The divine love that had already shone upon her would be with her; she would lift up her soul continually for help; Mr Tryan, she knew, would pray for her. If she felt herself failing, she would confess it to him at once; if her feet began to slip, there was that stay for her to cling to. Oh, she could never be drawn back into that cold damp vault of sin and despair again; she had felt the morning sun, she had tasted the sweet pure air of trust and penitence and submission.

These were the thoughts passing through Janet's mind as she hovered about her husband's bed, and these were the hopes she poured out to Mr Tryan when he called to see her. It was so evident that they were strengthening her in her new struggle – they shed such a glow of calm enthusiasm over her face as she spoke of them, that Mr Tryan could not bear to throw on them the chill of premonitory doubts, though a previous conversation he had had with Mr Pilgrim had convinced him that there was not the faintest probability of Dempster's recovery. Poor Janet did not know the significance of the changing symptoms, and when, after the lapse of a week, the delirium began to lose some of its violence, and to be interrupted by longer and longer intervals of stupor, she tried to think that these might be steps on the way to recovery, and she shrank from questioning Mr Pilgrim lest he should confirm the fears that began to get predominance in her mind. But before many days were past, he thought it right not to allow her to blind herself any longer. One day – it was just about noon, when bad news always seems most sickening – he led her from her husband's chamber into the opposite drawing room, where Mrs Raynor was sitting, and said to her, in that low tone of sympathetic feeling which sometimes gave a sudden air of gentleness to this rough man, 'My dear Mrs Dempster, it is right in these cases, you know, to be prepared for the worst. I think I shall be saving you pain by preventing you from entertaining any false hopes, and Mr Dempster's state is now such that I fear we must consider recovery impossible. The affection of the brain might not have been hopeless, but, you see, there is a terrible complication; and, I am grieved to say, the broken limb is mortifying.'

Janet listened with a sinking heart. That future of love and forgiveness would never come, then; he was going out of her sight for ever, where her pity could never reach him. She turned cold and trembled.

'But do you think he will die,' she said, 'without ever coming to himself? without ever knowing me?'

'One cannot say that with certainty. It is not impossible that the cerebral oppression may subside, and that he may become conscious. If there is anything you would wish to be said or done in that case, it would be well to be prepared. I should think,' Mr Pilgrim continued, turning to Mrs Raynor, 'Mr Dempster's affairs are likely to be in order – his will is…'

'Oh, I wouldn't have him troubled about those things,' interrupted Janet, 'he has no relations but quite distant ones –

no one but me. I wouldn't take up the time with that. I only want to...'

She was unable to finish; she felt her sobs rising, and left the room. 'Oh God!' she said inwardly, 'is not Thy love greater than mine? Have mercy on him! have mercy on him!'

This happened on Wednesday, ten days after the fatal accident. By the following Sunday, Dempster was in a state of rapidly increasing prostration, and when Mr Pilgrim, who, in turn with his assistant, had slept in the house from the beginning, came in, about half-past ten, as usual, he scarcely believed that the feebly struggling life would last out till morning. For the last few days he had been administering stimulants to relieve the exhaustion which had succeeded the alternations of delirium and stupor. This slight office was all that now remained to be done for the patient, so at eleven o'clock Mr Pilgrim went to bed, having given directions to the nurse, and desired her to call him if any change took place, or if Mrs Dempster desired his presence.

Janet could not be persuaded to leave the room. She was yearning and watching for a moment in which her husband's eyes would rest consciously upon her, and he would know that she had forgiven him.

How changed he was since that terrible Monday, nearly a fortnight ago! He lay motionless, but for the irregular breathing that stirred his broad chest and thick muscular neck. His features were no longer purple and swollen; they were pale, sunken and haggard. A cold perspiration stood in beads on the protuberant forehead, and on the wasted hands stretched motionless on the bedclothes. It was better to see the hands so, than convulsively picking the air, as they had been a week ago.

Janet sat on the edge of the bed through the long hours of candlelight, watching the unconscious half-closed eyes, wiping the perspiration from the brow and cheeks, and keeping her left hand on the cold unanswering right hand that lay beside her on the bedclothes. She was almost as pale as her dying husband, and there were dark lines under her eyes, for this was the third night since she had taken off her clothes, but the eager straining gaze of her dark eyes, and the acute sensibility that lay in every line about her mouth, made a strange contrast with the blank unconsciousness and emaciated animalism of the face she was watching.

There was profound stillness in the house. She heard no sound but her husband's breathing and the ticking of the watch on the mantelpiece. The candle, placed high up, shed a soft light down on the one object she cared to see. There was a smell of brandy in the room, it was given to her husband from time to time, but this smell, which at first had produced in her a faint shuddering sensation, was now becoming indifferent to her: she did not even perceive it; she was too unconscious of herself to feel either temptations or accusations. She only felt that the husband of her youth was dying, far, far out of her reach, as if she were standing helpless on the shore, while he was sinking in the black storm-waves; she only yearned for one moment in which she might satisfy the deep forgiving pity of her soul by one look of love, one word of tenderness.

Her sensations and thoughts were so persistent that she could not measure the hours, and it was a surprise to her when the nurse put out the candle, and let in the faint morning light. Mrs Raynor, anxious about Janet, was already up, and now brought in some fresh coffee for her, and Mr Pilgrim having awaked, had hurried on his clothes, and was coming in to see how Dempster was.

This change from candlelight to morning, this recommencement of the same round of things that had happened yesterday, was a discouragement rather than a relief to Janet. She was more conscious of her chill weariness; the new light thrown on her husband's face seemed to reveal the still work that death had been doing through the night; she felt her last lingering hope that he would ever know her again forsake her.

But now Mr Pilgrim, having felt the pulse, was putting some brandy in a teaspoon between Dempster's lips; the brandy went down, and his breathing became freer. Janet noticed the change, and her heart beat faster as she leaned forward to watch him. Suddenly a slight movement, like the passing away of a shadow, was visible in his face, and he opened his eyes full on Janet. It was almost like meeting him again on the resurrection morning, after the night of the grave.

'Robert, do you know me?'

He kept his eyes fixed on her, and there was a faintly perceptible motion of the lips, as if he wanted to speak.

But the moment of speech was forever gone – the moment for asking pardon of her, if he wanted to ask it. Could he read the full forgiveness that was written in her eyes? She never knew, for, as she was bending to kiss him, the thick veil of death fell between them, and her lips touched a corpse.

25

The faces looked very hard and unmoved that surrounded Dempster's grave, while old Mr Crewe read the burial service in his low, broken voice. The pallbearers were such men as Mr Pittman, Mr Lowme and Mr Budd – men whom Dempster had called his friends while he was in life; and worldly faces never look so worldly as at a funeral. They have the same effect of grating incongruity as the sound of a coarse voice breaking the solemn silence of night.

The one face that had sorrow in it was covered by a thick crape veil, and the sorrow was suppressed and silent. No one knew how deep it was, for the thought in most of her neighbours' minds was that Mrs Dempster could hardly have had better fortune than to lose a bad husband who had left her the compensation of a good income. They found it difficult to conceive that her husband's death could be felt by her otherwise than as a deliverance. The person who was most thoroughly convinced that Janet's grief was deep and real was Mr Pilgrim, who in general was not at all weakly given to a belief in disinterested feeling.

'That woman has a tender heart,' he was frequently heard to observe in his morning rounds about this time. 'I used to think there was a great deal of palaver in her, but you may depend upon it there's no pretence about her. If he'd been the kindest husband in the world she couldn't have felt more. There's a great deal of good in Mrs Dempster – a great deal of good.'

'I always said so,' was Mrs Lowme's reply, when he made the observation to her. 'She was always so very full of pretty attentions to me when I was ill. But they tell me now she's turned Tryanite; if that's it we shan't agree again. It's very inconsistent in her, I think, turning round in that way, after being the foremost to laugh at the Tryanite cant, and especially in a woman of her habits; she should cure herself of them before she pretends to be over-religious.'

'Well, I think she means to cure herself, do you know,' said Mr Pilgrim, whose good will towards Janet was just now quite above that temperate point at which he could indulge his feminine patients with a little judicious detraction. 'I feel sure she has not taken any stimulants all through her husband's illness, and she has been constantly in the way of them. I can see she sometimes suffers a good deal of depression for want of them – it shows all the more resolution in her. Those cures are rare, but I've known them happen sometimes with people of strong will.'

Mrs Lowme took an opportunity of retailing Mr Pilgrim's conversation to Mrs Phipps, who, as a victim of Pratt and plethora, could rarely enjoy that pleasure at first hand. Mrs Phipps was a woman of decided opinions, though of wheezy utterance.

'For my part,' she remarked, 'I'm glad to hear there's any likelihood of improvement in Mrs Dempster, but I think the way things have turned out seems to show that she was more to blame than people thought she was; else, why should she feel so much about her husband? And Dempster, I understand, has left his wife pretty nearly all his property to do as she likes with; that isn't behaving like such a very bad husband. I don't believe Mrs Dempster can have had so much provocation as they pretended. I've known husbands who've laid plans for tormenting their wives when they're underground – tying up their money and hindering them from marrying again. Not that I should ever wish to marry again; I think one husband in one's life is enough in all conscience,' – here she threw a fierce glance at the amiable Mr Phipps, who was innocently delighting himself with the facetiae in the *Rotherby Guardian* and thinking the editor must be a droll fellow – 'but it's aggravating to be tied up in that way. Why, they say Mrs Dempster will have as good as six hundred a year at least. A fine thing for her, that was a poor girl without a farthing to her fortune. It's well if she doesn't make ducks and drakes of it somehow.'

Mrs Phipps's view of Janet, however, was far from being the prevalent one in Milby. Even neighbours who had no strong personal interest in her, could hardly see the noble-looking woman in her widow's dress, with a sad sweet gravity in her face, and not be touched with fresh admiration for her – and not feel, at least vaguely, that she had entered on a new life in which it was a sort of desecration to allude to the painful past. And the old friends who had a real regard for her, but whose cordiality had been repelled or chilled of late years, now came round her with hearty demonstrations of affection. Mr Jerome felt that his happiness had a substantial addition now he could once more call on that 'nice little woman, Mrs Dempster', and think of her with rejoicing instead of sorrow. The Pratts lost no time in returning to the footing of old-established friendship with Janet and her mother, and Miss Pratt felt it incumbent on her, on all suitable occasions, to deliver a very emphatic approval of the remarkable strength of mind she understood Mrs Dempster to be exhibiting. The Miss Linnets were eager to meet Mr Tryan's wishes by greeting Janet as one who was likely to be a sister in religious feeling and good works, and Mrs Linnet was so agreeably surprised by the fact that Dempster had left his wife the money 'in that handsome way, to do what she liked with it', that she even included Dempster himself, and his villainous discovery of the flaw in her title to Pye's Croft, in her magnanimous oblivion of past offences. She and Mrs Jerome agreed over a friendly cup of tea that there were 'a many husbands as was very fine spoken an' all that, an' yet all the while kep' a will locked up from you, as tied you up as tight as anything. I assure you,' Mrs Jerome continued, dropping her voice in a confidential manner, 'I know no more to this day about Mr Jerome's will, nor the child as is unborn. I've no fears about a income – I'm well aware Mr Jerome 'ud niver leave me stret for that, but I should like to hev a thousand or two at my own disposial; it makes a widow a deal more looked on.'

Perhaps this ground of respect to widows might not be entirely without its influence on the Milby mind, and might do something towards conciliating those more aristocratic acquaintances of Janet's, who would otherwise have been inclined to take the severest view of her apostasy towards Evangelicalism. Errors look so very ugly in persons of small means – one feels they are taking quite a liberty in going astray – whereas people of fortune may naturally indulge in a few delinquencies. 'They've got the money for it,' as the girl said of her mistress who had made herself ill with pickled salmon. However it may have been, there was not an acquaintance of Janet's, in Milby, that did not offer her civilities in the early days of her widowhood. Even the severe Mrs Phipps was not an exception, for Heaven knows what would become of our sociality if we never visited people we speak ill of; we should live, like Egyptian hermits, in crowded solitude.

Perhaps the attentions most grateful to Janet were those of her old friend Mrs Crewe, whose attachment to her favourite proved quite too strong for any resentment she might be supposed to feel on the score of Mr Tryan. The little deaf old lady couldn't do without her accustomed visitor, whom she had seen grow up from child to woman, always so willing to chat with her and tell her all the news, though she was deaf, while other people thought it tiresome to shout in her ear, and irritated her by recommending ear-trumpets of various construction.

All this friendliness was very precious to Janet. She was conscious of the aid it gave her in the self-conquest which was the blessing she prayed for with every fresh morning.

The chief strength of her nature lay in her affection, which coloured all the rest of her mind: it gave a personal sisterly tenderness to her acts of benevolence; it made her cling with tenacity to every object that had once stirred her kindly emotions. Alas! it was unsatisfied, wounded affection that had made her trouble greater than she could bear. And now there was no check to the full flow of that plenteous current in her nature – no gnawing secret anguish – no overhanging terror – no inward shame. Friendly faces beamed on her; she felt that friendly hearts were approving her, and wishing her well, and that mild sunshine of good will fell beneficently on her new hopes and efforts, as the clear shining after rain falls on the tender leaf buds of spring, and wins them from promise to fulfilment.

And she needed these secondary helps, for her wrestling with her past self was not always easy. The strong emotions from which the life of a human being receives a new bias, win their victory as the sea wins his: though their advance may be sure, they will often, after a mightier wave than usual, seem to roll back so far as to lose all the ground they had made. Janet showed the strong bent of her will by taking every outward precaution against the occurrence of a temptation. Her mother was now her constant companion, having shut up her little dwelling and come to reside in Orchard Street, and Janet gave all dangerous keys into her keeping, entreating her to lock them away in some secret place. Whenever the too well-known depression and craving threatened her, she would seek a refuge in what had always been her purest enjoyment – in visiting one of her poor neighbours, in carrying some food or comfort to a sick-bed, in cheering with her smile some of the familiar dwellings up the dingy back lanes. But the great source of courage, the great help to perseverance, was the sense that she had a friend and teacher in Mr Tryan: she could confess her difficulties to him; she knew he prayed for her; she had always before her the prospect of soon seeing him, and hearing words of admonition and comfort that came to her charged with a divine power such as she had never found in human words before.

So the time passed, till it was far on in May, nearly a month after her husband's death, when, as she and her mother were seated peacefully at breakfast in the dining room, looking through the open window at the old-fashioned garden, where the grass plot was now whitened with apple blossoms, a letter was brought in for Mrs Raynor.

'Why, there's the Thurston postmark on it,' she said. 'It must be about your Aunt Anna. Ah, so it is, poor thing! She's been taken worse this last day or two, and has asked them to send for me. That dropsy is carrying her off at last, I dare say. Poor thing! it will be a happy release. I must go, my dear – she's your father's last sister – though I am sorry to leave you. However, perhaps I shall not have to stay more than a night or two.'

Janet looked distressed as she said, 'Yes, you must go, Mother. But I don't know what I shall do without you. I think I shall run in to Mrs Pettifer, and ask her to come and stay with me while you're away. I'm sure she will.'

At twelve o'clock, Janet, having seen her mother in the coach that was to carry her to Thurston, called, on her way back, at Mrs Pettifer's, but found, to her great disappointment, that her old friend was gone out for the day. So she wrote on a leaf of her pocketbook an urgent request that Mrs Pettifer would come and stay with her while her mother was away, and, desiring the servant-girl to give it to her mistress as soon as she came home, walked on to the Vicarage to sit with Mrs

Crewe, thinking to relieve in this way the feeling of desolateness and undefined fear that was taking possession of her on being left alone for the first time since that great crisis in her life. And Mrs Crewe, too, was not at home!

Janet, with a sense of discouragement for which she rebuked herself as childish, walked sadly home again, and when she entered the vacant dining room, she could not help bursting into tears. It is such vague undefinable states of susceptibility as this – states of excitement or depression, half mental, half physical – that determine many a tragedy in women's lives. Janet could scarcely eat anything at her solitary dinner; she tried to fix her attention on a book in vain; she walked about the garden, and felt the very sunshine melancholy.

Between four and five o'clock, old Mr Pittman called, and joined her in the garden, where she had been sitting for some time under one of the great apple trees, thinking how Robert, in his best moods, used to take little Mamsey to look at the cucumbers, or to see the Alderney cow with its calf in the paddock. The tears and sobs had come again at these thoughts; and when Mr Pittman approached her, she was feeling languid and exhausted. But the old gentleman's sight and sensibility were obtuse, and, to Janet's satisfaction, he showed no consciousness that she was in grief.

'I have a task to impose upon you, Mrs Dempster,' he said, with a certain toothless pomposity habitual to him. 'I want you to look over those letters again in Dempster's bureau, and see if you can find one from Poole about the mortgage on those houses at Dingley. It will be worth twenty pounds, if you can find it, and I don't know where it can be, if it isn't among those letters in the bureau. I've looked everywhere at the office for it. I'm going home now, but I'll call again tomorrow, if you'll be good enough to look in the meantime.'

Janet said she would look directly, and turned with Mr Pittman into the house. But the search would take her some time, so he bade her goodbye, and she went at once to a bureau which stood in a small back room, where Dempster used sometimes to write letters and receive people who came on business out of office hours. She had looked through the contents of the bureau more than once, but today, on removing the last bundle of letters from one of the compartments, she saw what she had never seen before, a small nick in the wood, made in the shape of a thumbnail, evidently intended as a means of pushing aside the movable back of the compartment. In her examination hitherto she had not found such a letter as Mr Pittman had described – perhaps there might be more letters behind this slide. She pushed it back at once, and saw – no letters, but a small spirit decanter, half full of pale brandy, Dempster's habitual drink.

An impetuous desire shook Janet through all her members; it seemed to master her with the inevitable force of strong fumes that flood our senses before we are aware. Her hand was on the decanter; pale and excited, she was lifting it out of its niche, when, with a start and a shudder, she dashed it to the ground, and the room was filled with the odour of the spirit. Without staying to shut up the bureau, she rushed out of the room, snatched up her bonnet and mantle which lay in the dining room, and hurried out of the house.

Where should she go? In what place would this demon that had re-entered her be scared back again? She walks rapidly along the street in the direction of the church. She is soon at the gate of the churchyard; she passes through it, and makes her way across the graves to a spot she knows – a spot where the turf was stirred not long ago, where a tomb is to be erected soon. It is very near the church wall, on the side which now lies in deep shadow, quite shut out from the rays of the westering sun by a projecting buttress.

Janet sat down on the ground. It was a sombre spot. A thick hedge, surmounted by elm trees, was in front of her; a projecting buttress on each side. But she wanted to shut out even these objects. Her thick crape veil was down, but she closed her eyes behind it, and pressed her hands upon them. She wanted to summon up the vision of the past; she wanted to lash the demon out of her soul with the stinging memories of the bygone misery; she wanted to renew the old horror and the old anguish, that she might throw herself with the more desperate clinging energy at the foot of the cross, where the Divine Sufferer would impart divine strength. She tried to recall those first bitter moments of shame, which were like the shuddering discovery of the leper that the dire taint is upon him; the deeper and deeper lapse; the oncoming of settled despair; the awful moments by the bedside of her self-maddened husband. And then she tried to live through, with a remembrance made more vivid by that contrast, the blessed hours of hope and joy and peace that had come to her of late, since her whole soul had been bent towards the attainment of purity and holiness.

But now, when the paroxysm of temptation was past, dread and despondency began to thrust themselves, like cold heavy mists, between her and the heaven to which she wanted to look for light and guidance. The temptation would come again – that rush of desire might overmaster her the next time – she would slip back again into that deep slimy pit from which she had been once rescued, and there might be no deliverance for her more. Her prayers did not help her, for fear predominated over trust; she had no confidence that the aid she sought would be given; the idea of her future fall had grasped her mind too strongly. Alone, in this way, she was powerless. If she could see Mr Tryan, if she could confess all to him, she might gather hope again. She must see him; she must go to him.

Janet rose from the ground, and walked away with a quick resolved step. She had been seated there a long while, and the sun had already sunk. It was late for her to walk to Paddiford and go to Mr Tryan's, where she had never called before, but there was no other way of seeing him that evening, and she could not hesitate about it. She walked towards a footpath through the fields, which would take her to Paddiford without obliging her to go through the town. The way was rather long, but she preferred it, because it left less probability of her meeting acquaintances, and she shrank from having to speak to anyone.

The evening red had nearly faded by the time Janet knocked at Mrs Wagstaff's door. The good woman looked surprised to see her at that hour, but Janet's mourning weeds and the painful agitation of her face quickly brought the second thought, that some urgent trouble had sent her there.

'Mr Tryan's just come in,' she said. 'If you'll step into the parlour, I'll go up and tell him you're here. He seemed very tired and poorly.'

At another time Janet would have felt distress at the idea that she was disturbing Mr Tryan when he required rest, but now her need was too great for that; she could feel nothing but a sense of coming relief, when she heard his step on the stair and saw him enter the room.

He went towards her with a look of anxiety, and said, 'I fear something is the matter. I fear you are in trouble.'

Then poor Janet poured forth her sad tale of temptation and despondency, and even while she was confessing she felt half her burden removed. The act of confiding in human sympathy, the consciousness that a fellow being was listening to her with patient pity, prepared her soul for that stronger leap by which faith grasps the idea of the Divine Sympathy. When Mr Tryan spoke words of consolation and encouragement, she could now believe the message of mercy; the water-floods that had threatened to overwhelm her rolled back again, and life once more spread its heaven-covered space before her. She had been unable to pray alone, but now his prayer bore her own soul along with it, as the broad tongue of flame carries upwards in its vigorous leap the little flickering fire that could hardly keep alight by itself.

But Mr Tryan was anxious that Janet should not linger out at this late hour. When he saw that she was calmed, he said, 'I will walk home with you now; we can talk on the way.' But Janet's mind was now sufficiently at liberty for her to notice the signs of feverish weariness in his appearance, and she would not hear of causing him any further fatigue.

'No, no,' she said, earnestly, 'you will pain me very much – indeed you will, by going out again tonight on my account. There is no real reason why I should not go alone.' And when he persisted, fearing that for her to be seen out so late alone might excite remark, she said imploringly, with a half sob in her voice, 'What should I – what would others like me do, if you went from us? Why will you not think more of that, and take care of yourself?'

He had often had that appeal made to him before, but tonight – from Janet's lips – it seemed to have a new force for him, and he gave way. At first, indeed, he only did so on condition that she would let Mrs Wagstaff go with her, but Janet had determined to walk home alone. She preferred solitude; she wished not to have her present feelings distracted by any conversation.

So she went out into the dewy starlight, and as Mr Tryan turned away from her, he felt a stronger wish than ever that his fragile life might last out for him to see Janet's restoration thoroughly established – to see her no longer fleeing, struggling, clinging up the steep sides of a precipice whence she might be any moment hurled back into the depths of despair, but walking firmly on the level ground of habit. He inwardly resolved that nothing but a peremptory duty should ever take him from Milby – that he would not cease to watch over her until life forsook him.

Janet walked on quickly till she turned into the fields, then she slackened her pace a little, enjoying the sense of solitude which a few hours before had been intolerable to her. The Divine Presence did not now seem far off, where she had not wings to reach it; prayer itself seemed superfluous in those moments of calm trust. The temptation which had so lately made her shudder before the possibilities of the future, was now a source of confidence, for had she not been delivered from it? Had not rescue come in the extremity of danger? Yes, Infinite Love was caring for her. She felt like a little child whose hand is firmly grasped by its father, as its frail limbs make their way over the rough ground; if it should stumble, the father will not let it go.

That walk in the dewy starlight remained for ever in Janet's memory as one of those baptismal epochs, when the soul, dipped in the sacred waters of joy and peace, rises from them with new energies, with more unalterable longings.

When she reached home she found Mrs Pettifer there, anxious for her return. After thanking her for coming, Janet only said, 'I have been to Mr Tryan's; I wanted to speak to him,' and then remembering how she had left the bureau and papers, she went into the back room, where, apparently, no one had been since she quitted it, for there lay the fragments of glass, and the room was still full of the hateful odour. How feeble and miserable the temptation seemed to her at this moment! She rang for Kitty to come and pick up the fragments and rub the floor, while she herself replaced the papers and locked up the bureau.

The next morning, when seated at breakfast with Mrs Pettifer, Janet said, 'What a dreary unhealthy-looking place that is where Mr Tryan lives! I'm sure it must be very bad for him to live there. Do you know, all this morning, since I've been awake, I've been turning over a little plan in my mind. I think it a charming one – all the more, because you are concerned in it.'

'Why, what can that be?'

'You know that house on the Redhill road they call Holly Mount; it is shut up now. That is Robert's house; at least, it is mine now, and it stands on one of the healthiest spots about here. Now, I've been settling in my own mind, that if a dear good woman of my acquaintance, who knows how to make a home as comfortable and cosy as a bird's nest, were to take up her abode there, and have Mr Tryan as a lodger, she would be doing one of the most useful deeds in all her useful life.'

'You've such a way of wrapping up things in pretty words. You must speak plainer.'

'In plain words, then, I should like to settle you at Holly Mount. You would not have to pay any more rent than where you are, and it would be twenty times pleasanter for you than living up that passage where you see nothing but a brick wall. And then, as it is not far from Paddiford, I think Mr Tryan might be persuaded to lodge with you, instead of in that musty house, among dead cabbages and smoky cottages. I know you would like to have him live with you, and you would be such a mother to him.'

'To be sure I should like it; it would be the finest thing in the world for me. But there'll be furniture wanted. My little bit of furniture won't fill that house.'

'Oh, I can put some in out of this house, it is too full, and we can buy the rest. They tell me I'm to have more money than I shall know what to do with.'

'I'm almost afraid,' said Mrs Pettifer doubtfully, 'Mr Tryan will hardly be persuaded. He's been talked to so much about leaving that place, and he always said he must stay there – he must be among the people, and there was no other place for him in Paddiford. It cuts me to the heart to see him getting thinner and thinner, and I've noticed him quite short o' breath sometimes. Mrs Linnet will have it, Mrs Wagstaff half poisons him with bad cooking. I don't know about that, but he can't have many comforts. I expect he'll break down all of a sudden some day, and never be able to preach any more.'

'Well, I shall try my skill with him by and by. I shall be very cunning, and say nothing to him till all is ready. You and I and Mother, when she comes home, will set to work directly and get the house in order, and then we'll get you snugly settled in it. I shall see Mr Pittman today, and I will tell him what I mean to do. I shall say I wish to have you for a tenant. Everybody knows I'm very fond of that naughty person, Mrs Pettifer, so it will seem the most natural thing in the world. And then I shall by and by point out to Mr Tryan that he will be doing you a service as well as himself by taking up his abode with you. I think I can prevail upon him, for last night, when he was quite bent on coming out into the night air, I persuaded him to give it up.'

'Well, I only hope you may, my dear. I don't desire anything better than to do something towards prolonging Mr Tryan's life, for I've sad fears about him.'

'Don't speak of them – I can't bear to think of them. We will only think about getting the house ready. We shall be as busy as bees. How we shall want Mother's clever fingers! I know the room upstairs that will just do for Mr Tryan's study. There shall be no seats in it except a very easy chair and a very easy sofa, so that he shall be obliged to rest himself when he comes home.'

26

That was the last terrible crisis of temptation Janet had to pass through. The good will of her neighbours, the helpful sympathy of the friends who shared her religious feelings, the occupations suggested to her by Mr Tryan, concurred, with her strong spontaneous impulses towards works of love and mercy, to fill up her days with quiet social intercourse and charitable exertion. Besides, her constitution, naturally healthy and strong, was every week tending, with the gathering force of habit, to recover its equipoise, and set her free from those physical solicitations which the smallest habitual vice always leaves behind it. The prisoner feels where the iron has galled him, long after his fetters have been loosed.

There were always neighbourly visits to be paid and received, and as the months wore on, increasing familiarity with Janet's present self began to efface, even from minds as rigid as Mrs Phipps's, the unpleasant impressions that had been left by recent years. Janet was recovering the popularity which her beauty and sweetness of nature had won for her when she was a girl, and popularity, as every one knows, is the most complex and self-multiplying of echoes. Even anti-Tryanite prejudice could not resist the fact that Janet Dempster was a changed woman – changed as the dusty, bruised and sun-withered plant is changed when the soft rains of heaven have fallen on it – and that this change was due to Mr Tryan's influence. The last lingering sneers against the Evangelical curate began to die out, and though much of the feeling that had prompted them remained behind, there was an intimidating consciousness that the expression of such feeling would not be effective – jokes of that sort had ceased to tickle the Milby mind. Even Mr Budd and Mr Tomlinson, when they saw Mr Tryan passing pale and worn along the street, had a secret sense that this man was somehow not that very natural and comprehensible thing, a humbug – that, in fact, it was impossible to explain him from the stomach and pocket point of view. Twist and stretch their theory as they might, it would not fit Mr Tryan, and so, with that remarkable resemblance as to mental processes which may frequently be observed to exist between plain men and philosophers, they concluded that the less they said about him the better.

Among all Janet's neighbourly pleasures, there was nothing she liked better than to take an early tea at the White House, and to stroll with Mr Jerome round the old-fashioned garden and orchard. There was endless matter for talk between her and the good old man, for Janet had that genuine delight in human fellowship which gives an interest to all personal details that come warm from truthful lips, and, besides, they had a common interest in good-natured plans for helping their poorer neighbours. One great object of Mr Jerome's charities was, as he often said, 'to keep industrious men an' women off the parish. I'd rether given ten shillin' an' help a man to stand on his own legs, nor pay half a crown to buy him a parish crutch; it's the ruination on him if he once goes to the parish. I've see'd many a time, if you help a man wi' a present in a

191

neeborly way, it sweetens his blood – he thinks it kind on you; but the parish shillins turn it sour – he niver thinks 'em enough.' In illustration of this opinion Mr Jerome had a large store of details about such persons as Jim Hardy, the coal carrier, 'as lost his hoss', and Sally Butts, 'as hed to sell her mangle, though she was as decent a woman as need to be', to the hearing of which details Janet seriously inclined, and you would hardly desire to see a prettier picture than the kind-faced white-haired old man telling these fragments of his simple experience as he walked, with shoulders slightly bent, among the moss-roses and espalier apple trees, while Janet in her widow's cap, her dark eyes bright with interest, went listening by his side, and little Lizzie, with her nankeen bonnet hanging down her back, toddled on before them. Mrs Jerome usually declined these lingering strolls, and often observed, 'I niver see the like to Mr Jerome when he's got Mrs Dempster to talk to; it sinnifies nothin' to him whether we've tea at four or at five o'clock; he'd go on till six, if you'd let him alone – he's like off his head.' However, Mrs Jerome herself could not deny that Janet was a very pretty-spoken woman: 'She aly's says, she niver gets sich pikelets as mine nowhere; I know that very well – other folks buy 'em at shops – thick, unwholesome things, you might as well eat a sponge.'

The sight of little Lizzie often stirred in Janet's mind a sense of the childlessness which had made a fatal blank in her life. She had fleeting thoughts that perhaps among her husband's distant relatives there might be some children whom she could help to bring up, some little girl whom she might adopt, and she promised herself one day or other to hunt out a second cousin of his – a married woman, of whom he had lost sight for many years.

But at present her hands and heart were too full for her to carry out that scheme. To her great disappointment, her project of settling Mrs Pettifer at Holly Mount had been delayed by the discovery that some repairs were necessary in order to make the house habitable, and it was not till September had set in that she had the satisfaction of seeing her old friend comfortably installed, and the rooms destined for Mr Tryan looking pretty and cosy to her heart's content. She had taken several of his chief friends into her confidence, and they were warmly wishing success to her plan for inducing him to quit poor Mrs Wagstaff's dingy house and dubious cookery. That he should consent to some such change was becoming more and more a matter of anxiety to his hearers, for though no more decided symptoms were yet observable in him than increasing emaciation, a dry hacking cough, and an occasional shortness of breath, it was felt that the fulfilment of Mr Pratt's prediction could not long be deferred, and that this obstinate persistence in labour and self-disregard must soon be peremptorily cut short by a total failure of strength. Any hopes that the influence of Mr Tryan's father and sister would prevail on him to change his mode of life – that they would perhaps come to live with him, or that his sister at least might come to see him, and that the arguments which had failed from other lips might be more persuasive from hers – were now quite dissipated. His father had lately had an attack of paralysis, and could not spare his only daughter's tendance. On Mr Tryan's return from a visit to his father, Miss Linnet was very anxious to know whether his sister had not urged him to try change of air. From his answers she gathered that Miss Tryan wished him to give up his curacy and travel, or at least go to the south Devonshire coast.

'And why will you not do so?' Miss Linnet said. 'You might come back to us well and strong, and have many years of usefulness before you.'

'No,' he answered quietly, 'I think people attach more importance to such measures than is warranted. I don't see any good end that is to be served by going to die at Nice, instead of dying amongst one's friends and one's work. I cannot leave Milby – at least I will not leave it voluntarily.'

But though he remained immovable on this point, he had been compelled to give up his afternoon service on the Sunday, and to accept Mr Parry's offer of aid in the evening service, as well as to curtail his weekday labours; and he had even written to Mr Prendergast to request that he would appoint another curate to the Paddiford district, on the understanding that the new curate should receive the salary, but that Mr Tryan should co-operate with him as long as he was able. The hopefulness which is an almost constant attendant on consumption, had not the effect of deceiving him as to the nature of his malady, or of making him look forward to ultimate recovery. He believed himself to be consumptive, and he had not yet felt any desire to escape the early death which he had for some time contemplated as probable. Even diseased hopes will take their direction from the strong habitual bias of the mind, and to Mr Tryan death had for years seemed nothing else than the laying down of a burden, under which he sometimes felt himself fainting. He was only sanguine about his powers of work: he flattered himself that what he was unable to do one week he should be equal to the next, and he would not admit that in desisting from any part of his labour he was renouncing it permanently. He had lately delighted Mr Jerome by accepting his long-proffered loan of the 'little chacenut hoss', and he found so much benefit from substituting constant riding exercise for walking, that he began to think he should soon be able to resume some of the work he had dropped.

That was a happy afternoon for Janet, when, after exerting herself busily for a week with her mother and Mrs Pettifer, she saw Holly Mount looking orderly and comfortable from attic to cellar. It was an old red-brick house, with two gables in front, and two clipped holly trees flanking the garden gate; a simple, homely-looking place, that quiet people might easily get fond of, and now it was scoured and polished and carpeted and furnished so as to look really snug within. When there was nothing more to be done, Janet delighted herself with contemplating Mr Tryan's study, first sitting down in the easy chair, and then lying for a moment on the sofa, that she might have a keener sense of the repose he would get from those well-stuffed articles of furniture, which she had gone to Rotherby on purpose to choose.

'Now, Mother,' she said, when she had finished her survey, 'you have done your work as well as any fairy-mother or godmother that ever turned a pumpkin into a coach and horses. You stay and have tea cosily with Mrs Pettifer while I go to Mrs Linnet's. I want to tell Mary and Rebecca the good news, that I've got the exciseman to promise that he will take Mrs Wagstaff's lodgings when Mr Tryan leaves. They'll be so pleased to hear it, because they thought he would make her poverty an objection to his leaving her.'

'But, my dear child,' said Mrs Raynor, whose face, always calm, was now a happy one, 'have a cup of tea with us first. You'll perhaps miss Mrs Linnet's tea time.'

'No, I feel too excited to take tea yet. I'm like a child with a new baby-house. Walking in the air will do me good.'

So she set out. Holly Mount was about a mile from that outskirt of Paddiford Common where Mrs Linnet's house stood nestled among its laburnums, lilacs and syringas. Janet's way thither lay for a little while along the high road, and then led her into a deep-rutted lane, which wound through a flat tract of meadow and pasture, while in front lay smoky Paddiford, and away to the left the mother-town of Milby. There was no line of silvery willows marking the course of a stream – no group of Scotch firs with their trunks reddening in the level sunbeams – nothing to break the flowerless monotony of grass and hedgerow but an occasional oak or elm, and a few cows sprinkled here and there. A very commonplace scene, indeed. But what scene was ever commonplace in the descending sunlight, when colour has awakened from its noonday sleep, and the long shadows awe us like a disclosed presence? Above all, what scene is commonplace to the eye that is filled with serene gladness, and brightens all things with its own joy?

And Janet just now was very happy. As she walked along the rough lane with a buoyant step, a half smile of innocent, kindly triumph played about her mouth. She was delighting beforehand in the anticipated success of her persuasive power, and for the time her painful anxiety about Mr Tryan's health was thrown into abeyance. But she had not gone far along the lane before she heard the sound of a horse advancing at a walking pace behind her. Without looking back, she turned aside to make way for it between the ruts, and did not notice that for a moment it had stopped, and had then come on with a slightly quickened pace. In less than a minute she heard a well-known voice say, 'Mrs Dempster', and, turning, saw Mr Tryan close to her, holding his horse by the bridle. It seemed very natural to her that he should be there. Her mind was so full of his presence at that moment, that the actual sight of him was only like a more vivid thought, and she behaved, as we are apt to do when feeling obliges us to be genuine, with a total forgetfulness of polite forms. She only looked at him with a slight deepening of the smile that was already on her face. He said gently, 'Take my arm,' and they walked on a little way in silence.

It was he who broke it. 'You are going to Paddiford, I suppose?'

The question recalled Janet to the consciousness that this was an unexpected opportunity for beginning her work of persuasion, and that she was stupidly neglecting it.

'Yes,' she said, 'I was going to Mrs Linnet's. I knew Miss Linnet would like to hear that our friend Mrs Pettifer is quite settled now in her new house. She is as fond of Mrs Pettifer as I am – almost; I won't admit that anyone loves her quite as well, for no one else has such good reason as I have. But now the dear woman wants a lodger, for you know she can't afford to live in so large a house by herself. But I knew when I persuaded her to go there that she would be sure to get one – she's such a comfortable creature to live with, and I didn't like her to spend all the rest of her days up that dull passage, being at everyone's beck and call who wanted to make use of her.'

'Yes,' said Mr Tryan, 'I quite understand your feeling; I don't wonder at your strong regard for her.'

'Well, but now I want her other friends to second me. There she is, with three rooms to let, ready furnished, everything in order, and I know someone, who thinks as well of her as I do, and who would be doing good all round – to everyone that knows him, as well as to Mrs Pettifer, if he would go to live with her. He would leave some uncomfortable lodgings, which another person is already coveting and would take immediately; and he would go to breathe pure air at Holly Mount, and gladden Mrs Pettifer's heart by letting her wait on him, and comfort all his friends, who are quite miserable about him.'

Mr Tryan saw it all in a moment – he saw that it had all been done for his sake. He could not be sorry; he could not say no; he could not resist the sense that life had a new sweetness for him, and that he should like it to be prolonged a little – only a little, for the sake of feeling a stronger security about Janet. When she had finished speaking, she looked at him with a doubtful, enquiring glance. He was not looking at her; his eyes were cast downwards; but the expression of his face encouraged her, and she said, in a half-playful tone of entreaty, 'You will go and live with her? I know you will. You will come back with me now and see the house.'

He looked at her then, and smiled. There is an unspeakable blending of sadness and sweetness in the smile of a face sharpened and paled by slow consumption. That smile of Mr Tryan's pierced poor Janet's heart: she felt in it at once the assurance of grateful affection and the prophecy of coming death. Her tears rose; they turned round without speaking, and went back again along the lane.

27

In less than a week Mr Tryan was settled at Holly Mount, and there was not one of his many attached hearers who did not sincerely rejoice at the event.

The autumn that year was bright and warm, and at the beginning of October, Mr Walsh, the new curate, came. The mild weather, the relaxation from excessive work, and perhaps another benignant influence, had for a few weeks a visibly favourable effect on Mr Tryan. At least he began to feel new hopes, which sometimes took the guise of new strength. He thought of the cases in which consumption patients remain nearly stationary for years, without suffering so as to make their life burdensome to themselves or to others, and he began to struggle with a longing that it might be so with him. He struggled with it, because he felt it to be an indication that earthly affection was beginning to have too strong a hold on him, and he prayed earnestly for more perfect submission, and for a more absorbing delight in the Divine Presence as the chief good. He was conscious that he did not wish for prolonged life solely that he might reclaim the wanderers and sustain the feeble: he was conscious of a new yearning for those pure human joys which he had voluntarily and determinedly banished from his life – for a draught of that deep affection from which he had been cut off by a dark chasm of remorse. For now, that affection was within his reach; he saw it there, like a palm-shadowed well in the desert; he could not desire to die in sight of it.

And so the autumn rolled gently by in its 'calm decay'. Until November, Mr Tryan continued to preach occasionally, to ride about visiting his flock, and to look in at his schools, but his growing satisfaction in Mr Walsh as his successor saved him from too eager exertion and from worrying anxieties. Janet was with him a great deal now, for she saw that he liked her to read to him in the lengthening evenings, and it became the rule for her and her mother to have tea at Holly Mount, where, with Mrs Pettifer, and sometimes another friend or two, they brought Mr Tryan the unaccustomed enjoyment of companionship by his own fireside.

Janet did not share his new hopes, for she was not only in the habit of hearing Mr Pratt's opinion that Mr Tryan could hardly stand out through the winter, but she also knew that it was shared by Dr Madely of Rotherby, whom, at her request, he had consented to call in. It was not necessary or desirable to tell Mr Tryan what was revealed by the stethoscope, but Janet knew the worst.

She felt no rebellion under this prospect of bereavement, but rather a quiet submissive sorrow. Gratitude that his influence and guidance had been given her, even if only for a little while – gratitude that she was permitted to be with him, to take a deeper and deeper impress from daily communion with him, to be something to him in these last months of his life, was so strong in her that it almost silenced regret. Janet had lived through the great tragedy of woman's life. Her keenest personal emotions had been poured forth in her early love – her wounded affection with its years of anguish – her agony of unavailing pity over that deathbed seven months ago. The thought of Mr Tryan was associated for her with repose from that conflict of emotion, with trust in the unchangeable, with the influx of a power to subdue self. To have been assured of his sympathy, his teaching, his help, all through her life, would have been to her like a heaven already begun – a deliverance from fear and danger, but the time was not yet come for her to be conscious that the hold he had on her heart was any other than that of the Heaven-sent friend who had come to her like the angel in the prison, and loosed her bonds, and led her by the hand till she could look back on the dreadful doors that had once closed her in.

Before November was over Mr Tryan had ceased to go out. A new crisis had come on: the cough had changed its character, and the worst symptoms developed themselves so rapidly that Mr Pratt began to think the end would arrive sooner than he had expected. Janet became a constant attendant on him now, and no one could feel that she was performing anything but a sacred office. She made Holly Mount her home, and, with her mother and Mrs Pettifer to help her, she filled the painful days and nights with every soothing influence that care and tenderness could devise. There were many visitors to the sick-room, led thither by venerating affection, and there could hardly be one who did not retain in after-years a vivid remembrance of the scene there – of the pale wasted form in the easy chair (for he sat up to the last), of the grey eyes so full even yet of enquiring kindness, as the thin, almost transparent hand was held out to give the pressure of welcome, and of the sweet woman, too, whose dark watchful eyes detected every want, and who supplied the want with a ready hand.

There were others who would have had the heart and the skill to fill this place by Mr Tryan's side, and who would have accepted it as an honour, but they could not help feeling that God had given it to Janet by a train of events which were too impressive not to shame all jealousies into silence.

That sad history which most of us know too well, lasted more than three months. He was too feeble and suffering for the last few weeks to see any visitors, but he still sat up through the day. The strange hallucinations of the disease which had seemed to take a more decided hold on him just at the fatal crisis, and had made him think he was perhaps getting better at the very time when death had begun to hurry on with more rapid movement, had now given way, and left him calmly conscious of the reality. One afternoon, near the end of February, Janet was moving gently about the room, in the fire-lit dusk, arranging some things that would be wanted in the night. There was no one else in the room, and his eyes followed her as she moved with the firm grace natural to her, while the bright fire every now and then lit up her face, and gave an unusual glow to its dark beauty. Even to follow her in this way with his eyes was an exertion that gave a painful tension to his face; while she looked like an image of life and strength.

'Janet,' he said presently, in his faint voice – he always called her Janet now. In a moment she was close to him, bending over him. He opened his hand as he looked up at her, and she placed hers within it.

'Janet,' he said again, 'you will have a long while to live after I am gone.'

A sudden pang of fear shot through her. She thought he felt himself dying, and she sank on her knees at his feet, holding his hand, while she looked up at him, almost breathless.

'But you will not feel the need of me as you have done... You have a sure trust in God... I shall not look for you in vain at the last.'

'No... no... I shall be there... God will not forsake me.'

She could hardly utter the words, though she was not weeping. She was waiting with trembling eagerness for anything else he might have to say.

'Let us kiss each other before we part.'

She lifted up her face to his, and the full life-breathing lips met the wasted dying ones in a sacred kiss of promise.

28

It soon came – the blessed day of deliverance, the sad day of bereavement; and in the second week of March they carried him to the grave. He was buried as he had desired: there was no hearse, no mourning coach; his coffin was borne by twelve of his humbler hearers, who relieved each other by turns. But he was followed by a long procession of mourning friends, women as well as men.

Slowly, amid deep silence, the dark stream passed along Orchard Street, where eighteen months before, the Evangelical curate had been saluted with hooting and hisses. Mr Jerome and Mr Landor were the eldest pallbearers, and behind the coffin, led by Mr Tryan's cousin, walked Janet, in quiet submissive sorrow. She could not feel that he was quite gone from her; the unseen world lay so very near her – it held all that had ever stirred the depths of anguish and joy within her.

It was a cloudy morning, and had been raining when they left Holly Mount, but as they walked, the sun broke out, and the clouds were rolling off in large masses when they entered the churchyard, and Mr Walsh's voice was heard saying, 'I am the Resurrection and the Life.' The faces were not hard at this funeral; the burial service was not a hollow form. Every heart there was filled with the memory of a man who, through a self-sacrificing life and in a painful death, had been sustained by the faith which fills that form with breath and substance.

When Janet left the grave, she did not return to Holly Mount; she went to her home in Orchard Street, where her mother was waiting to receive her. She said quite calmly, 'Let us walk round the garden, Mother.' And they walked round in silence, with their hands clasped together, looking at the golden crocuses bright in the spring sunshine. Janet felt a deep stillness within. She thirsted for no pleasure; she craved no worldly good. She saw the years to come stretch before her like an autumn afternoon, filled with resigned memory. Life to her could never more have any eagerness; it was a solemn service of gratitude and patient effort. She walked in the presence of unseen witnesses – of the divine love that had rescued her, of the human love that waited for its eternal repose until it had seen her endure to the end.

Janet is living still. Her black hair is grey, and her step is no longer buoyant, but the sweetness of her smile remains; the love is not gone from her eyes; and strangers sometimes ask,

Who is that noble-looking elderly woman, that walks about holding a little boy by the hand? The little boy is the son of Janet's adopted daughter, and Janet in her old age has children about her knees, and loving young arms round her neck.

There is a simple gravestone in Milby Churchyard, telling that in this spot lie the remains of Edgar Tryan, for two years officiating curate at the Paddiford chapel of ease, in this parish. It is a meagre memorial, and tells you simply that the man who lies there took upon him, faithfully or unfaithfully, the office of guide and instructor to his fellow men.

But there is another memorial of Edgar Tryan, which bears a fuller record: it is Janet Dempster, rescued from self-despair, strengthened with divine hopes, and now looking back on years of purity and helpful labour. The man who has left such a memorial behind him, must have been one whose heart beat with true compassion, and whose lips were moved by fervent faith.

NOTES

1. Methodism, a Non-conformist branch of Protestantism that developed from the teaching of John Wesley (1703–91). Methodism stressed that everyone could be saved and refuted the doctrine of predestination.

2. The pseudo-science of phrenology, which identifies character traits with features of the skull, was popular in the late eighteenth century.

3. Thomas Hobbes (1588–1679), English philosopher and author of *Leviathan* (1651), which described human nature as essentially pragmatic and self-seeking. His name subsequently carried connotations of atheism.

4. Not adhering to the Church of England.

5. Luke Byles derives the word correctly.

6. Antinomians asserted that moral law was not binding on Christians; the Anabaptists were any of several religious groups who recognised only the validity of adult baptism.

7. The Jesuits were members of the Society of Jesus, an order founded in 1534 to spread the Roman Catholic faith; the term Jesuit later came to mean a cunning, dissembling person.

8. A short, loose coat or cloak.

9. From *Night Thoughts* (1742–45), by Edward Young (1683–1765).

10. The art of boxing.

11. Independents were members of any sect, especially the Congregationalists, that allowed each local church free control over its own legislation and affairs, and therefore resisted formalised worship.

12. Salem is derived from the Hebrew 'shalom', peace.

13. Three Israelites who rebelled against Moses, and were swallowed up by the earth as punishment (Numbers 16).

14. See note 11.

15. A chapel located at a distance from the main parish church, for the convenience of more remote parishioners.

16. John Dryden (1631–1700), poet, critic and playwright, whose most ambitious work of translation was *The Works of Virgil* (1697); Hannah More (1745–1833), religious writer and philanthropist, who published *Sacred Dramas* in 1782; William Falconer (1732–69), Scottish poet and sailor, who produced the epic poem *The Shipwreck* in 1762; John Mason (1706–63), Non-conformist minister, who published his treatise *On Self-Knowledge* in 1743; *The History of Rasselas, Prince of Abissinia* (1759), a novella by Samuel Johnson (1709–84); Edmund Burke (1729–97), statesman and political philosopher, who wrote *On the Sublime and the Beautiful* (1757), a treatise on aesthetics.

17. An epic poem on the life of Christ, by Friedrich Gottlieb Klopstock (1724–1803).

18. An account (1832), by William Stephen Gilly, of the Swiss Protestant divine and philanthropist, Felix Neff (1798–1829).

19. *Father Clement* (1823), by the Scottish writer Grace Kennedy (1782–1825), is an anti-Roman Catholic novel that was enormously popular in the nineteenth century.

20. The doctrine of justification by faith, i.e. that salvation is granted according to faith rather than good works, was propagated by Martin Luther (1483–1546), and was one of the cornerstones of the Reformation.

21. *The Force of Truth* (1779) was an autobiographical account by Thomas Scott (1747–1821) of his conversion to true religious belief; Legh Richmond (1772–1827) was an Evangelical preacher, about whom Thomas Shuttleworth Grimshaw published a memoir in 1828.

22. *comme il faut*. As it should be (French).

23. A publisher of Evangelical literature, founded in 1799.

24. In the Bible, Rechabites were members of the family descended from Rechab, who refused to drink or grow wine or live in houses (Jeremiah 35). The term came to denote a teetotaller.

25. I have sinned (Latin).

26. The system followed in Independent sects of funding clergy by way of voluntary contributions from the congregation.

27. Latitudinarians conformed to Church of England forms, but held that strict Church governance was of little importance; Pantheism holds that the universe and God are one and the same.

28. Thomas Cranmer (1489–1556), Nicholas Ridley (d. 1555) and Hugh Latimer (d. 1555) were Protestant martyrs, burned at the stake in Oxford during the reign of Mary Tudor.

29. Long live the king (Latin).

30. Shadrach, Meshech (or Meshach) and Abednego were three young companions of Daniel, who were condemned to be burned by the Babylonian king Nebuchadnezzar, but survived the fiery furnace unharmed (Daniel 3).

31. The Puseyites, named for Edward Bouverie Pusey (1800–82), one of the leaders of the Oxford Movement, held that the Church of England was a direct descendant of the original Christian Church established by the apostles; the followers of Jacobus Arminius (1560–1609) believed that grace was granted to all believers, but that the individual was given free will to reject belief; Calvinism was at odds with Armininianism in that it held that salvation was granted only to some by a process of 'election', and that those to be saved would remain or 'persevere' in a state of grace until death; the Plymouth Brethren were a puritanical Evangelical movement that began in London, Dublin and Plymouth in the 1820s.

32. Henry Venn (1725–97), founder of the Clapham Sect and one of the leaders of the eighteenth-century Evangelical revival.

33. Johann Friedrich Overbeck (1789–1869), German painter and member of the Nazarene movement, who encouraged a revival of spirituality in art.

34. It is wonderful to bear children (Greek). From Sophocles' *Electra*.

35. Luke 15:7.

36. Henry Martyn (1781–1812), Protestant missionary in India and Persia. He died of the plague whilst working in Asia.

BIOGRAPHICAL NOTE

George Eliot was born Mary Ann Evans in Warwickshire in 1819. The youngest daughter of Robert Evans (a land agent) and Christina Pearson, she was a deeply religious child, and taught at Sunday school from the age of twelve. In 1828 she was sent to school in Nuneaton where she came under the influence of various Evangelicals, including the Rev. John Edmund Jones, a preacher who would later appear in a number of her novels.

Following her mother's death in 1836, Mary Ann (now Marian) became her father's housekeeper and companion, but continued to educate herself in her spare time. In 1841 she moved to Coventry and became acquainted with the religious freethinkers Charles and Caroline Bray. Their influence on her caused her to question – and reject – much of her Evangelical heritage, but the role of religion remained important to her and featured in many of her later works. Through the Brays, Marian was commissioned to translate Strauss's *Life of Jesus*, which appeared, anonymously, in 1846. As a result of this she met the publisher John Chapman who gave her a position on the *Westminster Review* in 1851. Around this time she moved to London and formed close friendships first with Herbert Spencer, who found her intimidating, and then with George Henry Lewes, with whom she lived until his death in 1878. The two never married as Lewes had previously married and had never divorced.

'The Sad Fortunes of the Reverend Amos Barton', the first of her *Scenes of Clerical Life*, appeared in *Blackwell's Magazine* in 1857 under the authorship of George Eliot; this was closely followed by 'Mr Gilfil's Love Story' and 'Janet's Repentance'. These were widely praised but speculation surrounded the identity of George Eliot, many supposing 'him' to be a clergyman. After much conjecture, she eventually stepped forward and revealed her identity.

Adam Bede appeared in 1859 and established her as a leading novelist of the day. This she followed up with *The Mill on the Floss* (1860) and *Silas Marner* (1861). *Middlemarch*, considered by many to be her masterpiece, was published in instalments in 1871–72, and *Daniel Deronda* in 1874–76. With these behind her, she was hailed as the greatest living novelist, and counted Henry James, Ralph Waldo Emerson, Ivan Turgenev and Queen Victoria among her admirers.

In 1878 Lewes died and Eliot formed a new attachment, marrying the forty-year-old John Walter Cross in 1880. This relationship distressed many of her friends, but brought about reconciliation with her brother Isaac with whom she had been estranged since 1857. Not long after her marriage, however, she died and, in 1882, was buried alongside Lewes.

SELECTED TITLES FROM HESPERUS PRESS

Author	Title	Foreword writer
Pietro Aretino	*The School of Whoredom*	Paul Bailey
Pietro Aretino	*The Secret Life of Nuns*	
Jane Austen	*Lesley Castle*	Zoë Heller
Jane Austen	*Love and Friendship*	Fay Weldon
Honoré de Balzac	*Colonel Chabert*	A.N. Wilson
Charles Baudelaire	*On Wine and Hashish*	Margaret Drabble
Giovanni Boccaccio	*Life of Dante*	A.N. Wilson
Charlotte Brontë	*The Spell*	
Emily Brontë	*Poems of Solitude*	Helen Dunmore
Mikhail Bulgakov	*Fatal Eggs*	Doris Lessing
Mikhail Bulgakov	*The Heart of a Dog*	A.S. Byatt
Giacomo Casanova	*The Duel*	Tim Parks
Miguel de Cervantes	*The Dialogue of the Dogs*	Ben Okri
Geoffrey Chaucer	*The Parliament of Birds*	
Anton Chekhov	*The Story of a Nobody*	Louis de Bernières
Anton Chekhov	*Three Years*	William Fiennes
Wilkie Collins	*The Frozen Deep*	
Joseph Conrad	*Heart of Darkness*	A.N. Wilson
Joseph Conrad	*The Return*	Colm Tóibín
Gabriele D'Annunzio	*The Book of the Virgins*	Tim Parks
Dante Alighieri	*The Divine Comedy: Inferno*	
Dante Alighieri	*New Life*	Louis de Bernières
Daniel Defoe	*The King of Pirates*	Peter Ackroyd
Marquis de Sade	*Incest*	Janet Street-Porter
Charles Dickens	*The Haunted House*	Peter Ackroyd
Charles Dickens	*A House to Let*	
Fyodor Dostoevsky	*The Double*	Jeremy Dyson
Fyodor Dostoevsky	*Poor People*	Charlotte Hobson
Alexandre Dumas	*One Thousand and One Ghosts*	

George Eliot	*Amos Barton*	Matthew Sweet
Henry Fielding	*Jonathan Wild the Great*	Peter Ackroyd
F. Scott Fitzgerald	*The Popular Girl*	Helen Dunmore
Gustave Flaubert	*Memoirs of a Madman*	Germaine Greer
Ugo Foscolo	*Last Letters of Jacopo Ortis*	Valerio Massimo Manfredi
Elizabeth Gaskell	*Lois the Witch*	Jenny Uglow
Théophile Gautier	*The Jinx*	Gilbert Adair
André Gide	*Theseus*	
Johann Wolfgang von Goethe	*The Man of Fifty*	A.S. Byatt
Nikolai Gogol	*The Squabble*	Patrick McCabe
E.T.A. Hoffmann	*Mademoiselle de Scudéri*	Gilbert Adair
Victor Hugo	*The Last Day of a Condemned Man*	Libby Purves
Joris-Karl Huysmans	*With the Flow*	Simon Callow
Henry James	*In the Cage*	Libby Purves
Franz Kafka	*Metamorphosis*	Martin Jarvis
Franz Kafka	*The Trial*	Zadie Smith
John Keats	*Fugitive Poems*	Andrew Motion
Heinrich von Kleist	*The Marquise of O–*	Andrew Miller
Mikhail Lermontov	*A Hero of Our Time*	Doris Lessing
Nikolai Leskov	*Lady Macbeth of Mtsensk*	Gilbert Adair
Carlo Levi	*Words are Stones*	Anita Desai
Xavier de Maistre	*A Journey Around my Room*	Alain de Botton
André Malraux	*The Way of the Kings*	Rachel Seiffert
Katherine Mansfield	*Prelude*	William Boyd
Edgar Lee Masters	*Spoon River Anthology*	Shena Mackay
Guy de Maupassant	*Butterball*	Germaine Greer
Prosper Mérimée	*Carmen*	Philip Pullman
Sir Thomas More	*The History of King Richard III*	Sister Wendy Beckett
Sándor Petőfi	*John the Valiant*	George Szirtes